DEDICATION

For Akiko, Akira and Kai.

DAVID BLAKE

THE DI TANNER SERIES

"Nor thieves nor the greedy nor drunkards nor slanderers nor swindlers will inherit the kingdom of God."
1 Corinthians 6:10

- PROLOGUE -

Saturday, 5th February

A LOUD SHARP snap from the wide open fireplace had Lawrence Hambleton blinking himself awake. With his head resting gently against the side of a dusty old wing-backed chair, he closed his eyes again to take in the still unfamiliar sounds of Long Gore Hall, its ancient timbers creaking above his head in the cold wintry wind. But there was something missing, and it took him a full second to work out what it was. The monotonous rumbling noise that had been playing in the background ever since he'd moved in the week before had come grinding to a halt. The generator must have packed-up, and for what would have been the second time that day.

Wondering how long it had been out for, his mind turned to the food he'd only just crammed inside the freezer.

Cursing quietly to himself, he lifted his head to glance around at the enormous shadow-filled living room, looking for the torch he'd been forced to carry around with him since realising the generator was far from reliable. Spying it lying on the floorboards, he pushed himself up, a hand taking a natural hold of the shotgun he'd been cleaning before falling asleep, when another sound tripped its way through the damp musty air. He didn't have to think twice to know what it was. It was the distinctive noise of glass breaking, or more accurately, one of Long Gore Hall's many dozens of windows being smashed.

As a welcome kick of adrenaline began coursing through his veins, he rose to his feet like a hungry lion, the beckoning scent of blood catching in its bristling nose.

Leaving the torch where it was, he brought the gun to bear on the door leading out to the foyer before inching his way over the dust-covered floorboards, his face wincing every time the ancient lengths of wood groaned under his burgeoning weight. When he reached the door, he nudged it open with the barrels of the gun to peer out into the oppressive gloom beyond. The vast musty foyer he was staring into was almost pitch-black, the light from the rising moon outside obliterated by decades of grime covering the still part boarded-up windows. As his eyes adjusted to the darkness, he cast them furtively around. From what he could make out, all the panes seemed intact.

With his mind questioning if it *had* been the sound of breaking glass he'd heard, or just his imagination playing games with him, another noise had him tilting his head to the pitch-black hallway leading down towards the kitchen. It was the unmistakable scraping noise of a chair being dragged over a hard tiled floor. Someone, or at least some*thing*, was inside his house.

Checking the gun was loaded, he snapped the barrels closed to begin inching his way forward, a steady finger resting gently against the shotgun's familiar curved steel trigger. As he reached the rectangular wooden doorway that led through to the kitchen, he nudged it open with his foot to cast his eyes fitfully over the shadows. The window was wide open, broken glass scattered on the floor. When he saw the drawer he'd left all his hunting knives in was hanging out from underneath the kitchen worktop, his heart began pounding deep inside his chest.

Traversing the shotgun's barrels across the room, a pair of dark brown eyes delved down into the darkest of shadows as a crooked smile played underneath his thin aquiline nose. It felt good to be hunting again, but he knew he had to be careful. He wasn't picking his way through South Africa's Kruger National Park, a gang of armed poachers lined up in his sights. He was where he grew up, the windswept barren lands of the Norfolk Broads. Back home he could shoot a poacher without so much as raising an eyebrow. He seriously doubted the British police would be quite so forgiving were he to shoot someone inside his ancestral home, even if they hadn't been invited.

'Whoever's in here,' he called out, his voice jarring against the cold silent darkness, 'you better know that I'm holding a Webley & Scott 12-gauge shotgun, both barrels of which are loaded. I'd also welcome the chance to use it. Bearing that in mind, I suggest you come out from wherever you're hiding with your hands where I can see them. I have no interest in making a charge against you for breaking and entering, but I do want you to get the hell off my property.'

He closed his mouth and waited, but there was no response.

'If you don't come out, I'll be forced to call the police.'

More silence.

'OK, fine. If that's how you want to play it.'

Hambleton was about to edge his way back the way he'd come when the flash of a blade sliced at the air just inches from his face. Jumping back, he didn't think, bringing the shotgun to bear on the shadow he could see lurking underneath.

- CHAPTER ONE -

DETECTIVE INSPECTOR JOHN Tanner brought his somewhat dated Jaguar XJS to a gradual halt at the end of an unlit pot-holed track, a pair of lopsided iron gates captured by the car's headlights blocking the way ahead.

'Looks like we're first on the scene,' he commented, peering into the distance at a moonlit stately home, the base of which was shrouded by long ethereal bands of ghostly white mist.

'I'm not exactly surprised,' he heard Detective Constable Townsend say, sitting in the passenger seat beside him. 'I mean...who'd want to come here?'

Tanner tugged at the handbrake to rest his hands on top of the Jag's over-sized leather steering wheel. 'Long Gore Hall,' he read out, staring up at the rusting iron lettering he could see arched between what was left of two crumbling brick walls.

Townsend leaned forward to follow his gaze. 'Sounds like something out of a horror film.'

'Looks a bit like one as well,' Tanner agreed, gesturing ahead to the hall itself, a soft yellow light glowing out from behind a handful of large rectangular windows, in front of which stood four immense Romanesque pillars.

'You'd have thought they'd have been able to come up with a slightly more cheerful name,' Townsend continued, shifting nervously in his seat.

'I suspect it was named after the marsh it was built in the middle of.'

'I'm sure it was, but even so.'

Tanner unclipped his seatbelt to reach for the door handle. 'Anyway, I suppose we'd better see if we can get those gates open.'

'You're not suggesting that we actually get out?' Townsend yelped, staring out of the passenger side window at tendrils of gently swirling mist that were already engulfing the car like a den of encroaching colourless snakes.

'Well, I think it's unlikely that they're going to open by themselves. Judging by the state of them, I think we'll be lucky if we can get them open at all!'

'Can't you nudge them open with the front of the car?'

Tanner looked at him before gazing forward again. 'Well, I would, of course, I'm just not sure which would give way first, the gates or the car's already dented chrome bumper.'

'Tell you what,' Townsend continued, sitting back in the Jag's soft cream leather seat, 'you do the gates and I'll stay here to guard the car.'

'From what?'

'Whatever's crawling around on all fours out there,' he replied, gesturing around at the stark barren landscape. 'Haven't you seen "An American Werewolf in London"?'

'Er...I believe it was me who lent you the DVD.'

'Then you'll remember what it said about full moons and mist covered moors,' Townsend continued, shifting his body to glance out through the rear window.

'It said to beware of the moon and stick to the path.'

'I'm fairly sure it was to beware of the moon and

whatever you do, don't get out of the car!'

'It was about two Americans on a hiking holiday.'

'Didn't they get out of someone's car at the beginning?'

'That was before they went into the pub.'

Townsend shook his head. 'Anyway, if they *had* been in a car, I'm fairly sure the barman would have told them to stay inside it.'

Tanner turned to offer Townsend a smile of parental amusement. Since Forrester had asked him to take their newest member of CID under his wing he'd been enjoying his company. The young detective constable had proven to have a razor sharp mind, and as his confidence had grown, an equally sharp sense of humour.

'Anyway,' Townsend continued, now staring ahead, 'fortunately for us, it looks like we won't need to.'

Tanner followed his gaze to see the shadowy figure of a tall thin man limping through the mist towards them dressed in the rather peculiar combination of a flat cap pulled down over his eyes, a long knitted scarf wrapped twice around his neck, and an old baggy cricket jumper.

'That must be the estate's owner,' Tanner muttered, making a note of the shotgun crooked over his arm. 'What was his name again?'

Townsend searched his coat for his notebook. 'A Mr Lawrence Hambleton,' he eventually replied. 'According to the newspapers, he arrived from South Africa last week after being left the estate by his grandfather.'

'Why not his parents?' Tanner enquired, raising an eyebrow.

'They were killed on safari. Mauled by a lion, apparently.'

'Nice.'

'For the lion, perhaps.'

Seeing the man set down the torch he'd been carrying to take a hold of one of the gates, Tanner stepped quickly out, leaving the car door open behind him.

'Detective Inspector Tanner, Norfolk Police,' he called, clawing out his ID to begin making his way over.

'Hambleton, Lawrence,' the man replied, with the hint of a South African accent.

'We hear you think you may have shot an intruder?'

'There are no maybes about it,' Hambleton stated, heaving up one end of the rusting heavy gate to begin dragging it back. 'The man came at me with a knife. I wasn't left with much of a choice.'

'Is he dead?'

'The last time I looked he was.'

Tanner stepped forward to give him a hand. 'I presume that was the gun you used?'

'It's the only one I brought with me.'

'From South Africa?'

With the gate open, Hambleton stopped to cast a pair of cool eyes over at Tanner. 'May I ask how you knew that?'

'My colleague said he read about you in the local news, how you inherited the estate from your grandfather.'

'And just how the hell did the newspapers find out?'

'Oh, they have their ways, believe you me. You must have mentioned it to someone at some point.'

'Only to my solicitor.'

'There you are then. Case closed.'

'Then I suppose I'd better learn to keep my mouth

shut.'

'But not before telling us what happened, I hope?'

'There's not much to tell, really. I'd nodded off in front of the fire when I heard a noise in the kitchen. When I went to take a look, this guy came at me from nowhere, so I shot him.'

'Fair enough,' Tanner replied, a little taken aback by the man's total lack of emotion. 'I take it you've been issued with a licence for that gun of yours?'

Hambleton glanced down at the shotgun still crooked over his arm. 'I have, but only for South Africa. Admittedly, had I known I'd end up shooting an intruder during my first week here, I'd have applied for a licence when I arrived.'

Tanner glanced over his shoulder to see Townsend still sitting in the car, his phone's screen lighting up his face. 'I presume it's alright if we drive down to take a look?'

'Be my guest. Just follow the road along. Somehow I'm not sure you'll be able to miss it.'

- CHAPTER TWO -

LEAVING HIS CAR next to an old dark green Range Rover, parked at the base of a short series of narrow moss-covered stone steps, Tanner and Townsend stepped out to stare up at the pillars they'd first seen from the estate's gated entrance.

'This place is huge!' Townsend exclaimed, having to tilt his head back to be able to see up to the mansion's roof. 'The guy must be minted!'

'I'm not so sure,' Tanner replied, his own eyes taking in the cracked masonry, rusting gutters, flaking paint, and the weeds he could see climbing over virtually the entire structure. 'It's going to need a lot of work.' Glancing over his shoulder to see the estate's new owner still limping in the darkness towards them, he turned back to continue. 'I reckon he'll need a shed load of cash just to make it habitable. The land is probably worth more than the house.'

'Sorry to have kept you,' they heard Hambleton eventually say, coming to a breathless halt beside them. 'It's my leg, I'm afraid. Sometimes I think life would be easier if the surgeon had just cut the damned thing off.'

Taking in the leg in question, Tanner offered him a look of empathetic curiosity. 'Was it a lion?'

'Poacher,' Hambleton replied, in a curt dismissive tone. 'In my experience, a far more dangerous species.'

'But you did lose your parents in a lion attack?'

Hambleton's shadowy face stiffened as he brought his dark brown eyes to bear on Tanner's. 'That's correct, Inspector...?'

'Tanner,' he replied. 'And my colleague, Detective Constable Townsend.'

'I suppose you read about that in the news as well,' Hambleton said, casting his eyes over at the ID Townsend was holding up. 'What else did they say about me, dare I ask?'

'Only that you arrived sometime last week.'

'Tuesday morning, to be precise.'

'And that you inherited the estate from your grandfather.'

'Correct again.'

'Did that come as a surprise?'

'What – my inheritance, or the state I found the place in when I arrived?'

'Well, both, I suppose.'

'Not the first, at least not really. I'm the last surviving Hambleton, so I'm not sure who else he'd have left it to. But I must admit, I wasn't expecting to find it in quite such a state. I've since found out that he'd spent the last ten years of his life stuck inside a nursing home, leaving it to the elements, as you can see.'

Casting his torch's beam up to the top of one of the tall stone pillars, he clicked it off to begin tapping it nervously against the top of his half-crippled leg. 'Anyway, you'd better come inside, and I'll show you where the body is.'

Tanner and Townsend offered each other a curious look before following him up the steps onto a large stone plinth upon which the stately pillars rested; a faint low rumbling noise growing louder with every step. When they reached a wide double-fronted door lined with dirt smeared window panels through which could be seen a warm inviting yellow light, they stopped to wait for the man to wrestle it open. The moment he did, the rumbling noise drifted away, leaving the light inside to flicker briefly before plunging them back into darkness.

'Bloody generator,' Hambleton cursed, stopping to switch his torch back on. 'For some reason it seems to keep cutting out.'

With both Tanner and Townsend each digging out their phones to turn on their respective torch apps, they followed the man through the door into what must have once been a truly resplendent foyer but was now nothing more than an empty hollowed-out chamber; a large cobweb-strewn chandelier hanging from the ceiling above.

'It's down here,' Hambleton continued, guiding them along a narrow hallway into an old Victorian kitchen, moonlight glancing in through a half-open sash window.

Seeing Hambleton stop where he was to train his torch down towards a grey flagstone floor, Tanner nudged himself inside to begin casting the light from his phone around. 'Didn't you say there was an intruder's body lying around here somewhere?'

'He was right there,' Hambleton muttered, his eyes staring down at the circular beam of light to the side of a large kitchen island.

Following his gaze, Tanner stepped cautiously over before crouching down to take a closer look. 'Well, there's blood,' he soon said. 'Quite a lot of it as well. He must have been slightly less dead than you thought.'

'But – I shot him in the chest – at point-blank range. There's no way he could have survived.'

Tanner stood slowly back up to swing his phone's light over the cold grey floor, just as the sound of a somewhat belated siren could be heard drifting in through the open window. 'The blood leads back to where he must have come in. There's more on the sill. I'd say he managed to get out. I think for your sake, we'd better try and find him before he bleeds out.'

'Why for my sake? The guy broke into my house to attack me with a knife.'

'That's as maybe, Mr Hambleton, but there's no sign of a knife here. I'm sorry to say this, but if he happens to die without us being able to find it, there's a strong possibility you'd be looking at a charge of manslaughter.'

- CHAPTER THREE -

WITH HAMBLETON LIMPING off to see if he could get the generator started again, Tanner left Townsend by the kitchen door to head back outside to find a number of police and emergency vehicles rumbling their way over the overgrown driveway towards him. Explaining what had happened to the first pair of uniformed constables he met; that an intruder had been wounded by a shotgun blast before fleeing the scene, he directed them to start a search of the grounds. With the arriving ambulance crew offering to join in the search, Tanner smiled to himself when he saw Dr Johnstone pull up behind them in his old Volvo Estate.

'You're a little early, I'm afraid,' he called out, watching the medical examiner climb slowly out.

'Is that your way of saying that the victim isn't dead?'

'At the moment, we're not sure.'

'I'm sorry?'

'It would appear that the intruder fled the premises after being shot, so we won't know if you'll be needed until he's been found.'

Johnstone let out an impatient sigh. 'Next time, would you mind telling whoever it was who called me to wait until there's an actual body? I was about to start watching the new series of, "I'm a Celebrity, Get

Me Out of Here!"'

Tanner offered him a bemused grimace. 'You don't actually watch that crap, do you?'

'You mean, do I enjoy watching a group of sex-starved wannabe celebrities constantly bickering with each other whilst being forced to eat worms, after which they have to suffer the humiliation of being voted out by the general public? Sorry, but – what's not to like?'

'You know,' Tanner replied, 'it does sound rather good. What time's it on?'

Johnstone glared down at his watch. 'About half an hour ago.'

'Oh well, never mind. You can always watch it on Catch-Up.'

'I suppose I'll have to. Anyway, I'm here now. Is there anything I can do, other than stand about twiddling my thumbs?'

'You could take a look at where the incident happened. Hopefully, it won't be long before he's found. He was apparently shot in the chest at point-blank range by a man with a rather large shotgun, so I can't imagine he'll be too far away.'

As the sound of yet another siren could be heard, Tanner led Johnstone up the stone steps into the still virtually pitch-black foyer. Guiding him down the hallway to find Townsend waiting patiently in front of the kitchen door, Tanner suggested he helped with the search before inviting the medical examiner inside.

'Well, there's certainly a fair amount of blood,' Johnstone eventually said, having spent a few moments surveying the scene with the aid of Tanner's torch. 'I don't suppose there's any chance we could have some more light?'

'It would appear that the place has yet to be

hooked up to the national grid, and the generator packed-up just after we arrived.'

'Oh well,' Johnstone shrugged, crouching down in a similar position to where Tanner had been. 'I'd estimate there to be about two pints worth of blood here, which wouldn't be fatal, but if the victim loses much more he's likely to go into shock. Another three or four and that would be it, I'm afraid. However, I'd say there is some good news. I don't think the person who shot him is the marksman they're making themselves out to be.'

'What makes you say that?'

Johnstone brought Tanner's attention to the side of the kitchen island where a semi-circular shadow could be seen. 'I'm no expert, but I'd say that's where the blast hit, the bulk of it at least. I'd say our victim was only caught by what I suppose could be described as a "glancing blow".'

- CHAPTER FOUR -

TANNER EMERGED BACK into the still pitch-black foyer to find Townsend directing a couple of police forensics officers towards the kitchen.

'I don't suppose the intruder's been found?' he asked, catching the young constable's eye.

'Not a sign. The blood trail leads out into the marsh. If he did wander out there, I can't imagine how he'll survive. I'm not sure how we'll be able to find him, either.'

Tanner glanced over his shoulder to find Hambleton standing behind him, a look of anxious concern etched out over his dark shadow-covered face.

'What does that mean – for me, I mean?' the man questioned, his hands held loosely down by his sides.

Tanner couldn't help but feel sorry for him. Assuming what he'd told them had been true, he'd barely set foot in the country and yet was now looking likely to be facing a charge of manslaughter, just because some idiot had broken into his house to make the ill-advised move of attacking him with a knife.

'Nothing yet,' Tanner eventually replied, struggling to maintain eye contact. 'Our medical examiner found a cluster of shotgun pellets embedded into one of the kitchen units. He's of the opinion that you only dealt the intruder a glancing blow. I think there's a high chance he'll live to tell the tale, so try not to worry.'

'That's easy for you to say. You're not the one who shot him!'

'Whilst you were being attacked in your own kitchen,' Tanner stated, before offering him what he hoped would be a reassuring smile. 'As long as he survives, I doubt you'll face charges.'

'And if he doesn't?'

'Let's cross that bridge when we come to it, shall we? Any luck with the generator?'

Hambleton shook his head. 'I've no idea what's wrong with the damned thing. The last time it stopped was because I'd forgotten to fill it up with diesel.'

'If it helps, I can ask someone to take a look at it for you?'

'That would be appreciated, thank you.'

There was an awkward moment of silence as Tanner considered how best to move the proceedings forward.

'So, anyway,' he eventually began, 'what are your plans for Long Gore Hall?'

Hambleton let out a world-weary sigh, his eyes glancing around at the surrounding shadows. 'Well, my intention had been to live here, but that was before I arrived to find the state it was in. In an ideal world I'd like to. It will probably depend on how much it's going to cost me to make it habitable. I grew up here, you see, before my parents dragged me off to South Africa, so the house holds what sometimes feels like a lifetime of memories.'

Tanner found himself following Hambleton's gaze with an uncomfortable frown. 'Good ones, I hope?'

'It's difficult to imagine, I suppose, what with the place looking like it does, but back in the day the house was truly resplendent. There was always something to do, some game to play. Just sliding down the banisters would keep me occupied for hours. There's even a hidden passageway, which always made playing hide and seek exceptional fun, especially as none of my friends knew where it was. But then my parents got the safari bug during a holiday out there, electing to spend the remainder of their days driving around in a beaten-up old Land Rover whilst taking pot-shots at the local wildlife.'

'I take it you didn't share their enthusiasm?'

'Killing animals for no particular reason? Not really. I doubt they'd have done the same thing now, but those were different times, when shooting animals for sport was considered normal, at least it was for those who could afford it. I suspect a part of me must have been left with an underlying sense of guilt for having done nothing but spend my formative years watching them kill some of the most majestic animals placed on God's good earth whilst doing nothing whatsoever to try and stop them. That was probably why I decided to devote the rest of my life to help try and protect what was left.'

'Despite what happened to your parents?'

'The lions were protecting the pride that my parents were attempting to kill. As difficult as it was for me to accept at the time, the truth of the matter was that they definitely had it coming. Anyway, I'm back in England now, and my grandfather has entrusted the estate to me, so my intention is to stay here and bring it back to its former glory, even if that means having to raise the funds in order to do so.'

'I take it that means you'll be around for a while?'

Hambleton turned back to face Tanner. 'Ah, I see what you mean. You'd prefer it if I didn't leave the country?'

'It would be appreciated,' Tanner replied. 'At least

until we've managed to locate your intruder. I'm afraid we'll also need to take a sample of your fingerprints and DNA. We have a police forensics unit on site, so we can do that now, if that's OK?'

Hambleton's shoulders slumped as his head rolled forward to leave him staring at the dusty bare-wooden floor. 'Yes, of course. Anything I can do to help.'

- CHAPTER FIVE -

Sunday, 6th February

TANNER STRETCHED HIS arms high above his head whilst opening his mouth to let out a loud self-indulgent yawn. Blinking against the sun's reflection, dancing over the surface of the River Yare outside the bungalow he was standing in, he took a moment to cast an admiring eye over towards his old Broad's cruising yacht, its bow peeking out from the purpose built moorings to the side of the modest single-storey building. With pride tugging at the corners of his lips, he tugged his dressing gown around his taut narrow waist to slide open the patio door.

Finding Christine curled up on a square black wicker chair in the farthest corner of a short narrow veranda, her body cocooned by a plump cream-coloured duvet as her eyes stared vacantly out at the river drifting effortlessly past, he took a reluctant step out to join her.

'Isn't it a little cold to be sitting out here?' he questioned, shivering slightly as his breath turned to clouds of instantly evaporating mist.

Christine closed her eyes to take in the low-lying sun. 'It's too nice not to, don't you think?'

'Er, no, I don't,' Tanner replied with a shudder. 'You do know that the temperature is barely above freezing?'

'Why don't you grab yourself a duvet and join me?' she replied, offering him an inviting smile.

'Well I would, of course, but it would appear that you have the only one, the same one I'd have been happily sleeping under had I not woken up to find someone had stolen it from under my very nose – literally!'

It was Christine's turn to shiver, nearly spilling her coffee as she did. Setting the mug down onto a table, she tugged the duvet around her shoulders to push herself up. 'Tell you what, how about I make breakfast as a penance. Besides, you're right, as nice as it is, it's far too cold to be sitting out here.'

Stepping back inside, Tanner watched her waft past him to enter the cosy two-bedroom bungalow they'd bought together only a few months before. The moment she and the duvet were through the door, he slid it closed to follow her over to where the kitchen stood, tucked neatly to the side of the small open-plan living area.

As she poured him out a coffee from the half-full carafe, she glanced up to catch his eye. 'So, what do you fancy?'

'Two of those, for a start,' Tanner replied, nudging himself up onto one of the stools in front of the breakfast bar.

'I meant to eat?'

Tanner reached over to flip open his laptop. 'I suppose that depends on what you're prepared to cook?'

'You know me. Any excuse to get the recipe book out.'

'How about a good old-fashioned full English?'

Christine spun around to pull out an old spiral-bound notebook from a drawer, scraps of paper and magazine cuttings hanging precariously out from its sides. 'I did that yesterday,' she replied, leafing through its dog-eared pages. 'How about ricotta hotcakes with bacon and rocket?'

Tanner raised an eyebrow. 'Sounds like an inedible spaceship.'

'Sorry – scrap that. I don't have the rocket. I can do zucchini tartine with warm mustard dressing, or maybe baked eggs with spinach, mushrooms, goat's cheese and chorizo?'

'Er...' he began, feeling his brain spin briefly out of control before slipping it safely into neutral. He loved the fact that Christine was an excellent cook, even if he didn't always like what she created, but at the end of the day he was a simple man with simple tastes, and would have been happy enough eating exactly the same thing, day-in, day-out. Besides, the concept of not knowing what was about to be presented to him, let alone if he was going to be able to eat it or not, would inevitably leave him with an unwelcome sense of mild anxiety.

'I don't suppose there's any chance you could just do a fry-up again?' he asked, his attention returning to the laptop screen as he navigated his way to the BBC's website.

'I know. How about spicy chickpeas with soppressata and eggs?'

'Apart from the fact that I've got no idea what suppresta is, I suppose I'd be happy enough to give it ago, if I have to, that is.'

'Don't sound too excited,' Christine replied, with obvious sarcasm.

Tanner shrugged. 'You know me. I'd be happy with baked beans on toast.'

'Don't worry, you'll like it. I promise!'

'Wasn't that what you said when you introduced

me to sushi?'

'Fair enough, I suppose. But honestly, how was I to know that you were going to react quite so badly?'

'It's raw dead fish!' Tanner exclaimed, as if the description alone was enough to justify what had been his admittedly somewhat over-dramatic adverse reaction.

'A delicacy that's enjoyed by millions of people throughout the world.'

'Most of whom live in Japan.'

'But does include several thousand who live right here in the UK,' Christine replied, unwrapping herself from the duvet to leave it draped over the back of a sofa.

'I have a theory about that.'

Rolling her eyes, Christine placed her head through an apron to spend a moment fastening its tie behind her back.

'Don't you want to know what it is?'

'Not particularly.'

'It's that nobody this side of the equator actually likes sushi,' Tanner began, regardless of whether Christine wanted him to or not, 'they just pretend to because they think all their friends do. I reckon it's a scenario best explained by the story about the emperor's new clothes. I don't know what it's called, but I assume there's some sort of special psychologists' word for it.'

'I believe you're referring to the social cognitive theory known as Groupthink.'

'OK, that's a little more Orwellian than I was expecting, but that aside, I'm fairly sure that if a single person were to be brave enough to stand up to publicly declare that sushi was in actual fact beyond disgusting, the entire British Japanese food industry would collapse, allowing everyone to get back to enjoying burger and chips.'

'And I suppose you'd like to nominate yourself for that job?'

'If it means not having to eat sushi again, I'd be delighted to.'

Christine lifted her head from out of her recipe book to fix her eyes onto Tanner's. 'Please remind me not to introduce you to any of my cooking friends. If they heard you say something like that I think they'd have you burnt at the stake.'

'Oh, I doubt it. They'd never be able to decide what to serve me with.'

Christine snorted through her nose before spinning around to start dragging various kitchen utensils from out of numerous cupboards and drawers.

'Speaking of psychological institutions,' Tanner continued, his attention returning to the BBC website, 'that place where you used to work is on the news.'

'You mean – Bradfield Hospital?'

'That's the one.'

'What about it?'

'Looks like one of the inmates managed to escape yesterday. Someone by the name of Jason Baines?'

Christine stopped what she was doing to turn slowly around, her mouth falling open as blood drained slowly from her face.

'I take it you knew him?' Tanner questioned, her reaction leaving him with a sense of concerned curiosity.

Her gaze drifted slowly out towards the river. 'Jason – he – he used to be one of my patients.'

'Is that good or bad?'

'Sorry – what was that?' she replied, shaking her head as if being woken from a dream.

'Is it good or bad,' Tanner repeated, 'that this Jason Baines character used to be one of your patients?'

'Well, he wasn't a problem when he was locked in his room,' she replied, her attention returning to what she'd been doing before, 'but if he's managed to escape, I'm not so sure.'

'What had he done to end up being there, anyway?'

'He murdered his parents. You must have heard about it. He cut them up with an axe.'

'Wasn't he the boy who'd only just turned sixteen, saying that they'd physically abused him throughout his life, keeping him locked inside their basement without so much as a window to look out of?'

'That's the one.'

'Christ, yes, I remember. I must admit thinking at the time that a part of me couldn't blame him for doing what he did.'

'I suspect most people thought the same thing.'

'Didn't he refuse to plead guilty, saying that someone even more deranged than both himself and his parents had broken into their house?'

'Something like that, but it was fairly obvious it was him. Apart from the physical evidence, he was already displaying all the signs of being a schizophrenic sociopath, and a highly intelligent one at that.'

'But surely that wasn't his fault. I'd have thought anyone would become a schizophrenic sociopath if they'd spent their entire life being physically abused by their parents whilst being locked inside a basement.'

'Assuming that you're referring to the old Nature versus Nurture argument, the jury's still out. Current thinking is that forty-nine percent of mental illness is influenced by genetics whilst fifty-one is accounted for by the environment in which the person is brought up. Either way, nobody felt that he was entirely to blame, given the actions of his parents, which was why he was sent to Bradfield Hospital instead of the nearest maximum security prison.'

Leaving the utensils she'd assembled on the worksurface, she skirted around the breakfast bar to join Tanner. 'What else does it say?'

'Not much. Only that the hospital is warning the general public not to approach him under any circumstances. They've also printed a mugshot of him.'

She leaned over his shoulder to stare at the screen. 'Well, that's not going to be much use. That was taken when he was arrested. He doesn't look anything like that now. Does it say how he managed to escape?'

'Only that it was yesterday evening between four and five.'

They both continued reading through the article before Christine stood up to shake her head. 'Anyway, they'd better find him soon. You really don't want to have Jason Baines on your doorstep, asking if he can borrow some milk. To be honest, I'm surprised you haven't been called in to help with the search,' she continued, making her way back around the counter.

'Well, it's Sunday for a start, and it's not as if he's wanted in connection with any of our current investigations.'

'But even so. If I was that police superintendent of yours – what was his name again?'

'Whitaker,' Tanner replied, spitting out his name as he'd just bitten into a maggot infested sandwich.

'If I was him,' Christine continued, 'I'd be more than a little keen to have him safely back in his room before he *is* wanted in connection with one of your current investigations.'

Finishing her sentence, they both glanced over towards the muffled sound of a phone, ringing from somewhere inside the main bedroom.

'I can almost guarantee that's your boss, telling you to come in.'

'Shit,' cursed Tanner, rising from his seat. 'Tell you what. How about we pretend that neither of us heard it?'

'To be honest, as much as I enjoy spending my Sundays with you, on this particular occasion, I think I'd rather you were out there helping to find him, especially bearing in mind the relationship we had.'

Tanner stopped to stare over at her. 'You were in a relationship with him?'

Christine let out an uneasy laugh. 'It was a doctor / patient relationship, at least it was from my perspective.'

'Are you saying he used to fancy you?'

'Well, I *was* better looking back then,' she smiled, self-consciously pulling a lock of hair down to cover the thin white scar running vertically down her forehead. 'Younger, too.'

'Did he actually say he did?'

'Pretty much all the time. But don't worry, I was hardly the only one. As is often the case with high-functioning sociopaths, he could be incredibly charming when he wanted to be. He subsequently had a small army of devoted followers who seemed to spend half their lives writing letters to him, most of which he'd happily respond to. I suppose it gave him something to focus his mind on.'

'So...I don't need to worry that he's escaped in order to head over here to ask for your hand in marriage?'

'Actually, now that I think about it, that was probably the reason why he did. He must have read about us buying a house together.'

Tanner stared over at her, his face taut with anxiety. 'But – it wasn't in the news.'

'I'm joking!' Christine stated, rolling her eyes. 'I doubt he's given me so much as a second thought – not since I left, at least.'

'Well, that's something, I suppose,' Tanner replied, just as his phone stopped ringing. 'Oh dear, what a shame. Looks like I missed the call.'

'I don't think you did,' Christine continued, turning her head towards the bedroom from where the muffled sound of Tanner's phone could be heard ringing once again.

- CHAPTER SIX -

WITH THE BROADS devoid of its normal hordes of summer tourists, and most of the residential population still tucked-up in bed, Tanner enjoyed a pleasant drive through the Norfolk countryside, arriving at Wroxham Police Station a little after ten.

Indicating to pull into the surprisingly full carpark, he was forced to wait at the entrance due to there being a bright orange Volkswagen Golf blocking the way ahead.

After waiting patiently for the car to do something other than remain stationary, he eventually lost his patience to lean briefly down on his horn. As the passenger door swung open, he watched a pair of shapely woman's legs swing out to stand slowly up. The moment he realised it was none other than DCI Forrester's attractive young niece, Detective Constable Sally Beech, he offered her an embarrassed wave as she smoothed down her virtually non-existent miniskirt to send him over a guilty smile. He was then forced to wait once again as she leaned her head back inside the car before finally standing up to nudge the door closed.

Backing up his XJS to allow the orange Golf to reverse around before driving slowly past, Tanner nodded over at the good-looking young man he could see behind the wheel, unable to help feel just a little bit envious. But the man he was looking at was either deliberately ignoring him, or was more likely too busy making sure he didn't scrape Tanner's car as he steered his way carefully out.

When he was finally able to drive in, Tanner parked in one of the few remaining spaces before stepping out to see Sally, standing on the pavement beside the station's entrance, waving at the other car as it sped quickly away.

'Boyfriend of yours?' he enquired, heading over towards her.

'Fiancé,' Sally replied, her translucent blue eyes still following the car down the road. 'But don't tell my uncle. He only proposed last night. I haven't even told my parents yet.'

'Oh, right. To be honest, I didn't even know you were in a relationship.'

Sally caught his eye with a guilty shrug before dropping them to the ground. 'I must admit, it's all happened rather quickly. I only met him last week.'

Tanner opened his mouth in surprise. About to offer her what he knew would be unwelcome words of wisdom, he forced himself to close it again. She wasn't his niece. She certainly wasn't his daughter. With a fairly good idea as to what her parents would have to say about it, no doubt Forrester as well, Tanner thought he may as well say something positive. 'Then it must be love!' he exclaimed, with a congratulatory grin.

Sally slowly raised her eyes to rest them gently on his. 'You don't think it's a little too soon?'

Tanner shrugged. 'A little, perhaps, but if you know, you know. Isn't that what they say?'

'And I *think* I know – but...'

'But you're not sure,' said Tanner, finishing the sentence for her. 'To be honest, I don't think you ever do. You just have to go with how you feel at the time. Saying that, I think most people give it a little longer than a week to decide. I assume there's no immediate rush?' he asked, finding himself glancing indiscreetly down.

'Nothing like that!' she exclaimed, her face blushing slightly as she pulled her coat around her slim narrow waist.

'Then if I were you, I'd give it some time. If you feel the same way about him in – say – six months, then why not?'

Sally pulled in a breath to stand up straight, as if an unseen weight had slipped silently from her shoulders. 'Thanks John, I mean, *sir*,' she corrected, smiling up at him. 'I think that was exactly what I needed to hear.'

'Anytime,' Tanner replied, stepping past her to heave open the door. 'Shall we go in?' he asked, holding it open for her. 'I understand our help is needed to track down a psychotic lunatic.'

'You mean *another* psychotic lunatic,' Sally replied, shaking her head as she made her way inside.

'I was thinking something very similar myself,' Tanner muttered, offering the back of her head an unseen wry smile as the door swung gently closed behind him.

- CHAPTER SEVEN -

HEADING STRAIGHT INTO Forrester's office as instructed, Tanner rapped his knuckles on the half-open door to find him standing in silence beside his desk, his phone's receiver pressed firmly against his ear.

Catching his eye for the briefest of moments, Tanner stepped inside to close the door quietly behind him.

'Yes, sir,' he eventually heard his DCI mutter, his mouth barely moving. 'I'll call you back the moment we have some news.'

Tanner waited for him to replace the receiver before approaching his desk. 'I take it that was Superintendent Whitaker?'

Forrester gave his head an uncertain nod. 'He seems to be under the impression that we've been dragging our heels on helping to track down this Jason Baines character.'

'That's a bit harsh!' Tanner exclaimed, tugging back the sleeve of his coat to stare down at his watch. 'We were only asked to join in the search about an hour ago.'

'A little, perhaps, but I suppose you can't blame him. He was the one who put Baines away.'

'Oh, right. I didn't know.'

'It was back when he was a DI,' Forrester continued, sinking down into his chair. 'With the fuss he's starting to make, I can only assume the guy must still be considered to be a particularly dangerous individual.'

'Something Christine would appear to be in agreement with.'

Forrester tilted his head. 'She knows him as well?'

'From her days spent working as a clinical psychologist. He was one of her patients. She was telling me about him whilst compiling a rather complicated multiple-choice questionnaire as to what I either did or didn't want to eat for breakfast.'

Forrester smiled over at him. 'I take it she's still obsessed with cooking?'

'Uh-huh,' Tanner replied, a forlorn expression rippling over his forehead.

'Is she still trying to get onto Bake Off?'

Tanner responded with an enervated nod. 'She applied again in December, but has yet to hear back. Between you and me, I'm really hoping she *doesn't* get on. She spends quite enough time in the kitchen as it is. I can't imagine what it would be like if she was accepted.'

'Well, you never know, it might help to get it out of her system.'

'I think it would be more likely to make it ten times worse.'

'Honestly, Tanner, I've got no idea what you've got to complain about. My wife hates cooking. She keeps telling me that if I want something other than Sainsbury's ready meals then I should make it myself. And there's you living with a part-time Cordon Bleu chef, ready to make you the sort of food you can only get in a Michelin starred restaurant, without even having to pay for it!'

Tanner gave his shoulders an apathetic shrug. 'I suppose. Anyway, what's the plan for tracking down this Jason Baines character?'

'Apart from going door-to-door with the one and only photograph we've been given,' Forrester began, sliding the mugshot Tanner had already seen on the BBC website towards him, 'I'm not sure what else we *can* do.'

Tanner turned it around to face him. 'I don't think that's going to help much. According to Christine, this was taken when he was first arrested. She said he looks nothing like that now. It would probably be more useful to start by attempting to get hold of a more recent picture.'

A knock at the door had them both looking up to find Townsend's face peering at them from behind it.

'Sorry to bother you,' he began, his eyes diving erratically between them. 'I just thought you should know that the interim forensics report has come in for last night's shooting.'

'Christ, I'd almost forgotten about that,' muttered Forrester, leaning forward over his desk. 'Anything of interest?'

'They've had a DNA match for the blood found at the scene. According to them, it belongs to the man we're supposed to be out looking for.'

'Who – Jason Baines?'

'The very same.'

Beaming a wide grin over at Tanner, Forrester clapped his hands together. 'Well, it looks like we're in luck, for a change. I'd better give Whitaker a call to let him know that one of our local residents had the good sense to shoot the man at point-blank range with a shotgun.'

Seeing him reach for the phone, Tanner cleared his throat. 'I'm sorry, sir, but before you do that, I'd probably better update you as to what was found at the scene.'

With one hand already holding the receiver against his ear, Forrester gave Tanner a look of wary suspicion. 'The body of Jason Baines, or did I miss something?'

'I think it was the estate's somewhat trigger-happy owner who missed something.'

'I don't have time for cryptic one-liners, Tanner.'

'Sorry, sir. Despite the property's owner admitting to having shot the intruder at point-blank range with an unregistered shotgun, I'm afraid it looked as if he only dealt the man a glancing blow.'

'I take it that means you didn't find a body?'

'Unfortunately, we didn't, at least not yet.'

Forrester slammed down the phone. 'For fuck's sake, Tanner! Why didn't you tell me that last night?'

'I'm sorry, sir, but news of what turned out to be nothing more nefarious than an injured intruder hardly seemed worthy of your time.'

'Then I suppose you'd better tell me what you did find?'

'Just a trail of blood, leading out the same way he'd come in.'

'Have you checked the hospitals?'

'Er...' Tanner began, wondering why neither himself nor anyone else had thought to do that, 'not yet, sir, no.'

Seeing the way Forrester was glaring at him, Tanner transferred his gaze over to Townsend.

'I can start ringing them all up now; if you like?' the young DC offered, coming gallantly to Tanner's rescue.

Muttering obscenities to himself, Forrester pushed himself up from his chair to make his way over to where a large map of the Norfolk Broads was fixed to the wall. 'There's probably not much point. He'd have to be bloody stupid to check himself into one. Where is Long Gore Hall, anyway?'

Tanner pushed his chair back to join him. 'It's – here, sir,' he said, lifting his hand to place a finger on the map, 'just about halfway between Hickling Broad and the coast.'

'And the nearest hospital?'

They both took a moment to study the map.

'It must be the one down the road,' Tanner eventually replied. 'Wroxham Medical Centre.'

'OK, well it seems unlikely he'd have been able to make it all the way there, not if he's nursing a shotgun wound.'

'He might have if he'd been able to flag down a car,' they heard Townsend propose behind them.

Forrester leaned his head in towards the map to begin studying it in more detail. 'It doesn't even look as if there are any roads around there he'd have been able to find one on.' Digging his hands into his pockets he took a half-step back. 'No, I think it's far more likely that he's either hiding out in the marsh somewhere or holed-up inside someone's house.'

'That's if he's still alive,' chipped in Tanner. 'Dr Johnstone estimated that there were about two pints of blood at the scene, so he may well have bled-out in a ditch somewhere.'

'Unfortunately, I don't think we can take the chance that he has. It's one thing having the possibility of some random intruder roaming about the Broads with a shotgun injury, but quite another when he's a psychopathic murderer who's already been convicted of killing his parents with an axe.'

Tanner turned to briefly glance over at Townsend before returning his attention back to his DCI. 'What do you want us to do?'

Forrester took another moment to cast his eyes over the map before spinning back to his desk. 'I think we'd better start by organising a press conference. We need to get the word out that Jason Baines is likely to be still on the loose, somewhere within the north-eastern region of the Broads. The fact that he's injured could quite possibly make him even more dangerous. Then we need to identify every house within walking distance of Long Gore Hall before driving around to each, asking if anyone's seen him whilst making sure he's not taking shelter inside any of their sheds or garages. However, before we do any of that, we're going to need a more up-to-date photograph.'

'I can drive up to Bradfield Hospital to see if they've got one on their system?' Tanner offered. 'It might also be useful to speak to some of the staff who were looking after him. According to Christine, Baines had quite a fan club. It's very possible that one of them lives nearby and that's who he's staying with.'

'OK, makes sense. Take Townsend with you, and make sure to call the minute you have some news.'

With an obedient nod, Tanner pushed himself up from his chair.

'And on your way out,' Forrester continued, 'if you can tell everyone else to start identifying every property within staggering distance of Long Gore Hall, I'll see if I can have a press conference set up for when you get back.'

Tanner turned down the edges of his mouth to give Forrester a grudging frown. 'By that I assume you want me to hold it?'

'Of course,' Forrester smirked, 'but only because I know how much you enjoy them.'

- CHAPTER EIGHT -

WITH TOWNSEND IN tow, after a short half-hour drive, Tanner pulled his car up outside Bradfield Hospital to find himself staring through the windscreen at a red and white barrier blocking the way ahead. After being forced to endure a series of security checks, they were eventually shown inside the main building where a stern straight-faced female receptionist ordered them to wait.

Within a few short minutes came the commanding voice of a tall wiry man, staring down at them through a pair of thin wire-framed glasses. 'I understand you're from the police?'

'Detective Inspector Tanner and Detective Constable Townsend,' Tanner replied, pushing themselves up from the chairs they'd barely made themselves comfortable on to begin digging out their formal IDs.

With his hands buried inside the pockets of a pristine white lab coat, the man stooped forward to study each one in turn before straightening himself up. 'I'm the Clinical Services Director,' he eventually announced, elevating his chin, 'Dr Michael Copeland. I assume you're here with news of our missing patient?'

Tanner cast his eyes around at the people occupying the chairs surrounding them. 'I don't suppose there's somewhere more private we can talk?'

'Sorry, yes, of course. Please, step this way.'

Following him down a peaceful carpeted corridor, they were soon ushered into a spacious office furnished with an opulent wooden desk to the side of a modern suite of brown leather sofas.

'Can I get you a coffee?' Copeland asked, offering them the two chairs placed at right angles to the desk.

Despite the enticing aroma filling the room, Tanner shook his head. 'Thank you, but we'd better push on.'

'I take it Jason hasn't been found?' Copeland began, as the three men eased themselves down into their respective chairs.

'Not yet, I'm afraid, but we believe we know his location, approximately, at least. He was caught breaking into Long Gore Hall yesterday evening, a somewhat neglected stately home just north of Hickling Broad. The owner said he came at him with a knife.'

'And he survived?' came Copeland's curious response.

'Fortunately, he had a shotgun with him at the time.'

Copeland's eyes briefly flickered between the two police officers. 'Sorry, but – are you telling me Jason is dead?'

'We believe he was only injured, managing to make his way out the way he'd come in. Whether he's since died of his wounds we don't, as yet, know. Until we do, we're proceeding on the basis that he's alive and well. We're subsequently organising a press conference to be held this afternoon whilst conducting door-to-door inquiries, asking if anyone's seen him.'

'Well, I'm glad to hear that you're taking the matter seriously. I assume you're here to ask for my help in some way?'

Tanner crossed one leg over the other. 'Firstly, we were wondering if you had a more recent photograph? We've been told that the one we've been issued with was taken when he was arrested, and that he's changed quite a bit since then.'

Copeland's attention drifted momentarily away. 'I suppose he has. He was only sixteen when he was brought in. Whether or not we have a more up-to-date one, I must admit, I don't know. It isn't customary for us to keep photographic records of our patients, but I'd be happy to ask.'

'We were also wondering if you'd have any idea as to where he might go – if he has either friends or family in the area?'

Copeland settled back into his chair to cast a cool pair of eyes over at Tanner. 'I assume you know what he did to his parents?'

'I was thinking more along the lines of cousins, uncles or aunts?'

'None that we've ever been made aware of.'

'Then how about admirers? We've been advised that there may have been quite a few.'

'Your source is correct again,' Copeland replied, resting his elbows on the arms of his black leather chair to steeple his fingers together. 'Jason has always attracted his fair share. More so when he was first admitted, after he'd been featured so heavily in the news. Whether or not they live locally, again I'd have to ask.'

'But you would know who they are?'

'We keep detailed records of everyone our patients are known to be interacting with, whether it's by letter, phone or through personal visits.'

'Has he had any visitors recently?'

'Not that I'm aware of, but again I'd have to check.'

'What about phone conversations? Are they monitored?'

'We have the ability to both listen to and record *any* conversation,' Copeland replied, spreading out his hands to reveal an overbearing grin. 'Whether or not we do will depend on who they're talking to. Calls to solicitors, for example, are never monitored.'

'How about mobiles?'

'For reasons which I'm sure you can appreciate, access to mobile phones are strictly prohibited.'

'But they do manage to find their way inside?'

'As I'm sure is the case with any secure institution, it has proven to be remarkably difficult to keep them out altogether. If it's not friends and family throwing them over the fence, it's members of staff found taking bribes to smuggle them in. Saying that, we do seem to have found a solution. We had a signal jamming device installed last year, which seems to be working.'

'And email?'

'Very few of our patients are allowed access to the internet.'

'Was Mr Baines one of them?'

Copeland paused for a moment. 'I believe he was recently granted access, but only to view certain websites. Certainly nothing that would allow him to communicate with the outside world.'

'Do you think you'd be able to provide us with a list of everyone he's been in contact with during the last six months?'

'From our phone records and the letters we know he's received,' he nodded. 'Also from conversations he's had with visitors in person. The one thing we're unable to monitor are conversations patients have with employees.'

'Is that a problem?'

'Normally it isn't, but Jason isn't a normal patient.'

Tanner exchanged a curious expression with Townsend before returning his attention back to the clinical services director. 'Are you telling us that he's had sexual relations with members of your staff?'

Copeland stared down at his hands, now clenched firmly together on top of his desk. 'As I mentioned before, Inspector, Jason has always been a bit of a charmer, which has led certain members of staff to believe that he had feelings for them. Of course, nothing could be further from the truth. One of the most dangerous aspects of a psychopath's behaviour is their inability to feel either empathy or guilt, leaving them happy to manipulate people to acquire whatever it is that they need at the time, in this particular instance, sex. The result of which is for us to spend a small fortune finding a suitable replacement.'

'You mean you fire them?'

'We don't have much choice. We can't have employees going about having sex with our patients. Apart from it being highly unethical, it can also be extremely dangerous.'

Tanner thought for a moment before opening his mouth. 'Has anything like that happened recently?'

'The last time was about five years ago, which is why I think it's unlikely to have been how Jason managed to escape.'

'So how did he?'

'One of our security guards made the mistake of allowing himself to become a little too friendly with him.'

'Is he alright?'

'A slight head injury, nothing more. As to whether

or not he'll remain in our service is another matter, but we won't know that until we've concluded our inquiry.'

'May I ask what you've found so far?'

'He managed to lure the guard in question into his room, apparently to look at something on his computer. He then knocked him unconscious, took his uniform and using an ID he'd somehow managed to forge, waltzed straight out the main gates, apparently without anyone raising so much as an eyebrow.'

- CHAPTER NINE -

ASKED TO WAIT back in reception whilst Dr Copeland made inquiries into the requested information, Tanner sank slowly back into the same chair he'd been sitting in before.

'Did any of that surprise you?' he heard Townsend quietly ask, re-taking the seat beside him.

'What, that their patients' hobbies seemed to include browsing the internet, chatting to friends on their mobile phones, and having sex with the hospital staff?'

'All of the above?'

Tanner sat back in the chair to fold his arms. 'Not really. I knew about the mobile phone problem. I was a little surprised that they allowed patients to access the internet. I know he said that they're only allowed to look at certain websites, but I'd be surprised if a high-functioning psychopath like our Mr Baines wasn't able to find a way around that.'

'What about them being able to have physical relations with members of staff?' Townsend asked, keeping his voice discreetly low.

'You mean SEX?' Tanner replied, deliberately raising his own.

As everyone in reception turned to stare at them, Townsend's youthful complexion turned an unsubtle shade of pink. Even the receptionist was scowling over at them.

'Thanks for that,' he muttered, his chin jammed into his chest.

Tanner began glancing innocently about the room whilst doing his best to keep a straight face. 'Sorry, did I say something I shouldn't have?'

Townsend slowly raised his eyes to make sure nobody was still looking at them before daring to continue. 'I suppose I just wasn't expecting it to have even been possible. I assumed that with this being a hospital for deranged lunatics, all the patients would be locked behind toughened glass.'

'I think it's more like your average prison, in that the inmates are only kept inside their rooms at night. The rest of the time they're probably allowed to wander about with relative freedom.'

'Is that really a good idea?'

'It probably depends on the individual.'

Noticing the receptionist was marching over towards them wearing a particularly stern expression, Tanner jammed his elbow into Townsend's arm to gesture over at her. 'Oh-oh,' he whispered, leaning his head in towards him. 'Looks like you're about to be asked to leave.'

The young detective constable looked up with a start, his face glowing once again. 'Why me?'

'Probably because you said the S. E. X. word out loud in the middle of a psychiatric hospital.'

'But – that was you!'

'Er...I don't think it was. Anyway, you're the one she's staring at.'

'Inspector Tanner?' they heard the woman enquire, coming to a halt directly in front of them.

'It wasn't me!' Tanner proclaimed, endeavouring to hide a devilish smirk. 'I don't even know what the word means!'

'I beg your pardon?'

'Oh, er, sorry. What was the question again?'

The receptionist scowled at him for a moment longer before handing him a slim plastic file. 'Dr Copeland asked me to give you this.'

'Right, of course,' Tanner replied, climbing to his feet to begin leafing through its contents. Unable to see any photographs, he scooped out a slim USB stick wedged into a corner. 'Is there a more recent photograph on this?' he enquired, holding it up.

'I believe you've already been told that we don't keep photographic records of our patients.'

'So, what's on here then?'

'Recordings of all the conversations he's had, either in person or over the phone since last September.'

'How about video footage?'

The woman hesitated. 'We *might* be able to provide you with something from our security cameras, but only with Dr Copeland's permission.'

'Then would you mind asking him for me?'

'Not immediately, I can't. He's in a meeting.'

Tanner let out an impatient sigh. 'I don't suppose you know how long he'll be?'

'I have no idea.'

'Then perhaps he can give me a call the moment he becomes available? If you're seriously expecting us to find this missing patient of yours, then we're going to need at least *some* idea as to what he looks like.'

- CHAPTER TEN -

ARRIVING BACK AT the station to find numerous TV camera crews busy setting up a complex array of film and recording equipment in the main carpark, Tanner left his car in one of the bays at the back of the building to make his way inside.

With Townsend left to fetch him a coffee, Tanner hurried over to Vicky's desk. 'I don't suppose there's any chance Jason Baines has been found lying dead in a ditch somewhere?'

'Not yet,' she replied, glancing up from her monitor. 'How did you get on at the hospital?'

'The one thing we needed was the one thing they didn't have.'

'So, no photograph then?'

Tanner shook his head. 'I asked if they had any video footage, thinking that we'd be able to print a frame off from that,' he continued, digging out his phone to stare down at the screen. 'It doesn't look like they've come back to me on that either.' Tucking his phone away he handed her the file he'd been given. 'They were at least able to provide us with a fairly comprehensive list of people he's been in contact with over the last six months. There's a USB memory stick in there as well, which should have recordings of all the conversations he's had.'

'Are they allowed to do that – record your

conversations?'

'Generally speaking, I think one waives one's rights to privacy when one decides to chop up one's parents with an axe.'

'Fair enough,' Vicky replied, casting her eyes down a long list of names. 'Has he really been in contact with this many people?'

'So it would seem. Apparently, he's a bit of a socialite. Anyway, I suggest we ask Sally to go through them to see if any of them live in the local area. It might be useful if she could start listening to the audio files as well. How's your list of residential homes coming along?'

Vicky closed the file to look up at her monitor. 'There are only fourteen houses in and around the Long Gore Marsh area, all of which are fairly isolated. We were just waiting for a photograph before driving over to visit them.'

'OK, I'll chase up the hospital, but I don't think you should wait. I'm fairly sure the local residents would know if they'd seen someone staggering about the place with blood seeping out from a hole in their torso.'

Vicky fetched up the file to climb to her feet. 'I'll give this to Sally. Are you ready for your press conference?'

Tanner glanced over his shoulder to see Forrester straighten his tie as he emerged out from his office. 'Not really,' he replied, 'but it looks like Forrester is.'

'All set?' the DCI boomed, marching his way over.

Tanner turned to face him with a particularly glum expression. 'Of course. I simply can't wait.'

'Cheer-up! You'll enjoy it once it starts.'

'I'll enjoy it more when it ends,' he muttered quietly to himself.

'How did you get on at the hospital?'

'We have a list of people he's been in communication with, together with recordings of all the conversations he's had over the last six months, but no photograph, I'm afraid.'

Forrester's cheerful expression evaporated to be replaced by his more normal indignant glare. 'You mean to say that we don't have a single thing to hand to the hordes of awaiting press?'

'Not in the form of a photograph, at least not of Jason Baines, but we've probably got some biscuits knocking about the place.'

'I'm not in the mood for your irreverent sarcasm, Tanner.'

'Neither am I, sir.'

Forrester took a moment to narrow his eyes at him. 'You could have at least told me before you left the hospital. You do realise that the press conference is about to start?'

'I was hoping they'd be able to send over some footage from a security camera, thinking that we could extract an image from that.'

'And have they?'

'Not the last time I looked.'

'And when was that?'

'About thirty seconds ago. I can chase them up if you like?'

Forrester lifted his arm to stare down at his watch. 'It's too late. We'll just have to make do with what we have.'

- CHAPTER ELEVEN -

'THAT WOULD HAVE gone a lot better had we been able to provide them with a more up-to-date photograph,' Forrester moaned, as he spun indignantly around on his heel to head back inside the station, leaving the assembled press-pack demanding to know when they were going to catch the notorious Jason Baines, and just exactly how the local population were supposed to keep their eyes open for an axe-wielding psychopathic murderer if nobody knew what he looked like.

'I've got no idea why they're blaming us,' responded Tanner, catching up to him as they made their way towards the main office. 'We did our job when we put him away.'

'That was you personally, was it?'

'Obviously not,' Tanner replied, clawing out his phone, 'but it's hardly our fault that he's managed to escape from the institution we had him safely locked up inside.'

'That's all well and good, Tanner, but that's not what Superintendent Whitaker is going to think, certainly not after he's watched that debacle on the six o'clock evening news.'

Entering the main office, Tanner stopped in the middle of the thoroughfare to stare down at his phone. 'Hold on, sir, the hospital has sent us an email. Looks like they've managed to find some video footage we can use.'

'That's just great. What are we supposed to do now, hold another press conference?'

'Not unless you want to?'

'Of course I don't bloody want to!'

Opening the attachment, Tanner began playing a grainy security camera video featuring a man being frog-marched underneath it, his shoulders hunched forward with his head facing the floor.

Forrester tilted the phone in Tanner's hand to stare down at the screen. 'Is that it?' he demanded, the moment it finished.

'Looks like it.'

'Well, that *was* worth waiting for.'

'He does look up at one point,' Tanner added, dragging it back to the beginning. 'If we freeze the frame when he does, we might be able to enhance the image, enough at least to send something off to the press.'

Forrester let out a world-weary sigh. 'Well, I suppose it's better than nothing.'

Hearing the sound of a woman clearing her throat beside them, they turned to find Forrester's niece, Sally Beech.

'Sorry to bother you,' she began, her mascara lined eyes focussed on Tanner's, 'but a call's come in about Jason Baines.'

'That must be some sort of a record,' Tanner replied, looking down at his watch. 'It normally takes unemployed time-wasters at least ten minutes before they start picking up the phones.'

'I think it's genuine,' Sally continued, glancing at her uncle before turning her attention back to Tanner. 'The caller says he saw him when he was shot inside the kitchen at Long Gore Hall.'

'Right, yes, of course. I suppose he was hiding

inside the fridge at the time?'

'He said he saw it happen through the window. More than that, he says he knows where he went afterwards.'

Forrester's eyes began boring down into Tanner's. 'Well? Aren't you going to take it?'

'I thought you wanted me to do something with this video?'

'I'd rather you spoke to someone who might actually know where he is?'

'Yes, sir, of course, but it's only going to be some pot-head with nothing better to do than to see just exactly how much of our time he can waste.'

'And you know that for a fact, do you?'

'Well, no sir, but...'

'Then may I suggest you take the call? Sally here can do something with that video, for all the good it will do.'

- CHAPTER TWELVE -

WATCHING HIM STOMP back to his office, Tanner turned to find Sally had been following his gaze.

'He's a bit grumpy today,' she commented, a quizzical frown knitting her otherwise unwrinkled forehead.

'Really? I hadn't noticed.'

'It's probably because its Sunday. I know he doesn't like working weekends.' She looked up at him with her customary flirtatious smile. 'Anyway, where do you want it?'

Tanner blinked to stare over at her. 'I'm sorry?'

'The call, silly.'

'Oh that!' he exclaimed, his shoulders dropping in relief.

'I have him on hold on my desk's phone, but I can transfer him over to yours if you prefer.'

'No, that's fine. I'll take him on yours. I doubt it will take long.'

Following her over, he perched himself on the edge of her desk to be handed the receiver.

'Detective Inspector Tanner speaking,' he began, his eyes drifting absently around the office. 'I understand you have news regarding Jason Baines?'

'I saw 'im,' came a slurred muffled voice from the other end.

Tanner covered the mouthpiece to catch Sally's

eye. 'The guy's drunk,' he whispered, rolling his eyes. 'Sorry, sir,' he eventually continued, 'you saw who?'

'The man you's look'n for. I saw 'im get shot by this other guy.'

'And where were you when this happened?'

'Right outside the kitch'n winda.'

'The one at Long Gore Hall?'

'That's right.'

'I see. I don't suppose you'd mind telling me what you were doing standing outside Long Gore Hall's kitchen window?'

'Don't ya want to know what 'appened after?'

'At this moment in time I think I'm more interested to find out what you were doing lurking about outside someone's private residence?'

'I saw him get up, as if nuff'n had happened,' the man continued.

'You mean, as if he hadn't been shot?'

'That's right. But it weren't like you said on the news. He never climbed out the same way he came in. He did come back to the winda, but then he turned back to follow the guy who shot 'im.'

'You're telling me he's still in the house?'

'All I'm say'n is that I didn't see 'im leave, and he ain't hurt, like you said. I saw 'im shot, square in the chest, but 'e weren't injured, like, at least 'e didn't look like 'e was.'

'OK, well, thanks for your call.'

A brief moment of silence followed before the man's voice came back over the line. 'Is that it?'

'For now, thank you.'

'But – you 'aven't even asked for me name?'

'That's OK. We have your number.'

'Oh, right.'

About to end the call, Tanner heard the man's voice again.

'There was somethin' else as well.'

Tanner glanced impatiently down at his watch. 'OK, go on.'

'When 'e took the knife out of the drawer, the one 'e used to attack the man with the shotgun – it's gonna sound funny, but 'e looked right at me.'

Tanner rose slowly to his feet. 'Sorry, what did you say?'

'The man inside the kitchen. He looked at me, and then – and then he winked, as if he already knew I was there.'

'No, before that. You said you saw him take a knife out of the drawer before attacking the man with the shotgun.'

'That's right. It was a big'un as well. Some sort of huntin' knife.'

Tanner began scrabbling around Sally's desk for a pen and something to write on. 'May I take your name please, sir?'

'It's Gibbs. Norman Gibbs.'

'And where are you calling from, Mr Gibbs?'

There was another pause from the other end of the line. 'What d'ya want to know that for?'

'If it's OK by you, would it be possible to stop by Wroxham Police Station at some point?'

'But – I ain't done nuff'in wrong.'

'It would only be for you to provide us with a statement.'

'I fought I just did.'

'Over the phone, yes, but we'll need something in writing for it to be official.'

'Wat do I care if it's official or not? I've told ya wat I know.'

'If the man you said you saw dies from his injuries, you're the only person who'll be able to tell us what actually happened, that he attacked the estate's owner with a knife.'

'I just told ya that the man weren't injured.'

'But if he was, and he dies, unless you can officially tell us what you saw, then the guy who shot him could be in a lot of trouble.'

Tanner waited in silence for a response, but the only thing he could hear was a car driving slowly past. 'Mr Gibbs, are you still there?'

More silence followed before the line went suddenly dead.

'He hung up!' Tanner exclaimed, staring at the end of the phone.

'What did he say?'

'That he saw Jason Baines rising from the grave to begin wandering the corridors of Long Gore Hall. At least something like that.'

'You still think it was a crank call?'

Tanner shook his head. 'He said he saw Baines take a knife out of a drawer before using it to attack the estate's owner.'

'And that means he was telling the truth?'

'We didn't mention anything about a knife to the press, or that a drawer had been left open. The only way he'd have known was if he saw it first-hand.'

Tanner replaced the receiver to grab the piece of paper he'd scrawled the man's name on. 'I don't suppose you know if anyone's spoken to Mr Hambleton today?'

'He called in this morning, asking if he could start using his kitchen again.'

'Well, at least we know that our escaped psychotic lunatic didn't creep into his bedroom last night to stab him to death. Do me a favour, will you?' he continued, handing her the scrap of paper. 'Can you see if you can find an address for our caller, and where he phoned us from? I think it might have been a public phone box, somewhere out in the sticks.'

'What makes you say that?'

'I heard a car drive past, but only one. Anyway, let me know the minute you have? I'll be in with your uncle.'

- CHAPTER THIRTEEN -

TANNER RAPPED HIS knuckles on Forrester's door to nudge it slowly open.

'Sorry to bother you, sir, but it looks like we have a witness for the shooting at Long Gore Hall.'

Forrester looked up at him with a curious expression. 'Was that the call Sally took?'

'It was, sir, yes,' Tanner replied, knowing what was coming next.

'Then it was a good job I told you to take it, wasn't it?'

'Absolutely, sir,' Tanner forced himself to say.

'Well?'

'Well – er – what, sir?' Tanner asked, for a moment wondering if he was seriously expected to say thank you.

Forrester let out an exasperated sigh. 'What did the caller say?'

'Oh, right. That he saw Baines attack Hambleton with a knife, just before Hambleton shot him.'

'And where did he say he went afterwards. That *was* the reason why you took the call, wasn't it?'

'He said he didn't leave.'

'What do you mean, he didn't leave?'

'After he was shot, he said Baines stood up, apparently uninjured, to follow Mr Hambleton inside the house.'

Forrester took a moment to study Tanner's face. 'I

thought you said it wasn't a crank call?'

'I'm fairly sure it was genuine. He knew about the knife, and that Baines took it from one of the kitchen drawers before attacking him, neither of which we told the press about.'

'But – he couldn't have simply stood up after being shot at point-blank range by a shotgun. What about all the blood?'

'I was going to ask him about that when he came in to give us a formal statement, but he refused to do so before hanging up. I've asked Sally to track down his address and where he called from. As soon as she has, I'd like to head out to see if I can find him.'

'Wouldn't it be a better use of your time to see if Baines *is* at Long Gore Hall, like the witness said?'

'I suppose that depends on how reliable he turns out to be. His speech was a little slurred, and I'm fairly sure he was calling from a public phone box. I was also curious to know what he was doing staring through someone's kitchen window on a Saturday evening. That, together with his rather unlikely description of what he saw take place...'

'If you're telling me he's some sort of homeless drunk, then why the hell are we even having this conversation?'

'Because, sir, if Baines dies from his wounds without a witness to say that the estate's owner had been forced to shoot him out of self-defence, then Hambleton is likely to spend the next ten years locked up for manslaughter, which I personally think would be a little unfair, given the circumstances. Besides, if Baines was wandering about inside Long Gore Hall, bleeding all over the place, I'd have thought Hambleton would have noticed him by now.'

'Unless Baines murdered him in his sleep, of course.'

'Sally said he phoned in this morning, asking if he could start using his kitchen again.'

Their conversation was interrupted by the very person they'd only just been talking about, her head emerging through the door with an apologetic frown.

'I've managed to locate where the witness called from,' she began, the bulk of her attention focussed on Tanner. 'It's a public phone box outside the Royal Oak, a small pub on the outskirts of Hickling.'

Tanner instinctively turned to stare at the map on the wall behind him. 'That's just down the road from Long Gore Hall.'

'I pulled up his file as well.'

'Whose file?' Tanner queried, turning back.

'The man who called. Norman Gibbs. He was convicted of drink driving about five years ago. His last known address was in Norwich, but that was before his conviction.'

Forrester caught Tanner's eye to glare over at him. 'So, the guy *is* a homeless drunk.'

'Maybe so,' Tanner continued, 'but we still need his statement. I can stop by Long Gore Hall after I've spoken to him if you like, just in case Hambleton has seen him?'

Forrester leaned back in his chair with an uncertain frown. 'OK,' he eventually replied, 'but I don't want you spending hours looking for this Norman Gibbs character in the vague hope that he's going to be a reliable enough witness to help Hambleton worm his way out of a manslaughter charge. Finding Baines has to be our number one priority!'

- CHAPTER FOURTEEN -

TANNER SAW THE person he was out searching for even before he'd found the phone box. The man was shuffling his way along the pavement towards Hickling village with what looked to be the entirety of his earthly possessions stuffed inside a giant plastic shopping bag.

Pulling up on the other side of the otherwise empty road, Tanner grabbed the notepad he'd brought with him to step quickly out.

'Mr Gibbs?' he called, crossing the road to dig out his ID. 'Detective Inspector Tanner. We spoke on the phone.'

'I didn't do nuff'n!' the man shouted over his shoulder, continuing to weave his way along the pavement.

'I'm not saying you did,' Tanner replied, forced into a run to catch up.

Stopping where he was, Gibbs swivelled himself around to stare back at Tanner, his eyes as red as his dirt-streaked face. 'Then what d'ya want?'

'I just need a statement from you,' Tanner continued, coming to a breathless halt. 'Then you can be on your way.'

'I told you wat I saw on the phone.'

Tanner put his ID away to show him the notepad, a pen tucked into its spiral binding. 'We just need something on paper with your signature on it, that's all.'

Gibbs stared down at the notepad. 'I don't see wat difference it would make.'

'It would mean a court would know someone saw what happened, and that we didn't just make the whole thing up.'

'I s'pose you want me in the dock, testifery'ing against that psycho-nutjob, the one I saw on the news.'

'Not at all, Mr Gibbs. We need a statement to help protect the man who shot him. Even if the pyscho-nutjob you're referring to is still alive, he's already been convicted. He wouldn't be at the trial. But if he dies,' Tanner continued, 'the man you saw shoot him could be charged with manslaughter.'

Gibbs lifted his eyes up to Tanner's. 'I – I don't understand?'

'You saw Jason Baines attack the home's owner with a knife. Your statement would prove that he was forced to shoot him out of self-defence.'

Gibbs shook his head to look away. 'None of that's my problem.'

'If you don't care, then why did you call?'

'Cus I thought it waz what I was supposed to do, as a public citizen. I didn't fink I'd 'ave to sign nuffin'

An idea came springing into Tanner's mind. 'If you did provide us with a formal statement, I'm sure Mr Hambleton would be very grateful. He's rich, you know.'

'How rich?' Gibbs asked with a penetrating gaze.

'He owns that big house you were at.'

'What, that pile of crap?'

'He's got cash as well,' Tanner added, without a single clue if he did. 'The guy's loaded!'

Tanner watched Gibbs eyes flicker with hesitant interest. 'OK, but I'm gonna need somethin' upfront.'

It was Tanner's turn to hesitate. 'Er...how much did you have in mind?'

'I s'pose a tenner should cover it.'

'How about five pounds now and the rest later?' he replied, digging out his wallet to remove a solitary blue note.

Gibbs gazed down at it with bulging eyes. 'Deal!' he eventually replied, his face cracking into a toothy grin. 'But I'm going to want another twenty after I've helped the guy get off.'

- CHAPTER FIFTEEN -

WITH GIBBS' SIGNED statement tucked safely inside the glovebox, Tanner continued his way on towards Long Gore Hall, arriving ten minutes later to find a dwindling band of overall-clad police forensics officers packing the last of their equipment into the back of their van.

Stepping out he called over to the nearest. 'Are you done?'

'Just about.'

Tanner took a moment to stare up at the vast pillared entrance, noting how it looked even more like a dilapidated ruin in the daylight.

With the rumbling sound of a diesel generator coming from somewhere inside the house, he caught the forensic officer's attention again. 'I don't suppose you've seen the owner around, Mr Hambleton?'

'He was in the kitchen, making himself something to eat. Not sure where he is now, though.'

Thanking him, Tanner made his way up the curved stone steps, in through the open front door to find the very person he was looking for, limping casually over the foyer dressed in what appeared to be the exact same clothes he'd been wearing the previous night.

'Mr Hambleton!' Tanner called out, raising a hand to help garner his attention.

Stopping where he was, the estate's owner turned to stare over at him with a quizzical frown.

Remembering just how dark it had been the night before, Tanner dug out his ID. 'It's Detective Inspector Tanner? We met last night?'

Hambleton brought a hand up to his forehead. 'Of course! Sorry. Forgive me. I didn't recognise you in the cold light of day; and when I say cold, I do of course mean bloody freezing.'

'At least I can hear you've managed to get the generator going.'

'Well, yes, but it doesn't make the place any warmer. I'm actually beginning to wonder if the only way to heat it up would be to set fire to it,' he added, with a self-amused smirk. 'Anyway, joking aside, I don't suppose there's been any sign of that man I was stupid enough to shoot last night?'

Tanner hesitated before answering. 'You haven't heard the news?'

'I'm not sure how I could have, being that I don't have a television, let alone internet reception.'

'We held a press conference earlier today, asking if anyone had seen him.'

'I take it that means you haven't?'

'Not yet, but a witness came forward shortly afterwards. He says he saw what happened – that the intruder came at you with a knife before you shot him.'

'Well, that's something, I suppose, although I'm not sure how he could have. I wasn't aware that there was anyone else here.'

'He said he was watching from outside your kitchen window.'

'What the hell was he doing out there?'

'Probably something similar to what your intruder was doing – looking for somewhere to crash for the night. Anyway, it at least means that we have a witness to verify what you said, that you shot the intruder in self-defence, something that could prove invaluable if he does happen to die from his injuries.'

'Then I suppose I should offer him my thanks. Does he have a name?'

'Norman Gibbs, but I shouldn't bother trying to find him in the phonebook. The last time I saw him he was weaving his way towards Hickling village with his worldly goods stuffed inside a plastic shopping bag.'

'You're telling me he's a homeless drunk?'

'So it would appear.'

'Right, I see. So, not the most reliable of witnesses then.'

'Possibly not, but I can assure you that one witness is considerably better than none at all, and it will be difficult for a prosecutor to prove that he was drunk at the time he was watching the events unfold through your kitchen window. I don't know about South Africa, but here in the UK you're innocent until proven guilty. The account from a first-hand witness should be enough to convince a jury that you acted in self-defence, whether that person is homeless or not.'

'Well, yes, I suppose.'

'We also have a name for your intruder. Jason Baines.'

Hambleton offered him a blank stare. 'Is the name supposed to mean something to me?'

'He escaped from Bradfield Hospital yesterday evening.'

'He *escaped?*'

'It's a secure psychiatric institution. Jason Baines is one of their patients. He was found guilty of killing his parents with an axe about ten years ago.'

Hambleton's eyes widened in horror. 'You mean to say that I had a psychotic axe-wielding murderer inside my house?'

'Unfortunately, it looks like you may still have.'

'I'm sorry?'

'The witness told us that he saw him push himself off the floor after you shot him to then follow you inside.'

'You mean – he's still here?' Hambleton questioned, his eyes darting into every shadowy corner. 'Jesus Christ! Couldn't you have told me that last night?'

'We only found out this afternoon, else I can assure you that we would have. Besides, we don't know for certain that he is. The forensics evidence indicates that he left the same way he came in. They also found about two pints of his blood all over your kitchen floor. If he is hiding around here somewhere I think he's far more likely to be worried about his own life than contemplating taking yours.'

'I'm not sure that makes me feel any better.'

'Anyway, I came over to ask if you've either seen or heard anything since last night to suggest that he might be here?'

'Well, no, but that's hardly the point. If there's even the vaguest possibility that he is lurking about, then I want the place searched, and I want it searched now!'

- CHAPTER SIXTEEN -

L EFT WITH LITTLE choice but to call in a police dog unit to conduct what turned out to be a fruitless search of the crumbling mansion, it wasn't until late in the evening when Tanner finally arrived home to find himself as tired as he was hungry.

Closing the front door he heard Christine's welcoming voice chime out around their modestly proportioned bungalow.

'Hello, darling. I'm in the kitchen!'

'No surprises there,' he mumbled quietly to himself, hanging up his sailing jacket to make his way inside.

Entering the open-plan living area he found Christine offering him a welcoming smile from behind the breakfast bar, her hands plunging repeatedly down into a large yellow mixing bowl.

'Are you hungry?'

'Starving! What's on the menu?'

'Risotto alla Milanese.'

'Sounds great!' he replied, rubbing his freezing cold hands together to glance over at the unlit fireplace. 'At least the first part does. Not sure about the second, but only because I've got no idea what it is.'

'It's just risotto with parmesan and saffron.'

Having previously thought saffron was something

dresses were made out of, Tanner nodded with sagacious pretence. 'Oh, right. Well, it still sounds good, *I suppose.*'

'OK, hold on. Let me finish what I'm doing and I'll get started. How was your day?'

'Long,' Tanner groaned, taking to a knee to turn the gas fire on. 'Yours?'

'I slept for most of it.'

'Lucky you. Did you see me on TV?

'I can't say I did. I assume it was about Jason?'

'Uh-huh,' Tanner replied, taking a moment to watch the flames begin licking their way around its fake coal before turning to stare about for the TV's remote. 'We found out that he was the person who broke into Long Gore Hall.'

'Isn't that that old run-down mansion, up near the coast?'

'That's the one.'

'I thought it had been abandoned years ago.'

'You really haven't been watching the news recently, have you.'

'I must admit, it's been a while. I assume someone is living there now?'

'A man called Lawrence Hambleton. He inherited it from his grandfather.'

'Lucky him!'

'I'm not so sure. Apart from how much it's going to cost him to have the place done up, he's only been there a week and he's already managed to line himself up for a possible manslaughter charge.'

'How on earth did he do that?'

'He shot the intruder at point-blank range with a shotgun.'

Christine stopped what she was doing to stare over at him. 'You mean...Jason Baines is dead?'

'At this stage we're not entirely sure. All we've

found of him so far is about two pints of his blood. Forensic evidence suggests that he left the same way he came in, through the kitchen window, heading out into the surrounding marsh, so there's every chance he's died from his injuries. But until we actually find a body, we're forced to assume he's still alive. That's what the press conference was about.'

Christine turned around to open the fridge. 'Any leads?'

'Only one so far,' Tanner continued, having found the TV's remote to collapse down into their modular sofa. 'A homeless guy by the name of Norman Gibbs *said* he saw the whole thing, but his version of events turned out to be just a little different from what we were expecting. He said Baines *didn't* leave the way he came in, but followed after Hambleton, the hall's new owner.'

With no response from Christine, he glanced around to see her standing motionless in front of the open fridge, staring at its burgeoning contents. 'Are you alright?' he eventually asked.

'We're nearly out of milk,' she suddenly stated, closing the door to return to the counter.

'Oh, right. Have we got enough for the morning.'

'What was that?' she asked, gazing over at him with a vacant expression.

'Milk?' Tanner repeated. 'Do we have enough for the morning?'

'Sorry,' she replied, shaking her head, 'just about. Don't worry, I'll get some on my way back from work. What were you saying?'

Tanner leant back against the sofa to turn the TV on. 'That this homeless guy said Jason Baines didn't leave the house, but got up to follow the new owner inside. He also said that he didn't seem to be injured, despite all the blood *and* the fact that he'd seen him being shot. When I told the estate's owner that he might have a psychotic axe-wielding murder wandering about inside his house, he freaked out.'

'I'm not surprised!'

'He wouldn't let me leave until I'd called in a dog unit to search the entire place. That's why I'm so late.'

'I take it you didn't find him?'

'Unfortunately not. After a lot of false leads the dog handlers eventually came to the same conclusion our forensics team had, that he must have wandered back out into the moors, but by that time the scent had gone, so we gave up and called it a day. Basically, it was a complete waste of time. All it proved was that our star witness was about as unreliable as he looked.'

- CHAPTER SEVENTEEN -

Monday, 7th February

T HE NEXT MORNING, Tanner awoke to find the temperature had plummeted overnight. What had up until then been a relatively mild winter had finally turned, transforming the view outside their bungalow into a magical carpet of frost, sparkling gently in the rays of a low rising sun. But what may have been beautiful to look at soon presented him with the normal practical difficulties. Firstly, his car's windows were covered in a thick layer of ice, forcing him to spend an unexpected ten minutes having to scrape it all off. He then had to drive into work along the virtually deserted country roads at what felt like a snail's pace, after having nearly come off on the very first corner due to an invisible patch of thick black ice. He subsequently reached Wroxham far later than he'd hoped, only to again be delayed by a news media van doing what ended up being a seven-point turn in the middle of the road outside the station, for no other reason than to find somewhere to park.

Finally able to steer into the station's carpark, he ditched his car between Vicky's and Cooper's to hurry inside. With coffee in hand, he'd only just plonked himself behind his desk to take a first tentative sip when a chilly breeze pricked the hairs on the back of his neck as someone tugged opened the main office doors behind him.

A moment later he caught sight of Forrester out of the corner of his eye.

'A word, if you will,' came the DCI's ominously low voice, his mouth just inches from Tanner's ear.

'*For fuck's sake*,' Tanner moaned, the moment Forrester had left to begin stomping his way over to his office. '*What have I done now?*'

Following on, he rapped lightly on the door to nudge it slowly open. 'You wanted to see me, sir?'

'Have you seen the Norfolk Herald?' Forrester barked, without any of the normal social pleasantries.

'I like to make a point of avoiding it, if at all possible,' Tanner responded, closing the door behind him.

Forrester shoved what Tanner assumed to be the latest edition over the desk. 'Well, unfortunately, I can't, not when I have Whitaker phoning me up, demanding to know which one of my staff members has been talking to the press.'

With his curiosity raised, Tanner eased himself down into a chair to swivel the newspaper around. 'Jason Baines Rises from the Dead,' he read out, laughing as he did. 'I'm sorry, sir, but I'm not sure what else you'd expect from such a ridiculous publication.'

'It's not what they've written that's the problem, it's where they got the story from.'

'No doubt from that homeless guy, Norman Gibbs.'

'If you bother to read it, you'll see that that can't be the case. They know everything: from Lawrence Hambleton not having a licence for his gun, to what Jason Baines' blood type is!'

'Well, it wasn't me.'

'I never said it was.'

'It wouldn't have been anyone from CID either,' Tanner continued. 'They all know better than to talk to the press.'

'What about that girlfriend of yours?'

'Excuse me, sir, but why do you automatically assume that I tell Christine everything that goes on here as if she's my bloody secretary, for her to then pick up the phone to the Norfolk Herald to offer them a blow-by-blow account?'

'Then who else would it have been?'

'I don't bloody know!'

A knock at the door had them both staring around to find Sally's pretty face, peering cautiously over at both of them.

'Er...sorry to bother you,' she began, her eyes resting on her uncle's, 'but there's a Dr Michael Copeland in reception, asking to speak to DI Tanner.'

'Who?'

Delighted to have found an excuse to leave, Tanner levered himself out of his chair to answer on Sally's behalf. 'He's the man in charge of the hospital Jason Baines escaped from. I'd better see what he wants. If he's come all the way over here, it must be important.'

- CHAPTER EIGHTEEN -

TANNER FOLLOWED SALLY out into reception to find Dr Copeland pacing up and down, his hands clasped firmly behind his back, but it took him a full moment to recognise him. In place of the shirt, tie, and pristine white lab coat he'd been wearing at Bradfield Hospital was a pair of jeans and a tatty crew-neck jumper, and instead of his former expression of smug superiority was a look of exhausted, angst-ridden fear.

'My son, David,' he blurted out, the moment he looked up to see Tanner. 'He didn't come home last night.'

Tanner came to a halt in front of him. 'What time was he supposed to?'

'He said around ten. He'd gone away for the weekend for a VEX Robotics competition his college was taking part in. I've been driving around all night trying to find him. I've been to see all his friends, but none of them have seen him. I – I didn't know where else to come.'

As the man's unshaven face began trembling uncontrollably, Tanner asked Sally to fetch him something hot to drink before leading him into the privacy of one of their interview rooms.

'When did you see him last?' Tanner eventually continued, closing the door to offer him a seat.

The doctor stood in the middle of the small

window-less room, staring blankly down at the chair being offered as if it wasn't there. 'Saturday morning, before he left,' he eventually began. 'We'd been arguing the night before. He'd come back stinking of cigarette smoke. I could smell it on his breath. He's only seventeen. I'd told him before about how dangerous smoking was, but he never listened. Not to me at any rate. The only person he ever did listen to was his mother.'

Tanner gently guided him down into the chair. 'May I ask where she is?'

'New York. She's an architect, working on some stupid over-sized tower block out there.'

Tanner answered a knock at the door to usher Sally quietly inside, a mug of steaming hot coffee held carefully in her hands.

'Which college does he go to?' Tanner asked, directing Sally to leave the mug on the table.

'The one in Walsham. It's only a short bus journey from where we live.'

'And where was this robotics competition?'

'Peterborough, but he sent me a text message when he arrived back.'

'Could he have stayed with friends last night to leave with them for college this morning?'

'I've already called the college. He didn't arrive for registration.'

'Is there any chance he could still be with his friends?'

'He'd have told me.'

'OK, well, could he have gone to see his mother?'

'His passport's still in the drawer beside my bed. Besides, he doesn't have enough money to buy himself a ticket. Not to fly to America.'

'Does he have any other family members he could be staying with?'

'None of them have either seen or heard from him.'

Seeing the first sign of tears begin welling up in his eyes, Tanner briefly turned to offer Sally a concerned frown. 'Try not to worry, Dr Copeland, he's most likely staying with a friend and just forgot to tell you. You know what teenagers are like!'

He watched Copeland look up to open his mouth. 'I – I think it might have been...' he began, before seemingly forcing it closed to shake his head as if either unwilling or unable to finish the sentence.

'You think it might have been who?' Tanner questioned, sinking down into the seat across the table from him.

The doctor screwed up his eyes. 'Jason,' he said, his voice barely a whisper. 'I think he might have taken him.'

Tanner gave Sally a curious look before returning his attention back to the man sitting opposite. 'I really don't think that's very likely, Dr Copeland. According to our forensics department, the man is currently staggering around Long Gore Marsh with a shotgun wound to his stomach, that's if he's alive at all. I think it's highly unlikely for him to have decided to take the opportunity to kidnap your son.'

'But the newspapers?' the doctor questioned, glancing up. 'They said something about him not being injured.'

'Assuming you're referring to the story currently running in the Norfolk Herald, I wouldn't take it too seriously if I were you. Besides, what possible reason would he have for escaping the walls of Bradfield Hospital to then kidnap your son?'

'Because he knows about him.'

'He knows about your son?'

'I was stupid enough to mention him during one of our sessions. It was a discussion about empathy. I even said where he was going to college. I think – I think he's going to use him to get back at me.'

'To get back at you for what?'

Tanner watched Copeland's knuckles whiten as he placed his hands around the coffee mug, a look of something akin to cruel obstinance dancing momentarily in his eyes. 'Treating the mentally ill isn't easy, Inspector. Matters of the mind rarely are. It's certainly nowhere near as straightforward as a normal surgical operation. It can take months, more often years of therapy, some of which can be painful in the extreme, at least from a psychological perspective. And don't forget, we're not just their therapists, we're their prison guards as well. He may never have shown it, but I knew he held a deep-seated resentment of me, one that I suspect grew to become hatred over the years, especially after he somehow found out that it was on my personal recommendation that the board declined his constant appeals for early release.'

'I still think it's unlikely he'd make a move to take your son. I'm sure he's alive and well somewhere. He might even be waiting at home for you as we speak.'

Copeland slowly shook his head. 'He's not. I asked the cleaner to wait, just in case he comes back.'

'But he could return at any minute. Tell you what, why don't you make your way home. Meanwhile, if you could let us have a photograph of him, I'll get the word out for everyone to start keeping their eyes open.'

- CHAPTER NINETEEN -

WITH SALLY SHOWING Dr Copeland out to his car, Tanner found himself once again at the door to Forrester's office.

'I'm afraid it looks like we may have another missing person on our hands,' he said, having nudged the door open to see his DCI lay the pen he'd been holding slowly down on the desk to begin aggressively rubbing his forehead. 'Dr Copeland's son, David. He didn't come back from a college trip yesterday. He thinks Jason Baines may have taken him.'

Forrester finally looked up with an irritated scowl, his skin hanging loosely from his jowls. 'Is that really very likely?'

'I must admit, at first I didn't think so, but now I'm not so sure. Copeland told him about his son during a therapy session, even mentioning where he went to college.'

'Jesus Christ! What the hell did he do that for?'

'I've got no idea, but he admits that it may have been a mistake.'

'*May* have been?'

'I'd have normally thought he'd have either run away or was staying at a friend's house, but with Baines having escaped the day before – well, it's an unsettling coincidence, put it that way.'

'Aren't you forgetting that Baines is supposedly nursing a gunshot wound?'

'Not if what Norman Gibbs said is true, and that he did follow Hambleton inside Long Gore Hall without any obvious injury.'

'Which we've already searched with a team of dogs, proving Gibbs to be about as reliable as your average politician.'

'There could still be some truth in what he said: that Baines isn't as injured as we're assuming him to be. If that is the case, then there is a chance that he's decided to take revenge on those he feels responsible for having him locked up. Dr Copeland certainly seems to be of the impression that he may be one of them.'

'I wasn't aware that he had anything to do with his conviction.'

'Maybe not, but he is responsible for him remaining inside. He just told me that it's because of his professional recommendations to the hospital's board of directors that Baines' numerous legal attempts to be granted early release have failed.'

'If that was true, then wouldn't Baines have taken him instead of his son?'

A haunting image of Tanner's daughter's body wedged itself into his mind. 'No doubt he understands that the most effective way to hurt someone is through their children.'

Forrester steepled his hands together in front of his mouth. '*If* Baines has taken Dr Copeland's son, what would you suggest we do?'

'According to him, he was at college last night. He'd been taking part in some sort of robotics competition. The teacher who took them may well have been the last person who saw him. I'd like to drive over there to have a chat.'

Forrester leant silently back in his chair with a sagacious frown.

'At the end of the day,' Tanner continued, 'if he's right, and it was his escaped patient who's taken his son, find him and we'll find Baines, leaving everyone happy, including Superintendent Whitaker.'

Hesitating for a moment longer, Forrester lurched suddenly forward. 'Very well. Have a chat with the teacher in question, maybe some of his classmates as well. Find out if any of them saw him being picked up. Meanwhile, I'll ask Sally to see if she can pull up any CCTV footage of the street immediately outside. Which college was it again?'

'The one in Walsham. It's only a half-hour drive from here, at least it will be without all the tourists.'

- CHAPTER TWENTY -

WITH A DAZZLING winter's sun helping to melt the ice from the largely deserted country roads, Tanner arrived at Walsham College far sooner than expected, only to be told that the teacher he needed to see was busy taking a class.

Forced to wait outside a classroom in a cold uninviting corridor, a sudden eruption of noise from inside had him being flattened against the wall as a small army of students burst out to bustle their way past, pushing and shoving each other as only students would.

Eventually able to elbow his way through, he found who he assumed to be the class's teacher inside, his eyes swollen by a pair of thick-lensed glasses. 'Mr Benison?'

'What is it?' the man demanded, wiping impatiently at a complex series of mathematical formulae scrawled out over a large ink-smeared whiteboard.

'Detective Inspector Tanner, Norfolk Police.'

The teacher immediately stopped what he was doing to stare nervously over. 'Oh! Sorry. I assumed you were one of my pupils. How may I help?'

'It's about someone I believe to be a student of yours, David Copeland?'

'David, yes. He's not in any trouble, I hope?'

'At this stage we're not sure. He was reported

missing this morning.'

'Oh dear. I'm sorry to hear that. Is he alright?'

Amused to hear such an illogical question coming from someone who clearly didn't lack at least a certain degree of intelligence, Tanner made sure to keep a straight face. 'Hopefully he is, but as I'm sure you can appreciate, we won't know until we find him.'

'No, of course,' Benison replied, rolling his eyes about inside his head as if giving himself a good telling-off. 'Stupid question. How can I help?'

'I've been told you look after something called VEX Robotics?'

The man's eyes became even more enlarged than they had been before. 'Indeed I do!' he exclaimed, with animated excitement. 'This year we've managed to make it through to the VEX National Championship! First time we've even come close!'

'And VEX is...?'

'It's an annual competition,' Benison continued, with an over-flowing abundance of enthusiasm. 'It's when schools up and down the country battle it out to discover who's built the best robot.'

'Right,' Tanner replied, feeling his brain begin to close down in much the same way as when Christine attempted to explain how one of her exotic dishes was made. 'A bit like Robot Wars, then?'

Benison glared over at him as if he'd just insulted his mother. 'A VEX robot has to accurately position as many pre-defined plastic objects as possible within a certain period of time. Robot Wars is just a silly television programme that seems to do nothing more useful than promote gratuitous violence.'

Tanner shook his head. 'Anyway, getting back to David. I was hoping you'd be able to tell me when you saw him last?'

'Sorry,' Benison replied, his gaze drifting up

towards the ceiling. 'It would have been when we returned from the Midlands heat last night.'

'Did he leave with anyone in particular?'

'Not that I noticed.'

'Do you know if there are any pupils he'd hang out with afterwards?'

'Unfortunately, there are only five students involved. It's always a bit of a struggle to find people capable of making a useful contribution. Whether they spend time together afterwards or not, I'm afraid I simply don't know.'

'But it is possible that he went off with one of them?'

'Actually, now that you mention it, I think I *did* see him afterwards, at least I think it was him.'

'Where was this?' Tanner enquired, his interest suddenly piqued.

'Just outside the carpark. I was loading some of the equipment we didn't need into the back of my car.'

'And where was he?'

'On the road, outside the school gates. He was talking to someone next to a car parked on the kerb. I remembered thinking they shouldn't be parked there. I'm sorry I didn't think of it sooner, it's just with the National Championship and everything.'

'Are you sure it was David?'

'I'm fairly sure it was, but it was dark. I suppose I could have been mistaken.'

'And the person he was talking to?'

'A man, I think. A little taller than David.'

'Did he seem injured in anyway?' Tanner continued, digging out his phone.

'Injured? Er, not that I noticed. Why?'

Tanner held out his phone to show the teacher the still image they'd taken from the security footage. 'Did he look anything like this?'

Benison took a moment to stare down at the screen. 'I'm sorry – I don't know. It could have been, but as I said – it was dark, and they were quite far away. To be honest, I didn't really look. I just assumed it was his dad picking him up.'

Tanner cast a concerned gaze out of the classroom window towards where an empty green playing field stood. 'His father was the person who reported him missing. Did you see him actually get into the car?' he continued, turning back.

'I think so.'

'And the car – did you see what it was?' Tanner questioned, his manner becoming increasingly agitated.

'I'm sorry, I'm not very good with cars. They all look the same to me. It was large and square if that's of any use. I suppose I should have been more vigilant. It's just such a common sight to see a student climbing into someone's car, I didn't give it a second thought.'

- CHAPTER TWENTY ONE -

BURSTING THROUGH THE college's main entrance into the cold uninviting air beyond, Tanner searched his coat to pull out his phone.

'Forrester, sir, it's Tanner. I've just been speaking to the person who teaches the missing boy's robotics class. He said he saw him being ushered into a car outside the school gates yesterday evening.'

Tanner heard the familiar creek of Forrester's chair from the other end of the line.

'Was he absolutely sure it was him?' came the DCI's eventual response.

'Not a hundred percent, but I think enough for us to proceed on the basis that it was.'

'What about the car's owner?'

'All he saw was a man talking to him beside it.'

'Was it Baines?'

'I'm sorry, sir, he didn't know, but I don't know who else it could have been.'

'Christ! I thought the man was supposed to be bleeding to death in a ditch somewhere. I don't suppose there's any chance it could have been a relative – the boy's mother, perhaps?'

'She's in New York.'

'Do we know that for a fact?'

'Well, no, but I'd have thought she'd have told her husband if she was flying back, certainly if she was doing so to simply pick up her son from college.'

'You don't have to be quite so condescending all the time, Tanner. It really isn't appreciated.'

'Sorry, sir, I just don't think it's likely to have been his mother.'

'But it is possible, though?'

'Well, yes, but...'

'Then we need to check to make sure before ruling it out altogether. That being said, I find myself having to agree with you. It does seem more likely to have been Baines. I don't suppose the teacher saw what car he was driving?'

'Only that it was large and angular, so probably some sort of old SUV, like a Range Rover, perhaps?'

'OK, I'll ask Sally to see if she's been able to dig out any CCTV footage. How soon can you get back?'

'Not long. There's hardly any traffic.'

'OK, good. I'll prepare something for us to read out to the press on your return.'

- CHAPTER TWENTY TWO -

MARTIN BENNETT STEPPED briskly up to the ancient base of St. Helen's church to tug a hand out from the warm depths of his winter coat's pocket. Placing it lightly on the church's jagged stone base to gaze briefly up to the top of its tower, he returned the hand to spin around, marching back the way he'd come.

This had become his lunchtime routine, ever since starting work as a volunteer at the Broads Wildlife Centre just two weeks before. He'd signed-up specifically to help keep a watchful eye over a pair of bitterns nesting at the furthest edge of Ranworth Broad. An invigorating stroll up to the church and back was just enough to stretch his legs and warm himself up before beginning his afternoon vigil.

One of the rarest breeding birds in the United Kingdom, the Norfolk Wildlife Trust were particularly keen to make sure nothing happened to disturb them, a tall order given where they had chosen to nest. Life would have been considerably easier for all concerned had they found somewhere inland, but the nest being so close to the water's edge meant there was a constant danger of someone motoring past, too fast and too close, unaware of what was there until it was too late. The various signs posted up at the entrance to the broad and on the approach to the nesting area could only do so much.

Most people took little notice. The only way was for someone to keep a constant eye on the nest, ready to warn boats entering the broad to keep well away from the area at the furthest end.

Stepping onto a raised wooden walkway that would eventually lead back to the broad, a familiar but wholly unwelcome sound drifted though the cold but otherwise tranquil still air. It was the low melodic rumble of a boat's engine.

Cursing, he launched himself into a run. Being the only person on duty that day, he knew it had been a risk to allow himself a lunchtime stroll, but until then it had been particularly quiet. The sound growing steadily louder was the first boat he'd either seen or heard all day.

With the wildlife centre just up ahead, he stopped to stare out over the water. There he could see the tell-tale ripples that a boat had indeed entered the broad not long before and was now navigating its way around its perimeter.

Swinging a satchel off his shoulder, he took to a knee to scrabble about for his field binoculars. Once found, he stood back up to focus them over the broad towards the bittern's nest. 'For Christ's sake!' he cursed, the moment the outline of a motorboat came looming into view, part hidden by an overhanging willow tree. Realising it had moored up alongside an old rotting jetty, just a few metres from the very nest he was supposed to be protecting, he removed the binoculars from his eyes to glance down at where the wildlife centre's flat-bottomed boat was tied, his mind whirling as to what was best to do. As much as he may have wanted to, blasting over the broad to start bawling out whoever he found behind the wheel of the boat was probably the worst thing he could have done.

He replaced the binoculars against his eyes. The boat was still there, at least what he could see of it, but there was no sign of anyone on board. 'What the hell are they doing?' he asked himself.

Realising he couldn't just stand there doing nothing, he came to a decision as to the best course of action; to motor slowly over, approaching the boat from the side furthest away from the nest in order to have a quiet but firm word with whoever it was he found onboard. At least that way he'd be able to make sure they left the jetty as quietly as possible, mitigating further disruption to the nesting bitterns.

Jumping down into the boat to start the engine, he set loose the lines to begin motoring as fast as he dared towards the far end of the broad, only to see the offending boat leaving the jetty to continue on with its journey, chugging slowly around the water's edge. The moment it emerged out from the shadows cast by the surrounding trees he shook his head to ease quickly back on the throttle. It was a Broads Ranger's patrol boat. They knew about the nesting bitterns and must have been doing a routine check.

Feeling both relieved and a little stupid, he waved over at the man he could see ducked inside the patrol boat's varnished wooden wheelhouse wearing the all too familiar uniform of a dark blue coat with a red life jacket hooked over his neck. But the man didn't wave back. He seemed too busy scanning the trees and shrubs crowding the water's edge. *He must be looking for that escaped psychotic lunatic*, Martin thought to himself, *but was it really necessary to go so close to the nesting birds, and why then feel it necessary to moor up?*

Keen to make sure that at least one of the parent bitterns was still there, he looked away from the passing patrol boat to bring the binoculars up to his eyes once again. Seeing the rounded top of a speckled brown head, just above a line of densely packed reeds, he let out a relieved sigh.

With the nest evidently safe, curious to know why the ranger had felt the need to moor his boat quite so close, still gazing through his binoculars he followed the edge of the reeds until his eyes rested on the blackened wood of the disused jetty. *Was there something there, lying on top of it?*

Doing his best to keep them steady against the gentle rocking of the boat, he looked again. There was definitely something there. What it was he couldn't be sure.

Becoming increasingly curious, he eased forward on the throttle, just enough to give him steerage way through the water. About thirty metres from the jetty he pulled the throttle back, raising his binoculars to look again. As he brought them into focus, his heart thumped hard in his chest. It was the crumpled body of a man, thick red blood oozing from its side.

Understanding why the Broad's Ranger had stopped before moving away, presumably to put an immediate call through to the police, Martin was about to do the same when something caught his eye. For a fraction of a second he thought he saw something on the body move. *Please don't tell me it was a rat*, he thought to himself, shuddering at the idea of seeing one of them feasting on the body's face.

Doing his best to control his breathing, he traversed the binoculars from the wound in the body's side, over to its feet, then back the other way, stopping to take in its ashen grey face. Grateful at least that its eyes were closed, he took a moment to study the line of dark congealing blood he could see running down from the corner of its contorted mouth.

Finding himself unable to look away, he continued to stare with morbid fascination, taking in every inch of the body's weather-beaten face, right up until the moment he saw its eyes blink themselves open to stare steadily down into his.

- CHAPTER TWENTY THREE -

'I DON'T FUCKING believe this,' moaned Tanner, storming his way into Wroxham Police Station to make a beeline for Forrester's office. Rapping his knuckles hard on the door, he waited impatiently to be called in before shoving it open.

'I don't think there's any need for us to read a statement to the nation's press,' he announced, turning back to glare out at the station's staff in the main office beyond.

'What on Earth are you going on about?' Forrester demanded, staring over at him with a look of irritated agitation.

Tanner closed the door to face him. 'The media parked outside. They already know about Copeland's son being taken, and that we think Jason Baines may have been responsible.'

Forrester took a moment to stare over at him. 'Are you sure?'

'They were yelling questions at me as I was coming in, demanding to know if Baines was injured or not, if we knew why he'd taken the Copeland boy, what we thought he was going to do to him, and if it was likely he'd be attempting to abduct anyone else. They even knew the boy's name, and that he was last seen at Walsham College on Sunday night.'

It was Forrester's turn to curse, his eyes drifting down towards his desk phone as if expecting it to ring at any moment. 'OK,' he began, taking a calming breath, 'I think it's obvious enough that someone here has decided to open up a direct line of communication with the press. What we need to know is who it is and why they've been stupid enough to start doing so.'

'I think we both know why,' commented Tanner. 'Someone's paying them.'

'But would anyone here really be dumb enough to accept, knowing what would happen if they were caught?'

Tanner caught Forrester's eye. 'I can think of one person.'

Forrester let out an exasperated sigh. 'Please don't tell me that you're about to accuse Cooper again?'

'Why not? He's the only one here both greedy and stupid enough to take money in exchange for information.'

'Based on what evidence? His past actions?'

'Well, frankly, yes!'

'May I take this opportunity to remind you once again, Tanner, that there's never been any evidence that he ever has, just a lot of office gossip and unjustified hearsay.'

'Where there's smoke there's fire, sir.'

'Said *nobody* in a court of law.'

'If it's not Cooper, then who else could it be?'

Forrester leant slowly back in his chair. 'Who else knew about what Dr Copeland told you – that he thought Baines would go after his son?'

Tanner was forced to stop for a moment to think. 'Nobody I can remember. I took him into the interview room alone. After that, I came straight here to talk to you.'

'You didn't mention it to anyone else?'

'Not that I can think of. Sally did come in at one

point, but only to bring the doctor in some coffee.'

'What about the duty sergeant?'

Once again Tanner was forced to think back to the time in question. 'We didn't discuss who he thought had taken his son when we were in reception. That only came out in the interview room. You don't think it could be Sally, do you?'

Forrester sent him an ominous foreboding look. 'You're not seriously suggesting that my niece – of all people – would accept a bribe from the press?'

'All I'm saying is that apart from you and me, she's the only one who knew what Dr Copeland said.'

'I'm sorry, Tanner, but you're going to have to look somewhere else. She's just not the type to go around accepting bribes from dodgy journalists. What about Vicky, or maybe even young Townsend?'

Tanner shrugged his shoulders with vague indifference. 'I'd say the same thing about them as you just said about your niece. Neither seem to be the type to start suddenly accepting bribes, at least not willingly.'

'You're saying that it might not be their choice?'

'I'm not saying anything, really, I just don't think it would be them. The only likely candidate I can think of is Cooper.'

Hearing a knock at the door, Tanner closed his mouth before turning to see Townsend's head appear around the side.

'Sorry to bother you,' the DC began, switching his gaze between Tanner and Forrester, 'I just thought you should know that we've had a call. A man's been found near the Broads Wildlife Centre. Sounds like he's been seriously injured.'

Forrester sat bolt upright in his chair. 'Is it Baines?'

'I'm sorry, sir. I don't know. All the caller said was

that it was an injured man. An ambulance has been sent, but I think they're going to have a problem with access. He was found on a disused jetty at the edge of Ranworth Broad, in an area surrounded by woodland. There's something else as well that the caller wanted me to make clear: that we needed to be especially careful as there's a pair of nesting birds nearby.'

'What?'

'Birds, sir, nesting nearby. Bitterns, to be exact.'

Forrester shook his head in disbelief before turning his attention back to Tanner. 'You'd better get over there, and take Townsend with you. If it is Baines, under no circumstances is he to get away. Handcuff him to the bloody ambulance if you have to.'

'I'm not sure the paramedics would approve.'

'Frankly, I don't give a shit.'

'And what about the bitterns?' Tanner queried, climbing to his feet.

'The who?'

'The birds, sir. They're on the endangered list. They're one of the rarest breeding species in the UK.'

'I'm sorry, Tanner, I thought our job was to protect the lives of Britain's *human* population. Had I known we were responsible for every other species as well, then I think we'd all be due a pay rise.'

'I'm only saying, sir, that if we're not seen to be doing all that we can to protect a pair of nesting bitterns on what is, after all, a nature reserve managed by the Norfolk Wildlife Trust, then the local community will be up in arms.'

'More so than if we allow an escaped psychotic lunatic to wander about the Broads coercing innocent teenagers into the back of a car?'

'Very possibly. You know how the British public

feel about our feathered friends.'

Forrester rolled his eyes in dismay. 'Fine! Do what you can not to disturb the precious birds, but if the injured man does turn out to be Jason Baines and he manages to get away, just because you spent two hours tip-toeing around some stupid nest in order to get to him, you're the one who's going to find yourself on an endangered species list!'

- CHAPTER TWENTY FOUR -

HAVING HELPED EACH other pick their way through a barbed wire fence, Tanner led Townsend out into a wide open clearing at the end of which lay Ranworth Broad, shimmering gently in a hazy winter's sun. On its very edge were four people, two paramedics and two uniformed police officers, all gathered around a small jetty on which lay someone Tanner assumed to be the injured person.

'This is a restricted area,' came the harsh whispered voice of a short rotund man appearing out of nowhere in front of them. 'Emergency personnel only!'

'We're CID,' came Tanner's curt response, digging out his formal ID to briefly take in the man's camouflaged coat and the binoculars hanging from his neck. 'Detective Inspector Tanner and Detective Constable Townsend. May I ask who you are?'

'I'm the person who called for the ambulance. Martin Bennett. I assume you're aware of the gravity of the situation?'

Tanner lifted his chin to peer over the man's shoulder at where the person still lay. 'All we know is that he's been seriously injured.'

'I meant,' Bennet began, his voice rising with suppressed hysteria whilst jabbing a finger over towards a pile of reeds situated close to the edge of the gently lapping water, 'that there's a pair of nesting bitterns right there!'

'Er...yes, of course. Sorry. Are they alright?' Tanner queried, struggling to maintain his professional demeanour.

Bennett brought his shoulders back to stand up straight, 'Well, yes, for now at least. The mother is still there. No sign of the father, though. Hopefully he's just waiting for you lot to bugger off before coming back.'

'And the injured man?'

'I've no idea,' Bennett replied, with dismissive disdain. 'But I wouldn't mind knowing what he was doing here. We spent hours erecting a barbed wire fence around the entire area.'

'We noticed,' Tanner muttered, glancing down at where he could feel one of the barbs had cut into his hand.

'Huge "Keep Out" signs as well, warning people about the nesting bitterns. Sometimes I wonder why we bother.'

'I must admit,' began Tanner, glancing over at Townsend, 'people can be exceptionally selfish about where they end up dying.'

'Well, he's not dead yet, more's the pity.'

Tanner sent the man an incredulous glare. 'Would you care to rephrase that?'

'I – I didn't mean that I wished he was dead – of course – I – I just meant that it's his fault. Judging by the injury, I reckon he must have cut himself when he was climbing over the fence.'

'You know that for a fact, do you?'

'Well, no, but I don't see how else he could have ended up here, all covered in blood. I've been on duty since eight o'clock this morning and I've only seen one other boat. He *must* have come over the fence.'

Tanner stopped where he was. 'Sorry, but which other boat was that?'

'The Broads Ranger's.'

'There was a Broads Ranger's patrol boat here?'

'Well, yes, but I thought you already knew that.'

'Forgive me, but how could we possibly have already known that?'

'I – I suppose I'd just assumed he'd called you. He was patrolling the broad when I came back from lunch. That's how I found the injured man, watching him through my binoculars. At first I thought it was just some idiot out for a joy-ride, or maybe even an egg collector. It was only when I saw him motor away from the jetty that I realised it was a Broads Ranger.'

'Excuse me,' came the whispered voice of one of the paramedics, making his way slowly up towards them whilst endeavouring to catch Tanner's eye. 'Are you from CID?'

Tanner responded with a single nod. 'How's the patient?'

'I think you'd better see for yourself.'

'Wait right there,' commanded Tanner, laying a hand down on Bennett's shoulder to barge his way past.

'I'm afraid there was nothing we could do,' the paramedic began, leading Tanner quietly over to where the man still lay. 'He was dead when we arrived.'

Coming to a stop about a foot away from the jetty, Tanner looked over at the body's dirt-streaked face, staring with unblinking eyes at the cold cloudless sky above.

'It's not Baines,' he muttered, seeing Townsend appear by his side.

Townsend took a moment to follow Tanner's gaze. 'How can you be sure?'

'Because this is our star witness, or at least he was. Norman Gibbs. The homeless guy who saw Baines being shot before apparently rising from the dead.'

Tanner's statement was met by a sombre silence as they continued staring at the man's face, as if knowing who he was added new gravitas to his passing.

'Any idea what caused that?' Tanner continued, bringing the paramedics attention to where thick coagulated blood could be seen seeping out from his stomach.

'I've never seen an injury like it before, at least not in the flesh, but if I was to hazard a guess I'd say it was a gunshot wound.'

Taking a firm hold of Townsend's elbow, Tanner led him quickly away. 'Call Forrester. Tell him who we've found and what we think has happened to him. Then call forensics and Dr Johnstone. Looks like we're going to need everyone down here.'

With Townsend nodding to immediately pull out his phone, Tanner's eyes scanned the clearing, looking for the man he'd spoken to earlier.

Finding him lurking under a tree, peering through his binoculars at something on the furthest side of the broad, Tanner shook his head with bemusement to start creeping his way over.

As he approached, Tanner watched the man raise the palm of his hand up to his face.

'I've just seen the male bittern,' he whispered, barely loud enough for Tanner to hear. 'He's over at the other end, hunting for fish.'

'I'm afraid, Mr Bennett, it looks like we're going to have to get this whole area cordoned off. A police forensics unit is going to need full access.'

Bennett lowered the binoculars to offer Tanner a look of confused animosity. 'I assume you're talking about where the injured man is?'

'I mean the entire area, Mr Bennett, which I'm afraid will have to include the location of your nesting birds.'

'I'm sorry, but you're not seriously suggesting that you need an entire police forensics team to start poring over an area that just happens to be where one of the rarest breeding birds in the whole of the UK is nesting, all because some idiot was stupid enough to catch himself whilst climbing over a barbed wire fence, one that was clearly marked with a sign saying, "NO ENTRY!" in large bold red letters?'

'To be honest, Mr Bennett, if it wasn't for two rather annoying factors, I'd be in complete agreement with you.'

'And what two factors are they, may I ask?'

'That, unlike my hand, the man's injury wasn't caused by him climbing over a barbed wire fence, it was caused by him being shot by a gun. And the fact that he's now dead means it's highly likely that this has become the scene of a murder investigation. So, unless you wish to be considered our prime suspect, being that you were the last person to have seen him alive, I suggest you start being a little more co-operative.'

Bennet's eyes grew wider with Tanner's every word as blood began draining rapidly from his face. 'But – I – I never went anywhere near him. I just saw him through my binoculars.'

'But you've already admitted to having been close enough to see his injury.'

'Well, yes, but only because he was still alive. If I hadn't seen him move, I'd have done the same thing the Broads Ranger did, drive immediately away.'

'Speaking of this so-called "Broads Ranger",' Tanner continued, digging out his notebook, 'I don't suppose you'd be able to tell me a little more about him?'

'Are you suggesting that I *didn't* see a Broads Ranger?'

'Not at all. I'm simply looking to clarify that it was one.'

'Why wouldn't it have been?'

'No particular reason. It's just that we didn't get a call from anyone saying they were. In fact, the only person who called in the incident was you.'

'Well, it wasn't a tourist's hire boat, I know that much.'

'Were you able to see who was behind the wheel?'

'Not close up.'

'But enough to know that that it was definitely a Broads Ranger?'

'Well, no, but he was wearing one of their dark blue coats with a bright red life jacket.'

'Did you see his face?'

Bennett thought for a moment. 'Just his hair. He was looking the other way when he drove past.'

'And...what colour was that?'

'Blond, tied at the back.'

Tanner stopped taking notes to stare over at him. 'I'm sorry, what did you say?'

'He had blond hair, tied at the back. Saying that, it was probably more grey than blond. Why – is he a friend of yours?'

- CHAPTER TWENTY FIVE -

TELLING THE NORFOLK Wildlife Trust Volunteer that he'd need to provide their forensics department with a sample of his DNA and fingerprints, Tanner finished their discussion by issuing him with a severe warning, that under no circumstances was he to mention anything about what he'd either seen or heard to the press, whether it was about the nesting bitterns or the body he'd found. If he did, then he *would* be placed under arrest as their prime suspect.

Having successfully put the fear of God into him, Tanner left him to his rare nesting birds to head off in search of Townsend.

'Were you able to get hold of Forrester?' he asked, finding him standing thoughtfully near the jetty where the body lay.

'Only briefly,' the young DC replied, glancing absently around. 'He said he'd get Sally to send Dr Johnstone down together with a forensics unit and a couple of squad cars.'

'Did you tell him that it wasn't our escaped parent-murdering psycho?'

'Uh-huh.'

'I assume he wasn't exactly bowled-over by the news.'

'He said he'd only just told Superintendent Whitaker that it was, so he was going to have to call him back to tell him otherwise.'

Tanner shook his head in bemused dismay. 'Why does he keep shooting himself in the foot like that?'

'I've no idea,' Townsend replied, his head tilting down to the black waterlogged mud surrounding the base of the dilapidated jetty. 'Speaking of feet, there's at least one set of footprints missing.'

'How'd you mean?'

'I've checked the tread pattern of the paramedics' shoes. You can clearly see them there,' Townsend continued, pointing them out with his hand. 'But there's no sign of the victim's, nor anyone else's. There are also no obvious signs on his skin or clothing to indicate that he was carried over the barbed wire fence, at least not the one we had to cross, which means he must have been dumped directly onto the jetty from the water. If that's the case, then it's in direct contradiction to what the wildlife centre volunteer said about not seeing any boats here all morning, apart from the one belonging to the Broads Ranger, of course.'

With what Bennett had only just told him about the person he'd seen behind the wheel of the patrol boat still whirling through his mind, Tanner found himself remaining silent.

'I'd be curious to know what Dr Johnstone has to say about how long he's been here for as well,' Townsend continued, 'I'm no expert or anything, but assuming he was shot somewhere else, it couldn't have been all that long.'

'Maybe another boat came through that the volunteer didn't see?' Tanner eventually proposed.

'Or maybe the body was dumped here by the guy in the Broads Ranger's patrol boat?'

The proposition was obvious enough. It was exactly the same idea Tanner had been forced to consider himself, but hearing Townsend say it out loud made his stomach churn with anxious uncertainty. 'Why would a Broads Ranger dump a body in the middle of a nature reserve,' he heard himself ask, 'especially as they'd have known the location was under constant observation thanks to the nesting bitterns?'

Townsend gave Tanner a look of consternated surprise. 'I'm not sure I was suggesting that it was, for that very reason. But I do think it would be worthwhile asking if any of their patrol boats have been reported missing recently. If the guy who shot him is going around pretending to be a Broads Ranger, it would certainly be a clever solution to being able to navigate around the waterways without anyone raising so much as an eyebrow to his presence, even to the point of being seen dumping the half-dead body of a man onto a disused jetty. It would also explain why he did so next door to a pair of nesting bitterns, being that he probably didn't have a single clue that they were there.'

'Yes, of course,' Tanner replied, in an apologetic tone. He'd been so caught up with the idea that it was Christine seen behind the wheel that he'd been unable to consider the more logical answer. 'I'll ask if they're missing a patrol boat. By the way, did you mention anything about this to Forrester when you spoke to him?'

'I didn't have a chance. As soon as he heard it wasn't Baines he seemed desperate to get me off the phone – probably to call Whitaker.'

'OK, good. Could you do me a favour and keep it that way, at least until I've made some enquiries?'

Townsend gave him a curious look. 'And between now and then?'

'I'm not sure we've got much choice but to wait

until Dr Johnstone shows up with the forensics team. At the very least we need to know if that is a gunshot wound. If it is, it wouldn't do any harm to know when it happened, and how long he's been here for either.'

- CHAPTER TWENTY SIX -

'SORRY I'M LATE,' Tanner called out, half his mind still back at the murder scene as he entered the welcome warmth of his riverside bungalow.

Having spent the remainder of the day unable to stop worrying about what the Wildlife Trust volunteer had told him, that the Broads Ranger he'd seen motoring away from the jetty where the body had been found bore a disturbingly close resemblance to Christine, he was now wondering how best to broach the subject as to where she'd been that day, and more to the point, if it had been her, why on earth hadn't she called the police?

'I'm afraid I've already eaten,' came Christine's voice, ringing out above the normal cacophony of pots and pans being rattled about. 'Shall I heat yours up now?'

As he stepped through to the living area to find her jamming plates down into the dishwasher, it was fairly obvious she was upset about something.

'Whenever is good for you,' he replied, catching her eye with a smile. 'How was your day?'

'Oh, you know, same old, same old. I heard on the news that a body had been found, so I knew you'd be late.'

'Jesus Christ,' Tanner mumbled quietly to himself, instantly scrabbling around for the TV remote. 'How the hell do they keep finding out so bloody quickly?'

'What was that?'

'We think someone at the station has been talking to the press.'

Christine glanced over at him whilst placing a plate heaped with food into the microwave. 'Is that a problem?'

'Unfortunately, yes, it is,' Tanner replied, turning on the TV to spend a few irritated moments searching for the news. 'We have to be able to control what's being shared with them. Holding information back can often be vital when working out who did what and when, especially when the inevitable crank calls start flooding in. Beyond that, if all the facts are made public, when we do eventually bring a suspect in for questioning, it's all too easy for them to concoct a story that fits neatly into the narrative that's already been broadcast, making it far harder for us to know if they're telling the truth. Worse still, it can put people's lives in danger, especially when the press use the information to start making up allegations of their own.'

'I'd no idea,' he heard her reply. 'Any idea who's been talking?'

With the BBC news on in the background, Tanner perched himself onto one of the breakfast barstools. 'If I had some spare cash, I'd put it on Cooper. Forrester, meanwhile, seems happy enough to assume it's you.'

'Me!' she exclaimed, catching his eye.

'Don't worry, he's not being serious, at least I don't think he is.'

'I should hope not! Besides, you're hardly here long enough to say more than three words to me, let alone spend hours going over the ins and outs of your investigations.'

'Yes, I know. Sorry again for being late.'

'You don't need to keep apologising,' she replied, dragging the plate out from the bleeping microwave to lay it steaming in front of him, 'not when you have a murder investigation to deal with. Speaking of which, any idea who the victim was?'

'Well, it wasn't Jason Baines, more's the pity.'

'I assume there's still been no sign of him?'

'Nothing that's been confirmed.'

'Then he must have died in a ditch somewhere.'

'We'll have to wait and see. Tell me, I don't suppose you know if any of your patrol boats have been reported missing recently?'

Christine turned to continue loading up the dishwasher. 'Not that I'm aware of. Should there have been?'

'It's probably nothing. There was a report of one motoring past where the body was found, at the far end of Ranworth Broad, just along from where those bitterns have been nesting.'

With Christine's mind appearing to have switched back into kitchen mode, Tanner sucked in a fortifying breath. 'I don't suppose you were anywhere near there today?'

'Near where?'

'Ranworth Broad, where those bitterns are nesting.'

'Not me. I've been on land management duty for over a week, cutting back the trees around Barton Broad. I thought I'd told you?'

'Sorry, you probably did,' Tanner replied, struggling to remember if she had or not. Telling himself that she must have, he re-opened his mouth to continue. 'I don't suppose there are any other Broads Rangers with hair similar to yours?'

'You mean, someone with flowing golden locks

who look as if they've just stepped off a fashion show catwalk?' Christine replied, closing the dishwasher door to shake her hair from side to side, as if advertising the latest clinically proven hair conditioning product.

'Er...I actually meant a man with long greying-blonde hair that normally looks as if it's been dragged through a hedge backwards.'

'Charming!'

'Seriously, though?'

'I suppose some of the men do have quite long hair. To be honest, I'd never given it much thought. Is it important?'

Tanner shrugged to stare down at the plate of steaming hot food. 'A witness said they saw a man in a Broads Ranger's patrol boat motoring away from the jetty where the body was found. There's no way he could have been there and not seen the body, but there's no record of him having called it in to the emergency services, which was odd, especially as the victim was still alive at the time. I'd have thought the least he would have done was to call for an ambulance.'

'Maybe his phone died?'

'OK, but aren't all your boats fitted with two-way radios?'

'Well, yes, but the range is pretty crap. If someone is more than half a mile away from another one, it's unlikely they'd be able to get through. Are you even sure it was a Broads Rangers patrol boat they saw? I mean, they do look pretty much identical to your own. They all used to be, after all.'

Tanner raised an intrigued eyebrow. 'I must admit, I didn't know that.'

'What did you think, we bought them from Argos? They're all your old stock. All we do to identify them as ours is to paint Broads Rangers down the side.'

- CHAPTER TWENTY SEVEN -

Tuesday, 8th February

AT WORK THE next morning, Tanner took a break from the tediously dull task of writing up his report from the previous day to make himself a coffee, returning to find Townsend waiting for him beside his desk.

'The preliminary forensics' report has come through for the body at Ranworth Broad,' the young DC began, as Tanner approached. 'The medical examiner's as well.'

Tanner planted himself down behind his desk to take a tentative sip from his coffee. 'Anything of interest?'

'Not much. Dr Johnstone has confirmed the victim's identity.'

'That was quick.'

'He had a criminal record,' Townsend continued, taking a slim file out from under his arm. 'Manslaughter from drink driving, which must have made him relatively easy to find.'

'I assume it *was* Norman Gibbs?'

'Uh-huh.' Townsend confirmed, browsing through the pages.

'Cause of death?'

'Bullet wound, as we thought. It pierced his abdomen leading to massive internal haemorrhaging.'

'Does it say when he was shot?'

'It says the injury occurred somewhere between three to four hours before his eventual death.'

'He lasted that long?'

'According to this, the bullet managed to miss every single one of his vital organs, so in a way he was very lucky.'

Tanner gave Townsend a curious look. 'I do hope you're joking?'

'I suppose I've always been a glass is half-full sort of a chap.'

'That's as maybe, but if you wake up one morning to find you've been shot in the stomach, then your glass is most definitely half-empty, no matter how much water is left in it.'

'Well, yes, but the fact that it missed all his vital organs did at least give him longer to live.'

'During which time he must have been in excruciating pain.'

'But alive, nonetheless, which is surely something to be grateful for, even if that time was filled with pain and suffering.'

Tanner took a moment to study his annoyingly handsome young face. 'Tell me, Townsend, what did you do before joining the Force?'

'I was at university.'

'Philosophy?'

'Law. I did Philosophy for "A" Level.'

Tanner nodded with sagacious understanding. 'Anyway, apart from attempting to establish if our victim was lucky or not, what else did they find?'

'Not much. He received the wound at another location, the lack of footprints in the mud meant that his body must have been dropped off from the water, and the murder weapon has yet to be found.'

'Is that it?'

'They discovered three DNA samples on both his clothing and the jetty his body was found on, one of which belonged to Jason Baines.'

Tanner narrowed his eyes at him. 'Couldn't you have told me that about five minutes ago?'

'The other belonged to the Wildlife Trust volunteer who found the body, Martin Bennett.'

'And the third?'

'Unknown.'

'Then it must have come from the boat seen motoring away.'

'The Broads Rangers' patrol boat?'

'If it was,' Tanner remarked. 'I spoke to Christine about that last night. She thinks the witness may have mistaken it for an old police boat. Apparently, all Broads Rangers boats used to be owned by the police. So it could be that Baines has managed to find himself one and is using it to creep around, pretending to be a Broads Ranger, which could explain why he's proving to be so difficult to find.'

'If that's the case, then where did the third DNA sample come from?'

'Whoever used the boat before he did. Don't forget, the transfer of DNA from one object to another is remarkably common.'

'So, it could be someone from the police?'

'If that's who was using the boat before, then why not?'

'Well, for a start, their DNA would have been on our database.'

'Then whoever used the boat before he did,' Tanner stated, his voice lifting with surly irritation. 'Either way, we need to find out if any police boats have been reported missing, either those in active use or ones that have been decommissioned.'

'Shouldn't we check to see if any Broads Rangers boats have been taken as well?'

'I've already asked Christine about that,' Tanner replied, glancing over to where Sally could be seen perched behind her desk, deep in conversation with someone on her mobile. 'She said they were all accounted for,' he continued, picking up his phone to dial her extension.

'The forensics report did mention something else which I thought might be of interest.'

'Uh-huh,' Tanner replied, lifting the phone to his ear.

'The third sample of DNA,' Townsend continued. 'They said it belongs to a woman.'

'Who the hell is she talking to?' Tanner muttered to himself, choosing to ignore Townsend to instead glare over at Sally.

'And I don't know if you've seen it or not,' Townsend continued, 'but the Norfolk Herald has a story running on the front page of their website. Not only does it name yesterday's victim as being Norman Gibbs, but it also says that we have a witness who saw a Broads Ranger's patrol boat motoring away from the scene, and that the person behind the wheel had greying-blond hair tied at the back. They also seem to have found out about the DNA we discovered, and that the unknown sample is that of a woman.'

Tanner slowly replaced the receiver into its cradle to begin staring down at the desk, leaving Townsend shifting his weight awkwardly from one foot to the other.

'I don't suppose there are any other woman with greying-blonde hair that's tied at the back who are currently working as a Broads Ranger, apart from Christine, of course?'

'Jesus fucking Christ!' Tanner eventually spat,

lifting his head to glare up at him. 'Who the hell keeps talking to the press?'

'Don't look at me!'

'Well, apart from the Wildlife Trust volunteer, you're the only person who knew, at least the part about the Broads Rangers' patrol boat.'

'Then it must have been the Wildlife Trust volunteer.'

Tanner took his mind back to when he told the witness what would happen if he talked to the press. Remembering the look of terror on his face when he'd threatened to arrest him as their prime suspect, he shook his head. 'No, it couldn't have been. He wouldn't have dared. Have you told anyone else?'

'Nobody, sir, at least no one outside the office.'

Tanner slowly rose to his feet to bring his eyes level with Townsend's. 'Let me ask you that again,' he began, his voice kept ominously low. 'Who *inside* the office did you tell?'

'Well, sir, I – er – might have mentioned something about it to Sally, in the kitchen, when I first came in this morning,' Townsend replied, the first signs of sweat rippling over his forehead.

Tanner continued to bore his eyes down into the young DC's. 'You know, I could have sworn I told you not to tell anyone.'

'I'm sorry, sir, but she has a way of wheedling information out of you. Five minutes alone in a room with her and she'll have uncovered your entire life story, from where you were born to how many people you've slept with, including their names, where they all live, and all their star signs. Actually, now that I think about it, it may be an idea to start using her to interrogate suspects.'

'This isn't funny,' Tanner muttered, his voice a harsh whisper as his eyes darted around the office. 'I can't have the press declaring to the world that the woman I'm living with is a crazed psychotic murderer.'

'Then I suppose it's a good job they haven't, sir.'

'Maybe not, but I doubt it will take them long to put the discovery of a woman's DNA together with the description of the person seen fleeing the scene in a Broads Ranger's patrol boat. The only reason they probably haven't already is because of the general stereotypical assumption that Broads Rangers are always men.'

'Er...just so you know, sir,' whispered Townsend, his eyes darting briefly over Tanner's shoulder, 'Forrester's on his way over, and it looks like he's got his grumpy trousers on.'

'Great - that's all I need,' Tanner moaned, turning his head to greet his DCI with a spurious smile.

'What's all this about a Broads Ranger's patrol boat seen leaving the murder scene yesterday, and a driver with greying-blond hair behind the wheel?'

'Yes, sir. It's all in my report.'

'Sorry, Tanner, but what report is that?'

'The one I was just putting the finishing touches to before emailing it over.'

'And yet its contents seem to have already found themselves featured on the front page of the Norfolk Herald's website. Can you explain to me how that is even possible?'

'Well, sir, I can only assume it's because whoever wrote the story is somehow able to type faster than me.'

'This isn't funny, Tanner!'

'That's exactly what I was telling Townsend, sir, less than thirty seconds ago.'

Forrester shot Townsend a furious glance before returning to drill his eyes down into Tanner's. 'At this rate, I may as well fire the entire bloody lot of you and employ a team of journalists instead. At least that way I'd know what was going on before having the humiliation of seeing the story appear on my Facebook newsfeed.'

'Feel free, sir, but to be honest, I doubt they'd accept. I'm fairly sure journalists get paid more than us. They probably have more sociable hours as well.'

'Then I suppose you'd better tell me what else is going to be in this report of yours before I fire you anyway?'

'Unfortunately, sir, not much more than you probably already know. Dr Johnstone's confirmed that the body is that of Norman Gibbs, the homeless man who witnessed the shooting incident at Long Gore Hall, that he was mortally wounded about four hours before his body was found, that he was most likely to have been carried there by boat, and that Jason Baines' DNA was found on both the body and the jetty it had been left on.'

'What about what they said about some unknown woman's DNA? Was that true?'

Tanner glanced surreptitiously over at Townsend.

'That is what the forensics report said,' the young DC replied, 'but as Tanner and I were just discussing, it was most likely to have been a contaminated sample, transferred from the patrol boat we think he must have used.'

'Do we know if any Broads Rangers patrol boats have been reported missing?'

Tanner shook his head. 'I've already checked, but there's a strong chance the witness was mistaken – that it was a police boat he saw, not a Broads Ranger's.'

'OK, then do we know if a police boat has been stolen?'

'I was about to ask Sally to find out when you came over, but she was on another call.'

They all looked over to where she was sitting, still busily chatting to someone on the phone, when they saw Cooper push himself up from his desk to begin hurrying his way over.

'A call's just come in,' he announced, tucking a wayward corner of his shirt back into his trousers. 'Someone thinks they just saw Jason Baines moor a boat up at the north end of Hickling Broad.'

'Was it a patrol boat?' Forrester enquired.

'I didn't think to ask. Are we expecting it to be?'

'I take it that means you're not following the Norfolk Herald on Facebook?'

'Sorry, sir, but I don't do Facebook.'

'Very sensible of you, Cooper.'

'I'm more of an Instagram type of guy,' he smirked. 'Facebook's for old people, isn't it?'

Forrester's gaze turned from mutual agreement to one of irritated dismay. 'I'm fairly sure plenty of young people still use Facebook.'

'Nobody I know,' he mumbled, partly under his breath.

'Never mind all that. Send the nearest squad car over to take a look. Then I suggest you get over there yourself; Vicky as well.'

Tanner waited for Cooper to spin away before opening his mouth. 'I assume you want Townsend and I to join them?'

'In a moment, but before you do, may I have a quiet word?'

- CHAPTER TWENTY EIGHT -

O PENING HIS DOOR for Tanner, Forrester followed him quietly inside. 'I just wanted a quick word in private about the woman's DNA found at yesterday's murder scene.'

Tanner hovered behind one of the chairs in front of his DCI's desk. 'To be honest, sir, Townsend's only just told me about it.'

'You haven't mentioned anything about it to Christine?'

'As I said, I've only just been told.'

'What about the description of the person seen behind the wheel of the patrol boat?'

With his hands clutching the back of the chair, Tanner shifted his weight from one foot to another. 'I know what you're about to say, but I can assure you that whoever was behind the wheel, it wasn't Christine.'

'And you know that for a fact, do you?'

'She was working up at Barton Broad yesterday, on a land management job.'

Forrester sank slowly down into his chair. 'I assume that means that you at least had the good sense to ask her?'

'When I heard the description of the person seen behind the wheel, and that of the boat they were helming, I wouldn't have been doing my job if the thought hadn't crossed my mind. So yes, I did ask her, but as I said, she was nowhere near the place, nor was there any reason for her to have been. Besides, we already have the DNA of the most likely suspect, discovered on both the body and the jetty it was found on. And now we've received word that the suspect in question has been seen climbing out of a boat at the top end of Hickling Broad, only a stone's throw away from Long Gore Hall, the place he was first seen. Bearing all that in mind, why we're even having this conversation is frankly beyond me.'

'There's no need to be quite so defensive, Tanner.'

'I wouldn't need to be if you didn't keep trying to implicate her in just about every serious crime that ever takes place around here.'

'Now that's not true, and you know it.'

'Isn't it? What about the time you were convinced she was a murder suspect when I first came back to work?'

'That's probably because she was, whether you were prepared to admit it or not.'

'And that she'd been going about planting evidence inside the boatshed at Coltishall in order to frame him for a murder you seemed convinced at the time she'd committed?' Tanner continued, his temper rising together with his voice.

'You mean, the one she gained illegal entry into, with your help I may add?'

'And now you're automatically assuming that it was her behind the wheel of the boat seen dumping a homeless drunk's body, having decided for some unknown reason to shoot him beforehand.'

'I think you need to calm down, Tanner.'

'It was only the other day when you were accusing her of being the one whose been talking to the press.'

'I could say something very similar about the way you're always accusing Cooper.'

'You mean, the person who was acting so suspiciously, even Professional Standards decided to investigate?'

'For which, Tanner, and for the very last time, the man was *fully* exonerated!'

'Whilst we're on the subject of whose been talking to the press, I think the time has most definitely come for you to start looking a little closer to home.'

'What the hell's that supposed to mean?'

'Your niece, Sally. You need to ask her about who she's been sharing confidential information with.'

'I've never heard anything so ridiculous in all my life,' Forrester began, his face darkening with embarrassed rage.

'It's not very nice when the shoe is on the other foot, is it?'

'I sincerely hope you have a damned good reason for accusing her of selling information to the press?'

'Townsend told her about the Broads Ranger's patrol boat being seen motoring away from the murder scene yesterday when he came into work this morning. Also about the description of the driver.'

'Why does that mean it was her? It could have just as easily been the witness at the scene, or anyone else who'd been there.'

'The only people the Wildlife Trust volunteer told were Townsend and me. Even if he had then gone and spoken to the press, he could never have known about what forensics said about a woman's DNA being found at the scene. Only someone here could have known about that.'

'Then why can't it be Townsend?'

'Well, it could, I suppose, but he's not the one whose been spending the entirety of their time recently doing nothing more productive than endlessly chatting to someone on her bloody mobile!'

Forrester joined Tanner in staring out through his partition window towards where Sally was sitting behind her desk, one hand holding her phone up to her ear, the other playing with her hair.

With a look of despondent desolation hanging from Forrester's face, Tanner decided to take a more diplomatic approach. 'To be honest, she's probably been doing it without realising.'

'How do you mean?'

'I saw she has a new boyfriend.'

Forrester peeled his eyes of his niece to gaze over at him. 'She does?'

'A good-looking young man driving a bright orange Volkswagen Golf. I saw him drop her off at work the other day. It may be worthwhile finding out what he does for a living, especially as she only met him a week ago, and the fact that he's already proposed.'

'He did what?'

'He proposed to her, a couple of days ago.'

'Jesus Christ! Do her parents know?'

'I've no idea.'

'You could have at least mentioned something about it to me.'

'She told me in confidence, but as the time they began going out with each other seems to coincide with when the press started knowing our every move, I thought it might be worth mentioning.'

'OK, well, I suppose I'd better have a word.'

As an awkward silence descended over the room, Tanner cleared his throat. 'I suppose Townsend and I had better be heading over to Hickling Broad.'

'Of course,' replied Forrester, his attention drifting back to his niece.

'Before I go, when you do get a chance to speak to Sally, if you could try to avoid mentioning that it was me who told you about her proposal of marriage, I'd be grateful. As I said, she did tell me in confidence.'

'Yes, of course. Don't worry, I'll make sure to be discreet.'

- CHAPTER TWENTY NINE -

WITH TOWNSEND STARING quietly out of the passenger window beside him, Tanner sped them over sweeping country lanes towards Hickling Broad without hardly saying a word. His mind was too busy contemplating recent events to be making idle conversation with someone born two decades before him, especially with what Forrester had just been saying to him about Christine. Could it really have been her behind the wheel of that patrol boat, he found himself constantly asking, and if so, why hadn't she called the police? There was no way she wouldn't have seen the body. Even if her mobile phone had died, or her two-way radio had been out of range, she'd have told someone. She certainly wouldn't have spent the previous evening lying to his face about where she'd been that day.

Hoping to God that the boat Jason Baines had been seen climbing out of was a long-discarded Broads Ranger's patrol boat, and that he'd also been seen wearing some sort of disguise, Tanner drew in a fortifying breath as a uniformed police officer came in to view, waving him into a small public car park.

Swinging his XJS into the nearest empty space, he turned off the engine to stare despondently over the steering wheel to where Vicky and Cooper could be seen, gazing down into a dark green flat-bottomed motorboat tied loosely to the end of a long narrow dyke.

'Well, it's not a patrol boat, Broads Ranger's or otherwise,' observed Townsend, following Tanner's gaze.

Tanner remained silent, his grip tightening around the top of the Jag's large leather steering wheel.

Seeing him remain where he was, staring vacantly out through the windscreen, Townsend turned to look at him. 'Are you alright, sir?'

Another moment of silence followed before Tanner reached over to open the car's wood-veneered glove box. 'Do me a favour, will you,' he began, taking out a hairbrush matted with strands of greying-blonde hair before diving back in for a clear plastic evidence bag, 'give this to forensics for me?' he continued, placing one inside the other. 'Unfortunately, it looks like I'm going to need to know if its DNA matches the sample found at yesterday's murder scene.'

Townsend recoiled from the bag as if it contained a deadly virus. 'But – doesn't that belong to...?'

'If that boat we can see down there had been a patrol boat of any description, believe you me, I wouldn't be doing this. However, as it stands, I don't see I have much of a choice. I need to know, one way or the other.'

Townsend lifted a reluctant hand to take the bag. 'Do you want me to say where I got it from?'

'If you could keep that to yourself for now, I'd be grateful.'

Seeing Townsend nod in response, Tanner reached for the door handle. 'Right then, I suppose we'd better see what our colleagues have found?'

- CHAPTER THIRTY -

'W HAT'VE WE GOT?' called Tanner, leading Townsend over to join Vicky and Cooper.

'Well, it's not a patrol boat,' Cooper replied, glancing up.

Tanner cast an irritated eye up at the hordes of other boats crammed along both sides of the narrow dyke. 'Anything else?'

'I reckon there's blood at the bottom,' Cooper added, gesturing down. 'I wouldn't want to bet against it belonging to that homeless guy we found yesterday.'

'I assume forensics has been called?'

Cooper nodded. 'They should be here any minute. The only other point of interest is the engine. Looks like one of those new electric ones. That must explain how he was able to motor into Ranworth Broad without being seen.'

'What about the person who made the call?'

'She's in the carpark behind us,' Cooper replied, directing Tanner's attention over to where two elderly women could be seen chatting to a uniformed policewoman, near the carpark's entrance. 'The one leaning over the Zimmer frame. Judging by how thick the lenses on her glasses are, I was surprised she was able to see anything at all!'

'You've already spoken to her?'

'Only briefly.'

'Was she sure it was Baines?'

'That's what she said.'

'I don't suppose she mentioned anything about what he was wearing?'

'I didn't ask.'

'What about his supposed injury?'

'Again – I – er...

'You didn't ask?'

Cooper gave Tanner an indifferent shrug. 'I assumed she'd have told me if he had been.'

'Did you at least ask her which direction he went after climbing out of the boat?'

Cooper opened his mouth only to close it again.

Shaking his head, Tanner turned to look at Townsend. 'Get some PCs to have this whole area cordoned off. I don't want so much as a mosquito going near that boat. Vicky and Cooper, if you can start coordinating door-to-door enquiries, asking if anyone's seen someone looking even remotely like Jason Baines ambling past their house, injured or otherwise, I'll see if I can have another word with our hopefully not too short-sighted witness.'

- CHAPTER THIRTY ONE -

TURNING ON HIS heel, Tanner made his way over to where he could see the policewoman begin escorting the two elderly women towards one of the cars.

'Excuse me!' he called out, digging around for his ID. 'Detective Inspector Tanner, Norfolk Police. May I have a word?'

His rapid approach was met by the steely gaze of the younger of the two women, doing her best to help her friend over the uneven gravel-lined carpark. 'Dorothy has already spoken to someone from the police, thank you.'

'Yes, sorry, I just have a couple more questions.'

'Well, if you must, but please be quick. She's been outside for far too long already.'

'It's alright my dear, there's no need to fuss,' her aged friend replied, pivoting herself slowly around to eventually gaze up at Tanner through a pair of large oyster-pink framed glasses. 'If the policeman needs to talk to me, then I'm sure I can put up with the cold for a little longer.'

'I wanted to ask again about the person you said you saw – Jason Baines?'

'That's right. He was climbing out of that little boat of his, just as we were coming back from our daily stroll. Isn't that right, Margery?'

'That's right,' her friend confirmed.

'I don't suppose you can tell me anything about him – what he was wearing, for example?'

Dorothy tilted one of her ears towards him. 'I'm sorry, my dear, I didn't quite catch that?'

'He's asking what the man was wearing,' her friend responded, lifting her voice.

'Oh, it was some of that awful green patterned clothing, wasn't it?' Dorothy continued, talking more to her friend than to Tanner. 'The sort you see fishermen wear, with those horrible blotches. What's it called?'

'I think they're called army fatigues,' her friend commented.

'I meant the pattern,' Dorothy replied, in a scolding tone. 'Something to do with large camels.'

'You're thinking of camouflage, my dear. Nothing to do with camels.'

'I'm fully aware of that, thank you, Margery. That's just how I was remembering the name. I'd imagined lots of giant camels plodding around the desert, all dressed up like soldiers. I'm afraid my memory's not what it used to be,' Dorothy continued, her attention returning to Tanner. 'Someone bought me a book for Christmas. Actually, I think it might have been for my birthday. Anyway, it was all about word association and how to use your imagination to help remember things. It really works, you know.'

Tanner was about to try and steer the conversation back to Jason Baines when he saw her reaching a frail trembling hand out towards him.

'Sorry, my dear, but who are you again?'

'Detective Inspector Tanner, Norfolk Police,' Tanner replied, endeavouring to hide his growing impatience. 'I was asking about the man you saw, climbing out of the boat.'

'Oh yes, that's right. It was Jason Baines. I never

thought I'd be seeing him again. We watched him tie up his boat to start wandering up the road towards Hickling Green, as if he didn't have a care in the world. Did you know he murdered his parents? Cut them up with an axe, he did.'

'And you're sure it was him?'

'Oh yes, quite sure, thank you,' she replied. 'As he stepped off the boat he looked straight at me. I'll never forget those eyes. Not until the day I die, which shouldn't be too long now,' she added, raising her hand again to cast a curious eye down at a watch that appeared to be as fragile as the wrist it was hanging from.

'Oh, please!' Margery laughed beside her. 'You've got a good few years left in you yet.'

'Good Lord, I hope not.'

'Am I to understand it that you've seen him before?' Tanner asked, stooping to try and catch Dorothy's eye.

'Only once,' she replied, making an effort to hold herself up straight. 'I was at Bradfield Hospital the day he arrived. I used to be a nurse there, you see. I remember him in particular because it was the very last day before my somewhat belated retirement. The moment I saw those eyes of his staring at me, I thought to myself just how grateful I was to be leaving.'

- CHAPTER THRITY TWO -

'ANY LUCK?' TOWNSEND asked, as Tanner made his way back to the end of the dyke.

'They saw him heading towards Hickling Green.'

'And they're sure it was him?'

'One of them recognised him from her days working at Bradfield Hospital. Where did Cooper and Vicky get to?'

'They went the same way.'

'OK, I'd better give them a call,' Tanner replied, searching for his phone. 'Apparently, Baines was wearing combat gear – probably trying to pass himself off as a fisherman.'

'Not a Broads Ranger?'

Happy to ignore the question, Tanner lifted his phone to his ear. 'Cooper, it's Tanner. Any sign of him yet?'

'One of the locals said he saw someone who might have been him,' came Cooper's breathless reply, 'but he wasn't sure. He wasn't injured, either.'

'Did he say what he was wearing?'

'Army type camouflage.'

'That's him! Tell me he saw which way he was going?'

'Up Sea Palling Road. We think he's heading for Long Gore Hall. He must have been hiding there all the time.'

'If he's been lurking about inside the house, Hambleton would have seen him. Besides, we've already searched the place. He must have found somewhere to shelter in the surrounding marshes. With any luck, that's where he's keeping Dr Copeland's boy as well.'

'OK, but if he's managed to get his hands on some camouflage gear, he's going to be virtually impossible to find.'

'You could be right. I'd better give Forrester a call. Hopefully, we'll be able to get another dog unit out.'

'It didn't work before.'

'Maybe not, but we have a fresh lead this time. Besides, I can't see how else we're going to find him. The marshes stretch out all the way to the sea.'

- CHAPTER THIRTY THREE -

WITH HIS HEAD slumped towards the ground, Tanner listened to the occasional innocuous bark from the police dogs in the distance as he trudged his way along a muddy unkept single track road. Glancing around to see the last of the winter's sun slip steadily over the edge of Norfolk's wide open horizon, he looked up to come to a sudden halt.

'Well that was a waste of bloody time!' he fumed, the words bringing Townsend to a standstill beside him, as they both stared up at the same lopsided gates they'd been parked in front of only a few days before. 'Those bloody dogs have led us all the way back to Long Gore Hall again!'

Tanner cast his eyes beyond the gates where they could see the hall itself, hovering above a delicate layer of pale ethereal mist. 'Hambleton must be over the moon to have us back.'

'It doesn't sound like he is,' Townsend commented, as the disgruntled echoes of raised voices merged together with the distant baying of the dogs. 'I'd say it was more like the exact opposite.'

Hurrying between the gates, it wasn't long before they could see Hambleton, standing at the top of the stone steps between two of the hall's giant towering pillars, levelling the barrels of his shotgun down at three Alsatians as their respective handlers fought desperately to keep them under control.

Hearing none other than Cooper's voice, yelling up at the estate's owner, Tanner opened his mouth to enter the fray. 'What the hell's going on here?' he demanded, glaring around at the various police personnel.

'Your colleagues are ordering me to give them full and immediate access into my home,' Hambleton replied, 'without so much as a by-your-leave, I may add.'

'The dogs came straight here,' stated Cooper. 'There was no hesitation. Jason Baines *must* be inside, but Mr Hambleton here is refusing to let us in.'

'I'm not playing this game again,' Hambleton continued. 'I've barely recovered from the last time you lot were here, pulling what's left of my home apart in a bid to look for someone who I've neither seen nor heard. If you insist on causing me further disruption, for no other reason than because your dogs have picked up what is obviously the same bloody scent, then you're going to have to produce some sort of a search warrant before I let anyone in, human or otherwise.'

'As I was trying to explain to Mr Hambleton,' Cooper continued, 'we don't need one, not when we're in active pursuit of a known criminal.'

'And as I was attempting to explain to your detective inspector, from the little I know about such matters, I'm fairly sure that the person would have needed to be seen entering the premises under discussion for that to be the case, which, as I understand it, nobody has, including myself, and I live here!'

Tanner turned to look at Cooper. 'I'm afraid Mr Hambleton does have a point.'

'But – the dogs – look at them! It's obvious he's

inside.'

Hambleton rested his finger on the shotgun's curved steel trigger. 'Those animals were behaving in the same dangerously uncontrolled manner before, during which time they found nothing but the contents of my fridge. I'm not having them inside again. And should they just happen to accidently-on-purpose slip their leashes, I won't hesitate to shoot them.'

With the dogs now snarling at Hambleton with ravenous agitation, Tanner took a tentative step forward, raising his hands as he did in a bid to try and placate the rapidly escalating situation.

'I understand what you're saying, Mr Hambleton, but we're only trying to help. As my colleague has said, something has led the dogs here, and the man we're after is now wanted in connection with murder. We also believe he's armed, making him someone who I'm sure you wouldn't want wandering about inside your home. So, for your own safety, it might be wise to let us have a quick look around.'

'Tell him we have the right to enter his property for that very reason,' blurted out Cooper, 'to prevent someone from being either injured or killed.'

Hambleton pivoted his gun around until it was pointing directly at Cooper's groin. 'As I said before, I haven't seen a single person anywhere near the place. Even if I had, I'm quite capable of looking after myself, as I hope is abundantly clear.'

'And now he's threatening to shoot me!' Cooper exclaimed, staring over at Tanner with a nervous laugh.

'Sorry, my mistake,' Hambleton smirked, traversing the barrels back to the dogs. 'I didn't realise it was aimed directly at your scrotal sack.'

'About your shotgun,' Tanner continued, 'I don't

suppose you've been able to get a licence for it yet?'

'I posted the application yesterday,' Hambleton huffed with belligerent indifference. 'You can confiscate it if you like, but then I wouldn't have anything to defend myself against the psychopathic murderer who's apparently hiding underneath my bed.'

A fractured silence fell over the group, marred only by the dogs still growling up at Hambleton.

With a sullen shake of his head, Tanner turned to look at Cooper. 'I suggest we leave Mr Hambleton to whatever he was doing before we so rudely interrupted him.'

'But – what about Baines?'

'If he is here,' Tanner responded, casting his eyes briefly up at the thick sinuous strands of ivy he could see clinging to the mansion's walls, 'then I suppose we'll just have to leave his fate, and that of Mr Hambleton here, in God's hands.'

- CHAPTER THIRTY FOUR -

Wednesday, 9th February

WITH THE DOGS picking up another scent, moments after being dragged away from Long Gore Hall, Tanner and his team continued searching the marshland late into the night. When the trail eventually went cold without anybody having had so much as a glimpse of Baines, he called Forrester to update him before sending everyone home. By the time he arrived back at his own, it was so late Christine had already gone to bed, leaving him a scrawled out note directing him towards something to heat up in the microwave.

The following morning he was so tired he fell straight back to sleep after his alarm went off. When he did eventually open his eyes, he barely had a chance to moan at Christine for not waking him up before she was out the door, leaving him scrabbling around the kitchen in search of something to eat before throwing on his suit to head off to work.

Arriving almost an hour later than he should have, he burst into an unusually quiet main office with the peculiar feeling that everyone was doing their best to avoid having to look at him. Even Sally glanced suddenly away the moment they had eye contact.

Assuming it was because Forrester had decided to take a stroll around the office whilst publicly berating him for his tardiness, he dived into the kitchen to pour himself a coffee before emerging to start staring about for Townsend. Unable to see him, he skulked over to where Vicky was sitting, staring at her monitor with an unusual amount of focussed attention.

'Morning,' he began, perching himself on the side of her desk. 'Everyone's very quiet.'

With Vicky responding with nothing more than a flicker of a smile, he began glancing nonchalantly around. 'I don't suppose you've seen Townsend, by any chance?'

'Forrester sent him out earlier.'

Tanner turned to look at her. 'What, on his own?'

Vicky shook her head. 'He went with Cooper.'

Tanner's head jolted back in surprise. 'And why the hell would Forrester send him out with Cooper?'

Vicky ducked her head down under the desk partition. 'Jesus, John, haven't you seen the news?'

'What news?'

'The front page of the Norfolk Herald, for a start.'

'Oh, right. What have they been saying now; that the Lock Ness Monster has been seen doing backflips in the middle of Barton Broad?'

'It's not just them. It's on the BBC's website as well.'

'What is?'

'Christine!' Vicky exclaimed, her eyes shooting up into Tanner's. 'They're saying she's the person who helped Jason Baines escape.'

'What?'

'And that she did so in order for him to help her murder the homeless guy, Norman Gibbs.'

'I've never heard anything so ridiculous in all my life! What possible reason would she have had for doing that?'

'I think it's because they found out who Norman Gibbs is.'

'Yes, we know who he is. Some homeless drunk who witnessed Hambleton shoot Baines, only for him to rise up from the dead.'

'He used to be a truck driver.'

'Yes, and...so what?'

'Before being convicted of drink driving.'

Tanner continued to stare down at her with uncomprehending bemusement.

'It was because of him that Christine lost her husband,' Vicky eventually continued, as if having to force the words out of her mouth. 'Her baby as well.'

Tanner stopped where he was, his mind lurching him back to the time he remembered mentioning his name to her.

'There's more, I'm afraid,' Vicky continued, closing a window on her computer to open up another. 'This is on the Norfolk Herald's website. They're saying she'd been caught having "relations" with Baines when she worked at Bradfield Hospital. That's why they had to let her go. They're also saying that they've been writing love letters to each other ever since.'

Whilst she'd been talking, blood had been slowly draining from Tanner's face, leaving the skin around his eyes saggy and grey.

Swallowing hard, he forced himself to open his mouth. 'You never told me where Cooper and Townsend went?'

'I'm sorry, John. Neither of them wanted to, not even Cooper. Forrester gave them a direct order.'

'Without even having the decency to tell me first?'

'He said he didn't have any choice.'

A guilty shadow fell over Vicky's face as she glanced away, leaving Tanner glaring over at Forrester's office. 'We'll see about that!' he spat, shoving himself off the edge of her desk.

'John, don't!' she called, but to no avail. He was already halfway over the office floor, charging his way towards the DCI's door.

- CHAPTER THIRTY FIVE -

'COME IN, WHY don't you,' Tanner heard Forrester mutter, as he burst into his office to come to a standstill in front of his desk, his body shaking with uncontrollable rage. 'Would you care for a coffee? A cream bun, perhaps?'

'You know why I'm here.'

'Then you know why I had no choice.'

'You've sent Cooper, of all people, to arrest Christine, the woman I just happen to be in a relationship with, just because of what some idiot wrote in the Norfolk Herald?'

'Er, no, Tanner. I sent Cooper out to bring her in for questioning based on evidence we collected at the murder scene.'

'What evidence?'

'The woman's DNA. It's a direct match with Christine's.'

'And how the hell do you know that?'

'Because of the sample you gave to Townsend.'

Tanner ground his teeth into a venomous snarl. 'I gave that sample to him in confidence.'

'For Christ's sake, Tanner, you don't go around handing out murder suspect's DNA samples "in confidence".'

'So, he told you then?'

Forrester let out an exasperated sigh. 'Forensics called me first thing this morning. They told me that a sample he'd provided matched one found at the scene. I brought him in here to ask him where he got if from. At first, out of some form of misplaced loyalty, he refused to say. I had to threaten to have him arrested for attempting to pervert the course of justice, reminding him that it was a civil law offence, one that carried a maximum penalty of lifetime imprisonment, before he eventually broke down and told me.'

Tanner remained ominously silent, like a ticking time bomb waiting to explode.

'What the hell were you thinking?' Forrester continued. 'Giving an impressionable young junior officer evidence in a murder investigation, telling him not to let anyone know where he got it from? Have you completely lost your mind?'

'This is *my* investigation,' Tanner growled.

'That doesn't give you the right to do whatever you damned well like with total disregard for the law you're supposed to be upholding, let alone encouraging someone else to do the exact same bloody thing!'

'I asked him not to mention anything because I didn't think it would have been Christine's DNA.'

'Then why did you give it to him?'

'Because I wanted to be sure it wasn't.'

'And yet here we are, having proved beyond all reasonable doubt that it is.'

'That's as maybe, but just because her DNA was found at the scene doesn't mean she had anything to do with his murder.'

'It means she was there, Tanner.'

'It means her DNA was there, not her.'

'Despite the fact that we have an eyewitness saying she was?'

'We have a volunteer birdwatcher telling us he saw

a man with long grey hair behind the wheel of a patrol boat of some sort.'

'If I remember correctly, his description was that the driver had greying-blond hair, and that the person was behind the wheel of not just any patrol boat, but specifically one belonging to a Broad's Ranger. If that's not enough, we now know that the murder victim was the person directly responsible for the death of both her husband and child, that she'd been fired from her position at Bradfield Hospital for being caught having sex with the very man everyone's been out looking for, a man she's apparently continued to stay in touch with long after her forced departure from the criminal psychiatric hospital he was being kept locked inside, *and* whose DNA was found alongside hers at the murder scene. If that's not evidence enough, Tanner, then I'm not sure what is!'

Doing his best not to listen to the facts Forrester was laying out in front of him, Tanner's mind careened around in ever decreasing circles, desperately trying to come up with some sort of an explanation that would instantly clear Christine of all possible suspicion, when he heard Forrester's desk phone burst suddenly into life.

'Forrester!' the DCI stated, snatching up the receiver.

Seeing his eyes narrow as they slowly lifted up into his, Tanner prepared himself for the worst.

Ending the call, Forrester gently replaced the receiver back into its cradle. 'That was Cooper.'

Tanner held his breath.

'Your presumed-innocent girlfriend didn't show up for work today.'

'That's absurd! She left before I did. And no, she wasn't dragging an unfeasibly large suitcase behind her.'

'Then she must have heard the news on the way in, that she was wanted in connection with the murder of the man responsible for the death of both her husband and child.'

'If that was the case, she'd have called me,' Tanner continued, his hand frantically digging around for his phone.

Forrester waited patiently for him to check for either missed calls or messages. 'Well?'

'No,' he eventually replied, putting it away with a nonchalant shrug, 'but all that means is that there was no need for her to. She often doesn't see anyone when she arrives at work. She simply takes her allocated boat to wherever she needs to be that day.'

'Do you know where that would be?'

'I have an idea,' Tanner replied, turning to leave.

'Under the circumstances, I think it's probably better if you let us take it from here.'

Tanner stopped in front of the door. 'You're seriously expecting me to tell you where she is so that you can send Cooper out to arrest her?'

'I'm sorry, Tanner, but I can't let you go chasing after her.'

'I won't be chasing after her as she hasn't run away. I just need a chance to talk to her.'

'To warn her that she's about to be arrested? I'm sorry, Tanner, but I can't let you do that.'

'You're forgetting, *sir*, that I'm still the SIO for this investigation.'

'You can't possibly imagine that that's still the case?'

'You're telling me I'm not?'

'Your girlfriend is now one of the prime suspects. You're not even on the team, let alone leading it.'

'You're expecting me to stand here and do nothing?'

'No, Tanner, I'm expecting you to go home and do nothing.'

Tanner shook his head. 'I'm sorry, sir, but that's not going to happen.'

'It *is* going to happen because I *said* it's going to happen. And if I find out you've made any effort to warn her, whether by phone, email, or any other form of communication, you'll be facing disciplinary charges. Is that clear?'

'Then I suppose I'll just have to ask her family and friends to instead,' Tanner grimaced at him with sarcastic glee, before tugging open the door to storm out, leaving Forrester slamming his fist down on his desk to bellow hopelessly after him.

- CHAPTER THIRTY SIX -

'CHRISTINE?' TANNER CALLED out, gently closing the door to their riverside bungalow before standing silently in the hallway, actively listening to nothing but a faint electrical buzz coming from the fridge in the kitchen.

Calling her name again, he peeled off his coat to conduct the briefest search of the rooms. She wasn't there. Neither did he expect her to be. She was at work, oblivious to the fact that half the Norfolk Constabulary were out looking for her in connection with the murder of some idiot homeless drunk. And why was she still at work and not attempting to flee the country? Because she had nothing to do with it. The idea she'd done any of what the newspapers had said was beyond ridiculous. Admittedly, he didn't know how her DNA had ended up at the scene where the body had been found, but as he'd told Forrester, it was hardly conclusive. The transfer of DNA from one object to another happened all the time. The fact that the body belonged to the person who'd been behind the wheel of the truck that had overturned on the motorway, the ensuing pile up killing her husband and child, had to be just one of those bizarre coincidences. As to the idea that she'd helped Jason Baines escape from a psychiatric hospital after a five year affair was the stuff of pure fiction. Even if she had managed to fall under his enigmatic spell during her time there, it was ancient history. She wasn't some bored housewife, so desperate for a man's attention that she'd spend her days exchanging love letters with some deranged parent-murdering psycho-nutjob.

Taking a seat at the kitchen's breakfast counter he dug out his phone once again to stare hopelessly down at its screen. Nobody had called. He didn't know if that was good or bad. He checked the sound was on full volume before opening his contacts list, his finger hovering over Christine's name. *Why couldn't he call her?* he asked himself. *Just to say hello?*

Of course, he already knew the answer, at least as to why he shouldn't. As a member of CID who up until half an hour before had been the SIO for the murder investigation she'd somehow become implicated in, any attempt to make contact with her at such a critical time would most definitely be seen as attempting to pervert the course of justice. Even if he said nothing more innocuous than to ask her how her day was going, it would make no difference. The timing of the call would leave Professional Standards forced to assume it had a more illicit purpose: to warn her that the police were out looking for her.

'Fuck it,' he eventually muttered, tapping on her name to lift the phone to his ear. Realising he didn't have a single clue as to what he was going to say, he was about to hang up when he heard it click through to voicemail.

'Hi Christine, it's – er – John,' he eventually began, instantly regretting having opened his mouth. As his imagination whisked him off to a dock inside a Magistrates' Court, forced to listen to the recording he was about to make, he cursed quietly to himself. 'Just calling to ask – er – what time you think you'll be back today? Call me when you get a chance. Bye for now.'

Ending the call he cursed again. 'That was just about the dumbest thing I've ever done in my entire life,' he muttered out loud.

Ditching the phone on the counter, he slid off the stool to make himself some coffee before deciding to take another look around the house, this time to see if there was any sign that she'd done as Forrester had suggested, packed a bag to do a runner.

Entering their bedroom, he cast his eyes over the dressing table. Everything seemed to be there, but if he was to be honest, he wouldn't know if anything wasn't. He turned his attention to the wardrobe, opening the doors for her side to find it crammed full of clothes. Again, it was difficult to tell if anything was actually missing.

He was about to close the door to take a look inside the bathroom when an old shoebox caught his eye on the shelf at the top, its lid held down by a pale blue ribbon.

Remembering what Vicky had told him about what the Norfolk Herald had said, how she'd apparently been exchanging love letters with Jason Baines since the time she'd left, he reached up to lever the box out with his fingers. With more than a twinge of guilt, he sat down on the edge of the bed to stare nervously down at the box. He didn't need to open it to know what was inside. Its weight and feel was enough for him to know that it was crammed full of letters and cards, probably dating back to when she was a teenager.

With the feeling that he didn't have much of a choice but to look inside, he glanced up at the open bedroom door, half-expecting to see Christine standing there, glaring at him with her hands placed firmly down on her hips. Unsure as to exactly why, he got up to close the door before making his way back to the bed. There he took a moment to remember how the ribbon had been tied before easing the bow apart to prise open the lid.

It was as he'd imagined, piled high with literally dozens of old letters and cards. He could even see the dog-eared corners of photographs sticking out from the bottom.

Filled with a sickening sense of self-loathing, he lifted out the first to slowly unfold it in his hands.

"My dearest Christine," it began.

His hand fell limp to his lap, the letter slipping through his fingers to float gently down to the floor, like a petal detaching itself from a dying rose. He didn't need to read the rest. The flamboyantly signed name he glimpsed at the end was enough for him to know that for once the story in the Norfolk Herald had been true.

- CHAPTER THIRTY SEVEN -

Thursday, 10th February

WITH A HEAD full of dreams, Tanner flickered his eyes open only to close them again a split second later. The brain inside his skull was thumping in pain, and the light streaming through the glass patio doors felt like it was burning out the backs of his retinas.

The moment he remembered where he was, what he'd found the day before, and how much he'd been drinking afterwards, a wave of nausea surged up from his stomach.

Forcing himself off the settee, he stumbled over to the kitchen sink to retch briefly before his body spasmed and convulsed to be violently sick.

Gasping for breath, he stared down at the contents of his stomach with shameful revulsion. With the putrid stench making him retch again, he turned on the tap to clear the bowl when he heard the chiming sound of the doorbell, echoing its way around the house.

'Go away,' he groaned, rinsing his mouth out with the water cascading from the end of the tap.

Assuming it was either the postman or some idiot wanting to sell him something he didn't want, he remained where he was for a moment, staring down at the sink whilst listening to the growing sound of silence. It wasn't Christine, he knew that much. Even if she'd forgotten her key, there was one hidden around the side of the house.

For the first time since he'd opened his eyes his thoughts turned to her. Had she come back the evening before, or had she been arrested to spend what would have been a terrifying night locked inside one of Wroxham Police Station's holding cells?

Retching once more, he heard the doorbell chime out again, this time to be followed by the voice of a man, hollering out his name. It took a full moment for him to realise who it was.

Taking a fortifying breath, he pushed himself up from the sink to look inside the bedroom. She wasn't there, nor had she been. Turning around, he weaved his way towards the front door, as if on a ship being tossed about on the open sea. There he could see a pair of dark brown eyes, staring at him through the open letterbox.

'Cooper?' he questioned.

The eyes blinked in confirmation before the letterbox rattled itself closed. 'Can I come in?' his voice came again.

'If you're looking for Christine, she's not here.'

'It's not about her.'

Tanner hesitated before asking a question that only half of him wanted to know the answer to. 'Did you find her?'

'Not yet, but it's possible that she's gone to stay with her parents.'

'Then what the hell are you doing here?' Tanner demanded, a feeling of relief swerving off into a pit of tortured resentment.

'Haven't you seen the news?'

Tanner grabbed hold of his wrist, momentarily wondering where his watch had gone. 'I've – I've only just got up. Why? What happened?'

'It's Superintendent Whitaker's son. He's gone missing.'

'What?'

'He disappeared last night. We have a witness saying they saw him getting into a car outside a local pub. The man seen helping him matches Baines' description.'

'Jesus Christ!' Tanner exclaimed, lurching forward to open the door to find Cooper staring at him with great bags hanging down from his eyes.

'They want me to be the new SIO,' he said, smiling nervously as he dug his hands into his pockets.

'OK, well, with me gone, I'm not surprised.'

'I've told them I don't want to.'

Tanner offered him a curious expression. 'I thought you'd have jumped at the chance?'

Tanner watched Cooper's bottom lip tremble ever-so slightly. 'It's – it's too much,' he began, glancing briefly away. 'Not with the Superintendent's son missing as well. Now he's asking for you.'

'Whitaker wants me back as the SIO?'

Cooper nodded in response.

'Well, good luck with that!'

It was Cooper's turn to look confused. 'I – I thought – what with Christine and everything...'

'That was before I found out that the story the Norfolk Herald printed was true. She *had* been exchanging love letters with Jason fucking Baines. I found one yesterday, when I got home, stuffed into an old shoebox at the top of the wardrobe.'

'But – that doesn't mean she helped him escape. It doesn't mean they murdered Norman Gibbs together, either.'

'Who – the man convicted of being directly responsible for the death of her husband and child?'

Tanner watched Cooper stare imploringly at him before blinking his eyes to the ground.

Feeling almost sorry for him, Tanner re-opened his mouth. 'Listen, if you really think it's too much, just tell them that they'll have to bring someone in from outside.'

'Whitaker has already said he wants someone with local knowledge. That's why he's asking for you. He was furious when Forrester told him he'd taken you off the investigation.'

'But he did so for good reason. I can't be seen leading something involving the woman I was in a relationship with.'

'Whitaker doesn't care about that. He just wants his son found.'

'What about Forrester?'

'I'm not sure he has much of a choice. He has to do what Whitaker tells him.'

'Does Forrester know you're here?'

Cooper shook his head.

'Look, Cooper, I appreciate you coming around like this and everything. Had I not found that letter I'd have probably accepted. But now...' Tanner looked away, his gaze disappearing into the distance. 'I'm sorry,' he eventually continued, 'but it's a no, I'm afraid.'

Cooper stood tall to force a smile at him. 'Of course, I understand. Thanks at least for listening. If you happen to change your mind, we're holding a briefing at eleven o'clock this morning. Whitaker will be there, as will half-a-dozen or so of his subordinates from HQ.' Tucking a hand inside his black city coat he pulled out a folded A4 file to hold out in front of him. 'I brought you a copy of the missing person's report, just in case you said yes.'

'Well, I'll take a look,' Tanner replied, taking the

file, 'but please don't expect to see me there.'

- CHAPTER THIRTY EIGHT -

WITH THE FRONT door closed, Tanner turned to make his way back inside, desperate for a coffee and something for his relentlessly thumping head. Discarding the missing person's report onto the nearest sofa, he put the kettle on to begin pulling open the various cupboards and drawers in search of some pain killers. Unable to find any, he cursed out loud. He knew they had some. He'd bought two packs himself only the week before. They just weren't in any of the usual places.

Assuming Christine must have hidden them somewhere during one of her frantic tidying-up sessions, he made his way into the bathroom, wrenching open the cabinet doors above the sink to start poking around inside. 'For fuck's sake, Christine,' he moaned to himself, his head feeling like it was about to explode, 'what the hell have you done with them?'

As he shifted some form of overpriced skin rejuvenating cream to one side, a pair of nail clippers slipped off the shelf, hitting the edge of the sink to disappear into the bin on the floor which was already filled to the brim. For a full moment he was tempted to just leave it there before realising that if he did, he'd only be left having to buy another pair.

With disgruntled resignation, he eased himself down to begin picking his way through its contents, doing his best not to think about some of the objects he was having to touch. After a minute of fruitless searching, he was about to resign himself to buying a new pair when something caught his eye, lying half-hidden underneath an empty bottle of mouthwash. 'What the hell?' he questioned, instantly forgetting about his aching head and the fact that it was stuck halfway inside a bathroom bin. The object he was looking at was familiar enough, he just hadn't seen one for what must have been well over twenty years.

Carefully lifting it out, he stared down at the small rectangular panel where two short pink lines could be seen running vertically down. With his heart picking up an uncertain beat, he dived back inside the bin, looking for the package it must have come in. With it clamped between the fingers of a trembling hand, he rose unsteadily to his feet to prop himself up against the edge of the sink. There he turned the empty box over in his hand, his eyes becoming transfixed to the pictorial diagram found on the back.

Two lines pregnant, one line not.

- CHAPTER THIRTY NINE -

THE MOMENT TANNER stepped into the open-plan office at Wroxham Police Station, packed to the rafters with police personnel, every head in the room seemed to turn to stare over at him.

Seeing Cooper come spluttering to a halt at the opposite end, his skin pale, his forehead glistening with sweat, Tanner sent him a reassuring smile.

With Cooper clearing his throat to continue the briefing that had evidently already started, Tanner straightened his tie to begin creeping surreptitiously around the edge of the room, heading for the white board at the end, to the side of which he found DCI Forrester.

'Sorry to sneak in like this,' Tanner whispered, taking a moment to gaze over at the long bony face of Superintendent Whitaker, standing in the midst of a small group of unfamiliar police officers on the opposite side. 'I've brought in some evidence which I think will help to clear the name of at least one of the suspects.'

'Thank you, Tanner,' Forrester replied, taking a firm hold of Tanner's arm to lead him behind a nearby filing cabinet. 'I'm sure we all appreciate your help, but I was under the distinct impression that you were no longer involved in this investigation.'

'Yes, sir, of course, but that was before I discovered that the woman everyone's been assuming has been in league with Jason Baines could well be in as much danger as everyone else.'

'I take it you mean Christine?'

Tanner nodded, taking out the shoebox he'd found from under his arm. 'I found these yesterday, inside her wardrobe,' he continued, removing the lid to show him the letters inside. 'Half of these were written to her by him, spanning a period from the time she left Bradfield Hospital up until about two months ago.'

Tanner watched Forrester's face cloud with confusion as his eyes darted briefly over at Whitaker before taking in the letters. 'Surely these only prove what the newspapers have been saying,' the DCI eventually responded, bringing his attention back up to Tanner, 'that they'd been maintaining a relationship long after she'd been told to leave.'

'I must admit, that's what I thought as well, but that was before I sat down to actually read them. From what Baines writes, it's clear that the relationship was only one way. They also indicate that Baines was furious at Christine for not having made more of an effort to keep her position at the hospital. He was even more pissed-off with Dr Copeland for having fired her in the first place. What's also clear is that she only sent a handful of letters back in return, each one explaining how much she regretted what had happened between them.'

'I see. So, you have the letters she wrote as well, do you?'

'Well, no,' Tanner replied, glancing down, 'but it's obvious what she'd written from reading his replies.'

'What the hell's going on here?' came Whitaker's harsh low voice, his ferret-like face appearing suddenly beside them.

'DI Tanner has brought in what he's describing as

evidence that Christine Halliday – the woman he's currently cohabiting with – hadn't been quite so involved with Jason Baines as the newspapers have been claiming.'

'Good! Then he can be reinstated as the SIO.'

Forrester balked at his response. 'I'm, er, sorry, sir, but I really don't think it's as simple as that. There's still the fact that she knew the murder victim, being that he was directly responsible for what happened to her husband and newly born child. And then, of course, there's her DNA.'

'I thought we'd already been over this. Forensics found it where his body was found, *not* where he was murdered.'

'Well, yes, but...'

'Which anyone could have left there, including our prime suspect, Jason Baines, who I hope I don't have to remind you is the same man seen offering a lift to my now missing son. If Detective Inspector's Tanner's girlfriend is now in the clear, then I want *him* leading the investigation, not that stuttering buffoon you have out there at the moment.'

As shocked as he was embarrassed to have heard the superintendent make such cruel and inappropriate remarks against one of their own, Tanner stole a glance over at the man being discussed, still addressing the gathered crowd in the hope that he hadn't heard.

'I can assure you, *sir*,' he heard Forrester continue, 'that DI Cooper is more than capable of leading this investigation.'

'I do hope you're joking. I'm not sure I've ever met anyone *less* capable. Either way, I'm not taking the chance. Not when it's the life of my son we're talking about. I want DI Tanner, and that's the end of it.'

'If you say so, sir,' Forrester responded, with more

than a hint of irreverence.

'I do say so, thank you very much,' came Whitaker's biting response, as the sound of someone's desk phone could be heard trying to compete with Cooper's wavering voice. 'Now, with that settled, you need to update Tanner on the role my men are going to play.'

Tanner transferred a curious look from Whitaker to his DCI. 'Which men are those?'

'The ones standing on the other side,' Forrester replied, gesturing over. 'They're a unit of specialised firearms officers.'

Tanner's head jolted back in surprise. 'Is that really necessary?'

Whitaker stared down his aquiline nose at him as if he was of no more significance than a decomposing fly. 'There's a deranged psychotic lunatic on the loose, one who's not only in possession of a handgun, but has already shown that he's not afraid to use it. To be honest,' he continued, his look of disdain shifting over to Forrester, 'I can't quite believe you hadn't requested an armed unit before.'

Tanner watched Forrester's face darken with what he could only assume was embarrassed rage.

'I suppose you should also know,' Whitaker continued, his eyes still boring into Forrester's, 'that I've decided to give them a shoot to kill order as well.'

'B-but...' spluttered the DCI, 'he's not some sort of radicalised Middle Eastern terrorist!'

'I suppose that depends on your definition. As far as I'm concerned, a convicted armed psychopath more than qualifies.'

The sound of someone clearing their throat to their side had them turning around to find young DC Townsend, shifting awkwardly from one foot to the other. 'Sorry to bother you, sirs,' he began, the bulk of his attention focussed on Forrester, 'but another body's been found.'

Whitaker's face went as white as a sheet. 'It's n-not my...my...' he began – the words barely able to stumble out of his mouth.

'I'm sorry, sir,' Townsend continued, his eyes resting sympathetically on the superintendent's, 'they didn't say.'

- CHAPTER FORTY -

TANNER CRANED HIS neck to gaze down at the body of an over-weight middle-aged man dressed in a charcoal grey suit, a twisted leg hanging over the edge of an industrial-sized wheelie bin parked at the back of a restaurant in Stalham. 'Well, at least it's not Whitaker's son,' he eventually commented, glancing about at the various emergency personnel. 'He's not still here, is he?'

'He left the moment he found out it wasn't,' Townsend replied, following his gaze.

'Do we know who found the body?'

Townsend nodded towards a smartly dressed young woman waiting at the corner of the pub, talking quietly to a female police constable. 'Miss Melissa Heywood. She's the restaurant's manager.'

'OK. Why don't you head over to take her statement?'

Townsend was about to spin away when Tanner saw Dr Johnstone's old Volvo Estate turning into to the carpark. 'Actually, hold on. Let's have a chat to our medical examiner first, shall we?'

A few moments later they heard Johnstone's voice, stepping out to begin trudging his way over. 'What do you have for me today? An actual body, I hope.'

Tanner waited for him to come closer before opening his mouth. 'At a guess I'd say he's been shot, in much the same way as our previous victim.'

Coming to a standstill between them, Johnstone pushed his glasses up the bridge of his nose to peer over the edge of the bin. 'OK, well, if you can stand back a little, I'll take a closer look.'

Before doing so, Tanner gestured with a hand to highlight a mark on the body's forehead. 'You may want to be careful of that. From what I can see, I'd say it was a partial fingerprint.'

Johnstone leaned forward. 'Looks like you could be right about that.'

'Excuse me!' came the forthright voice of the restaurant's manager, calling over to them from where she was standing, 'but I don't suppose there's any chance I can get back to work now?'

Leaving Johnstone to begin his examination, Tanner led Townsend towards her. 'Sorry to have kept you. Miss Heywood, isn't it?'

'That's right,' the lady nodded.

'I understand you found the body?'

'He was one of our customers, at least he almost was.'

'Almost?' Tanner queried, coming to a halt in front of her.

'That man...' the woman began, her eyes darting briefly over at the body, 'he came into the pub, before...before...'

'Was he on his own?'

'He was, but he was booked to have lunch with someone else.'

'And what happened to them?'

'He'd already called in to cancel. He must have forgotten to tell his friend.'

'I bet he was pleased about that.'

'Not exactly. After having a go at me he stormed out, moaning about having had his afternoon wasted.'

'And then you found him here?'

'Just after he left I heard a loud bang coming from the carpark. I thought it might be some of the local boys letting off fireworks. They've been doing so ever since Bonfire Night. So I came out to tell them to clear off. That's when I saw...' The young woman's eyes drifted over to the body again.

'Did you see anyone else?'

'I – I don't think so,' she replied, 'although, to be honest, I'm not sure I really looked. As soon as I saw him I just turned immediately around to come straight back inside.'

'I don't suppose you knew his name?'

'I'm sorry, he didn't say.'

'He wasn't a regular?'

The woman shook her head.

'How about the person who made the reservation?'

'We should do,' she replied, unwrapping her arms from the tablet held tight against her chest, 'unless someone's already deleted it.'

Tanner waited for her to check with impatient expectation.

'A Mr Lawrence Hambleton,' she eventually replied, lifting her head.

Tanner raised a curious eyebrow at Townsend.

'We have an address for him,' she continued, 'if that's of any use?'

'I don't think that will be necessary,' Tanner replied, smiling back, 'but thanks anyway.'

Making sure they had her contact details, Tanner gave her permission to return to her work when he saw Johnstone endeavouring to garner their attention.

'Marcus Brooke,' they heard him say as they headed back. 'Your friend in the bin,' he added, holding up an evidence bag with a business card floating inside. 'I found this in his suit's outer breast pocket. Assuming it belongs to him, he's the senior partner for a local conveyancing firm, one by the name of Glanville & Brookes.'

'I think I know it,' chirped Townsend, 'at least, I've walked past it a few times. It's the one just down the road.'

'Any sign of a wallet?'

'Not yet, but I can't say I've had much of a look. I was examining the wound when I just happened to see the card.'

'Was I right – about him being shot?'

'I don't think there's any doubt about that. Close range, as well.'

'But not by a shotgun?'

'A shotgun? Er, no. If the culprit had used one of those, I doubt there'd be much left of him.'

'And I assume that was the cause of death?'

'I'd be very surprised if it wasn't, but as always, I won't be able to confirm that until I get him back to the lab.'

'Before you do, I don't suppose you could make that partial fingerprint a priority?'

'That shouldn't be a problem. I'll instruct forensics as soon as they get here.'

- CHAPTER FORTY ONE -

'SO, MR HAMBLETON calls to arrange to have lunch with the senior partner of a local conveyancing firm, only to cancel it at the last minute without bothering to tell him, leaving the senior partner in question to be shot in the carpark by the person we can only assume to be Jason Baines?' commented Townsend, in a confused questioning tone whilst following Tanner towards his car.

'I'd have to agree, it doesn't make much sense, unless of course it wasn't Hambleton who made the reservation.'

'You're thinking it was Baines?'

'It would make more sense.'

'It would?'

'Well, a little.'

Reaching the car, Townsend stopped beside the passenger door to start scratching his head. 'Even if it was Baines pretending to be Hambleton, why would he want to lure the senior partner of a conveyancing firm out to a public restaurant in order to shoot him in the carpark around the back?'

'I only said it made more sense,' Tanner replied, in a curt irritated tone as he stopped to pull out his phone. With still not having heard from Christine, he found himself having to force his mind back to the task at hand. 'But only because Baines is a more likely candidate to go around shooting people in carparks for no apparent reason than Hambleton is.'

'But he'd still need some sort of a motive.'

'We don't know that he doesn't,' Tanner replied, unlocking the door to heave it open, 'which is why we're going to pay a visit to the victim's conveyancing firm.'

'If that's the plan, then I don't think we'll need the car. It's the next street down. There's nowhere to park down there, either.'

- CHAPTER FORTY TWO -

STEPPING OFF STALHAM high street to immediately enter the small stuffy offices of Glanville & Brookes Solicitors, Tanner and Townsend approached the unwelcoming face of the dark haired lady they found peering over her glasses at them from behind an uncluttered reception desk.

'Detective Inspector Tanner and Detective Constable Townsend, Norfolk Police,' Tanner announced, as they each dug out their respective IDs. 'We'd like to speak to someone about Mr Brookes; if we may?'

The lady lifted her glasses to study the IDs being presented to her with an aloof supercilious expression. 'Mr Brookes isn't here,' came her eventual response, returning the glasses to the bridge of her nose.

'Which is why I'm asking to speak to someone about him, not to him,' Tanner replied, swallowing the words of a more sarcastic response.

'And his business partner, Mr Glanville, is in a meeting.'

'Then I think it may be necessary to interrupt him.'

The lady took a moment to study Tanner's face. 'May I ask what could possibly be so important?'

'As I mentioned earlier, it concerns Mr Brookes.'

'Are you telling me he's been arrested?'

'It's nothing like that.'

'Then what is it?'

'At this precise moment in time we're not at liberty to say.'

'I'm sorry, Inspector, but I'm not prepared to interrupt Mr Glanville's meeting unless you tell me.'

Tanner let out a capitulating sigh. 'We believe that the body of Mr Brookes is currently half-hanging out of an industrial-sized wheelie bin around the back of The Granary, the restaurant one street down from yours.'

The woman's mouth fell open as the colour drained from her already washed-out face. 'I'm sorry – but – what did you say?'

'Are you asking me to repeat it?'

But there was no need. The receptionist was already picking up the phone.

'I'm most dreadfully sorry to interrupt you, Mr Glanville,' they heard her begin, her eyes darting furtively between them, 'but there are a couple of policemen down in reception asking to speak to you with regards to Mr Brookes. It would appear that something dreadful has happened to him.'

- CHAPTER FORTY THREE -

BEING ADVISED THAT he'd be straight down, Tanner and Townsend took the seats offered to them to begin listening to the sound of floorboards creaking above their heads. Within less than a minute, a bald-headed man with a chubby red face came charging through a side door to send a disturbed questioning glare over at them before turning his attention to the receptionist. 'You said something has happened to Marcus?'

Tanner pushed himself up to his feet. 'May I assume you're Mr Brookes' business partner, Mr Glanville?'

'That's right,' the man replied, pivoting himself around. 'Now, can someone please tell me what's happened to Marcus?'

'Is there somewhere more private we can talk?' Tanner asked, his eyes flickering over towards the receptionist.

'I'm sure Mrs Finch doesn't mind.'

'I'm sure she doesn't, but even so.'

'Oh very well,' Glanville huffed, rolling his eyes to begin leading them back through the door he'd only just come out of, 'but I really don't have long. I have a client waiting for me upstairs.'

Ushering them through to a spacious office on the same floor, one that must have been reserved for more formal meetings, Glanville closed the door to place himself behind a chair at the end of a large oval table. 'OK, so can you now please tell me what this is about?'

Without being offered a seat, Tanner drew in a breath. 'A body was found earlier this afternoon. It has yet to be formally identified, but at the moment we believe it to be your business partner, Mr Marcus Brooke.'

For the longest moment Glanville just stared at Tanner with a blank mystified expression, before eventually shaking his head. 'I'm sorry, Inspector, but you must be mistaken. Marcus was only here a couple of hours ago.'

'Before leaving to attend a luncheon appointment?'

'Well, yes, but...'

'At the Granary restaurant, the one at the end of the high street?'

Glanville pulled out the chair to sink slowly down, his eyes remaining fixed on Tanner's. 'Are you sure it was him, I – I mean, I know he had a heart condition.'

'With regret, at the moment we don't believe his death was from natural causes.'

'I'm sorry, I don't understand?'

Keen to avoid having to offer a more detailed description of the suspected cause, Tanner gestured for Townsend to take a seat before following suit. 'We've been told he'd gone there to have lunch with someone?'

'Well, yes. To meet one of our clients, a Mr Hambleton.'

'I don't suppose you know what the meeting was supposed to be about?'

'We'd been appointed by his grandfather to manage his estate. He passed away a few months ago, leaving his grandson as the sole beneficiary. I believe

Mr Hambleton asked to meet with Marcus to discuss the possibility of putting it up for sale.'

'You mean, Long Gore Hall?' Tanner queried, catching Townsend's eye.

'And the land surrounding it,' Glanville confirmed. 'I assume you're familiar with the estate?'

'We met Mr Hambleton there a few days ago,' Tanner continued, his attention returning to the solicitor sitting at the end of the table. 'I must admit, he didn't leave me with the impression that his intention was to sell.'

'From what I understand, he was somewhat disappointed by the state he found it in. He's probably reached the conclusion that he can't afford to have it brought back to its former glory, which is hardly surprising.'

Tanner took a moment to glance about the room. 'Did you hear the news; that your client was reported to have shot an intruder there?'

'Someone did mention something about it. Is it relevant?'

'Was it Mr Hambleton who told you?'

'I believe it was Marcus. I've yet to meet Mr Hambleton,' Glanville continued, turning to gaze wistfully out of the window, 'but if Marcus really is dead, then I suppose I'm going to have to, along with all his other bloody clients. Christ! Are you sure it's Marcus?'

'As I said before, Mr Glanville, we've yet to make a formal identification, but we are proceeding on the basis that it is. With that in mind, I don't suppose he has any family living nearby?'

'Not that I'm aware of. His parents passed away some time ago. I think he has a brother knocking about the place somewhere. Not sure exactly where though.'

'What about a family of his own?'

'He never married. Never met the right girl, apparently.'

'Then I don't suppose there's any chance that you'd be able to help us?'

Glanville looked up at Tanner with a startled expression. 'You want me to identify his body?'

'You don't have to, of course, but it would certainly save us some time.'

'Well – I could – I suppose,' the solicitor mumbled, shifting uncomfortably in his seat. 'May I finish my meeting first?'

'Of course. There's no immediate rush. I'll send a police officer around to escort you over.'

With Glanville getting up to show them out, Tanner stood up with Townsend to catch his eye. 'Whilst we're here, I don't suppose you've ever heard of a man by the name of Jason Baines?'

'You mean, the patient who recently escaped from Bradfield Hospital?'

Tanner nodded in response. 'Did Mr Brooke know him, by any chance?'

'Not that I was aware of. Why?'

'He's never been a client of yours?'

'Good Lord, no! We're a conveyancing firm. We don't do criminal law. Even if we had to, I'm not sure I'd even know where to start!'

- CHAPTER FORTY FOUR -

'I'M NOT SURE that was much help either,' Tanner commented, stepping out of the solicitors' office to immediately pull out his phone.

'You didn't think it was odd that Hambleton would appear to have changed his mind about selling Long Gore Hall?' Townsend queried, as they began making their way back to the restaurant.

Having still not received a single message from Christine, Tanner put the phone away with a sense of both growing concern and mounting frustration. 'Not really,' he eventually replied. 'To be honest, I thought he was mad not to have put it up for sale the moment he stepped inside. He probably had a builder around, telling him how much it was going to cost to do the place up.'

'Do we still think Baines shot the guy we found in the wheelie bin? I mean, other than what they'd heard about in the news, neither the victim nor his business partner seemed to know anything about him.'

'That's only what Glanville told us. For all we know, Brookes was gay, and was one of the seemingly many people who Baines had been exchanging love letters with.'

'So I suppose Brookes wrote to him last week, telling him he'd met someone else, which was why Baines escaped, to exact his revenge?' proposed

Townsend, in a dubious tone.

Townsend's somewhat flippant suggestion only served to divert Tanner's mind back to Christine. 'Unfortunately, as unlikely as that may sound, at this stage we just don't know. All we do know is that two people are dead, two more are missing, my girlfriend is being hunted down by my very own police department, and there's an escaped psychopath on the loose going around shooting seemingly random people for no apparent reason.'

'He's not the only one who's armed,' commented Townsend, rounding a corner to see Whitaker's firearms officers stepping down from the back of a van, each with a particularly lethal-looking semi-automatic carbine rifle slung over their shoulders.

'Jesus fucking Christ!' Tanner exclaimed, stopping where he was to stare over at them with agitated bemusement. 'That's all we bloody need!'

Seeing Dr Johnstone zip up his coat as he hurried towards his car, he shot Townsend an irritated scowl. 'Looks like I'm going to have to have a word with Whitaker's men, but don't let Johnstone go before I've had a chance to talk to him.'

'Understood,' Townsend replied, as Tanner turned up the collar of his coat to begin storming his way over towards the nearest and tallest of the armed officers.

'Excuse me!' he called out, catching the man's eye, busily handing out magazine cartridges to the surrounding men. 'May I ask what the hell you think you are doing?'

'Superintendent's orders,' the square jaw man replied, meeting Tanner's gaze with a pair of narrowing eyes. 'And you are?'

Tanner quickly dug out his formal ID. 'Detective Inspector Tanner. I'm the SIO for this investigation, which means that I'm in charge, not Superintendent bloody Whitaker. Now I suggest you re-collect those magazines of yours, climb back into your van and bugger off.'

'Can't do that, I'm afraid,' the man replied, taking the last remaining magazine to load into the receiver of his own semi-automatic carbine. 'The Super's given us direct orders to start conducting door-to-door enquiries in search of the missing patient, Mr Jason Baines.'

'I see. And if someone opens the door who you think might know something they don't at first appear willing to tell you, what are you going to do, threaten to line them up against a wall and shoot them?'

'As the missing patient is now wanted in connection with no less than two gun-related murders, we've been told not to take any chances.'

'We'll see about that,' Tanner muttered, pulling out his phone to give Forrester a call, only to see Johnstone open the boot of his car out of the corner of his eye to place his medical bag inside. 'Shit,' he cursed, under his breath, glancing about in search of Townsend, wondering why he wasn't stopping him from leaving.

Putting his phone away, Tanner turned his attention back to the armed officer. 'I'm afraid I'm going to need confirmation from my DCI before I can let you start poking guns at the local population.'

'You're welcome to call him, but as I said before, our orders come from HQ.'

Tanner drew in a calming breath. 'Can you at least give me five minutes before you leave?'

'You have as long as it takes for us to get ready. Best I can do, I'm afraid.'

With still no sign of Townsend, Tanner hurried over to where Dr Johnstone was tugging opening his driver's side door. 'Are you all done?' he called out, his voice stopping the medical examiner's head from disappearing inside.

'Ah, Tanner. I was hoping to catch you before I left.'

'I don't suppose you found anything else?'

'Only the victim's wallet. The credit cards inside bore the same name as on the business card.'

'No other injuries?'

'Nothing obvious. I'd be surprised if the cause of death isn't as it appears. I should be able to have a full post-mortem report for you by lunchtime tomorrow.'

Curious to know why he'd wanted to speak to him if he had nothing new to add, Tanner turned his head to gaze over to where he could see the armed officers looking as if they were about to leave. 'OK, that's fine. Give me a call if you find out anything before then.'

Stepping away to continue making the call to Forrester, he heard Johnstone calling after him.

'You should probably know that I had that fingerprint sent off for priority analysis, as requested.'

Having already forgotten about it, Tanner stopped to send Johnstone a questioning look. 'Did they say how long it would take to come back with a result?'

'They already have.'

'That didn't take long.'

'I wanted to let you know the result first,' Johnstone continued, as he began glancing surreptitiously about, 'before it becomes public knowledge.'

Johnstone's words and behaviour had Tanner's heart thumping hard in his chest. 'Before *what* becomes public knowledge?'

'I'm sorry, John,' the medical examiner continued, his eye's turning to rest gently on Tanner's, 'apparently, the result came up almost immediately. It was a direct match.'

Tanner continued to stare over at him as his stomach began to churn. 'You're not seriously about to tell me that it belongs to Christine?'

'I'll sit on it for as long as I can,' Johnstone replied with a solemn nod, 'but at the end of the day, there's nothing I can do. It will have to be included in my final report.'

- CHAPTER FORTY FIVE -

WITH HIS MIND becoming numb to the world around him, Tanner wasn't even aware that Johnstone had driven away when he heard the sound of Townsend's voice, calling to him as if through a distant fog.

Seeing his head suddenly appear beside him, Tanner jumped with a start. 'Jesus Christ, Townsend! Is it really necessary to sneak up on me like that?'

'Er...sorry, sir. I just wanted to apologise for having failed to stop Dr Johnstone. I was having to deal with some mad old woman demanding to know if we were under attack by a group of militant terrorists.'

'By who?'

'Militant terrorists, sir,' Townsend repeated. 'I think she was a little perturbed to see an armed police unit march straight past her.'

'Shit!' Tanner cursed, lifting himself up onto the balls of his feet. 'Don't tell me they've gone already?'

'About five minutes ago. Didn't you get a chance to speak to them?'

'I told them to climb back into their van and bugger off,' came Tanner's simmering reply. 'Unfortunately, they wouldn't listen, not to me at any rate. According to them, they're under direct orders from Whitaker.'

'But – aren't you the SIO?'

'That's what I thought. Anyway, the thing I'm really struggling to get my head around is what he thinks he's going to achieve by having a group of armed police wandering about the place.'

'I'd assumed it was because Baines is armed as well.'

'I'm sure it is, but with his son being one of the two missing boys, I'd have thought he'd be keen to minimise the risk of him becoming an innocent casualty. Assuming he was, sending out an armed police unit to find the man who took him would appear to be somewhat counterintuitive.'

'Maybe he doesn't see it that way.'

'Evidently not,' Tanner replied, turning his head to begin gazing wistfully off into space.

'Did Johnstone have anything else to add?'

'Huh?'

'Dr Johnstone? I saw you talking to him.'

'Oh, nothing important. Listen, I don't suppose I could ask you to do me another favour?'

Townsend's hands slunk slowly down into his pockets. 'Er...to be honest, sir, I'm not sure I should. I assume you heard what happened last time; that Forrester had me in his office, accusing me of attempting to pervert the course of justice?'

'Don't worry about Forrester. His bark is far worse than his bite.'

'It is?'

'Listen, I have to find Christine. I think the fastest way to do that will be to locate her car. If I give you her number plate, can you go back to the station and plug it into the ANPR for me? If that doesn't come up with anything, start phoning the local carparks and train stations. Whilst you're at it, you may as well request access to her phone, email, social media, and bank accounts.'

Townsend raised an uncertain eyebrow as he began digging around for his notebook. 'Is it alright if I ask Sally to help?'

'I'd rather you didn't. Actually, I'm going to insist that you don't! If you need help, try Vicky. Oh, and one more thing, if you do find her car, can you please make a point of *not* telling Forrester?'

Townsend stopped taking notes to look slowly up at Tanner.

'And definitely not Whitaker,' Tanner added. 'The last thing I want is for him to order his bloody firearm officers to begin searching for her as well.'

'I'll do the best I can, but if I get dragged into Forrester's office again...'

'Don't worry, I'm sure that won't happen.'

'But if it does?'

'OK, if he does, which he won't, then I'll suppose you'll have to tell him.'

Nodding in reluctant agreement, Townsend returned to his notes. 'And how about you?'

'I'm going to see if I can figure out who saw her last, assuming it wasn't me, that is.'

- CHAPTER FORTY SIX -

WITH THE SUN already setting fast, Tanner tore along the country lanes heading for Potter Heigham, to where the Broads Rangers' patrol boats were moored.

Arriving to see one chug sedately up the gently flowing river towards him, he stepped onto the pontoon to wait at the end. When he thought he recognised the bearded middle-aged man whose head was leaning out the side of the wooden wheelhouse, he held up a hand as a greeting whilst racking his brain in an effort to remember his name.

As the boat slowed to a crawl, Tanner watched him climb onto the side to begin making his way towards its pointed bow. There he crouched down to fetch up a mooring line from off the deck before standing tall to face him.

'Eve'n, John,' the man eventually called, his nonchalant Norfolk accent affable enough.

'Richard, isn't it?'

'On a good day. Any chance you could give me a hand?'

'Of course,' Tanner replied, taking a step back to catch the rope as it spiralled its way through the air.

'I assume you're look'n for Christine?'

Tanner nodded to start taking in the slack, leaving Richard treading lightly back to the wheelhouse. 'I don't suppose you've any idea where she might be?'

'I suppose that depends on who's ask'n,' the Broads Ranger replied, re-taking his position behind the wheel. 'I assume you know that we've had your lot down here already, asking something very similar.'

'You told them that you didn't know where she was, as she hadn't shown up for work that day.'

'Consider'n we'd all 'eard the news as we'd been com'n in; that you lot were out look'n for her in connection with that escaped psycho, Jason Baines, as well as the murder of that Wildlife Trust volunteer, I think that was just about all we were prepared to say. So anyway, if you're here with your Detective Inspector's hat on, you'll probably find my answer is going to be someth'n very similar.'

'I'm here as her friend!' Tanner stated, with firm resolution.

Steering the boat into the space between the pontoon and the boat moored up on the other side, Richard cast a wary eye over at him. 'Despite the paper say'n that you're the one in charge of the investigation?'

'As it turns out, I'm not as "in charge" as I thought, and the guy who is has just sent out an armed police unit to begin door-to-door inquiries. At the moment, they're only looking for Baines, but from what I found out today, that's going to change, and I don't have long before it does. I don't particularly wish to imagine what could happen if the police open fire on him whilst he's holding a knife to Christine's neck. If you know anything, anything at all...?'

As the boat came to a gradual stop, Tanner waited in hopeful silence for Richard to step off to start looping the boat's stern-end line around the cleat at the pontoon's furthest end.

'Fair enough,' he eventually replied, standing up to take Tanner in, 'but I can't say I know much more than what I told your colleagues.'

'But you do know something?'

'Only that she didn't exactly *not* turn up for work that day. She arrived as normal, maybe a little late, but only about five minutes. I was here with everyone else, get'n the boats ready. As I said, we'd all 'eard the news on the way in, so we were obviously talk'n about her. So when we saw her arrive in that car of hers, none of us were quite sure what to say. Fortunately for us, as it turned out, we didn't 'ave to.'

'How do you mean?'

'She stepped out to wave over at us before going over to talk to someone who must've been wait'n for her in the carpark.'

Tanner drew in a fortifying breath. 'Did you see who it was?'

'Not clearly. He was behind the wheel of some over-sized four-by-four. But if I was asked to hazard a guess, I'd say it was the man you were look'n for.'

'Jason Baines?'

Richard nodded.

'What happened then?'

'They talked for a bit, then she climbed in and they drove off.'

'I don't suppose you heard what they were talking about?'

'The only thing I 'eard her say was the name of that place he'd escaped from.'

'Bradfield Hospital?'

'That's the one.'

'Did she say anything to you before they left.'

'Not a word. It was as if she'd forgotten we were even there.'

'And the car he was driving?'

'It was one of them Range Rovers. One of the older models.'

'Colour?'

'Dark green.'

'I don't suppose you made a note of the number plate?'

Richard snorted with laughter. 'Not a chance! We were too busy wondering where she was head'n.'

Tanner turned to begin staring about. 'If you said she arrived here as normal, then where's her car?'

'I've no idea. It was gone by the time we got back.'

- CHAPTER FORTY SEVEN -

LEAVING THE BROADS Ranger to finish tying up the boat, Tanner hurried back to his car to hear the demanding tone of his phone ring from inside his coat. In the increasingly vague hope that it might have been Christine, he stopped to pull it out. But it wasn't her. It was someone calling from Wroxham Police Station's main office number. With the assumption that it was Townsend, he answered the call. 'Tanner speaking!'

'Tanner, it's Forrester.'

'Shit,' he cursed, holding the phone away from his mouth.

'I was just wondering where you are,' he heard his DCI continue, 'being that I've just seen Townsend waltz into the office without you?'

'I'm out looking for Baines, sir, like everyone else.'

'I see. Then why isn't Townsend with you?'

'I – er – thought he'd be of more use searching for him online.'

'And how's he supposed to do that when the man in question doesn't have an online presence, being that up until five days ago he was safely locked up inside a psychiatric hospital?'

'I – I thought he'd be able to start checking through some CCTV camera footage.'

'To look at what? Every street in the whole of Norfolk?'

'Er...not exactly.'

'Then where, *exactly?*'

Determined not to have to tell him that neither of them were looking for Baines, but Christine instead, Tanner was forced to start choosing his words very carefully. 'We had a lead, sir.'

'Pray, do tell.'

'Someone thought they saw him behind the wheel of an old Range Rover.'

'And you're only just telling me this now?'

'Well, yes, sir, but in fairness, we've only just found out ourselves, and they weren't exactly sure it was him.'

'Who wasn't?'

Tanner cursed again. The more he said, the closer he was coming to having to mention Christine, so further implicating her in what was now a double-murder investigation. 'I was talking to a Broads Ranger,' he eventually continued. 'He said he saw Baines driving out of the carpark in Potter Heigham, where they keep their patrol boats.'

'When was this?'

'Yesterday morning.'

'You mean, the same time Christine reportedly "disappeared"?'

Standing firm, Tanner drew in a breath. 'They saw her talking to him.'

'To Jason Baines?'

'Yes, sir.'

'Jesus Christ, Tanner!'

'Apparently, she then climbed into his car before being driven off, but that doesn't mean they're working together, nor that they've re-kindled their supposed previous carnal relationship,' Tanner heard himself blurt out, as if trying to convince himself as well as his DCI. 'For all we know, he's kidnapped her in the same way he's thought to have taken Whitaker's son and the doctor's son.'

'That's as may be, Tanner, but neither Whitaker's son, nor Doctor Copeland's has had their DNA found at the scene of a murder, with the victim being the person responsible for the death of both her husband and child.'

Taking cold comfort from the fact that Forrester didn't know about her fingerprint having been found on the dead solicitor as well, Tanner wrestled to find something else to say in her defence, but nothing was coming to mind. Even for him, it was becoming increasingly hard to believe that she was anything less than a willing accomplice to Baines' murderous intent.

'Anyway,' he heard Forrester continue, 'you said you had a lead?'

Recalling the description of the car, Tanner remembered what he'd been thinking about before taking the call, and the location it had been leading him to. 'Yes, sir. The car the Broads Ranger saw. He said it was a dark green Range Rover. One of the older models. It's the same car I've seen parked outside Long Gore Hall. The same colour as well.'

'Sorry, I'm confused. You're now saying Hambleton was seen picking up Christine?'

'Not at all. I'm simply saying that it was his car, at least it might have been.'

'Yes, Tanner, "might" being the operative word. Do you have any idea how many dark green Range Rovers there are in Norfolk? Just about every man and his wife has one!'

'Not quite, sir.'

'OK, maybe not *every* man, but most of the wives do. Just because a witness saw one hardly means it was Hambleton's.'

'But it's a lead, nevertheless.'

'You're not seriously thinking about going over there to ask him if he drove over to Potter Heigham yesterday morning to pick up your estranged girlfriend, possibly with the intention of selling her to the highest bidder?'

'I was thinking more along the lines that Baines may have stolen it,' Tanner replied, struggling to appreciate Forrester's sarcasm.

'No doubt he did, but from Hambleton?'

'I'm fully aware that it's a longshot, thank you, sir, but the connection is there, leaving me with no choice but to follow it up.'

'Surely, if it had been stolen, he'd have reported it?'

'Then there's the restaurant table reservation.'

'The what?'

'I haven't had a chance to tell you, but it was Hambleton who booked the table to meet with the now murdered solicitor, cancelling the reservation just moments before he arrived.'

After an uncomfortably long silence, Tanner eventually heard Forrester let out a heavy sigh of reluctant capitulation. 'Very well, but if you arrive to find his car is still parked out the front, and that it has been since the last time he used it, I'd be grateful if you could leave the poor man alone to find something slightly more productive to be getting on with, like trying to find out if anyone else has reported having had their dark green Range Rover stolen, for example.'

- CHAPTER FORTY EIGHT -

ARRIVING AT THE twisted rusting gates that marked the boundary of the Long Gore Hall estate, Tanner ground his teeth with frustration as he looked ahead to see not one, but two cars parked outside, one a bright red Mini, the other being the same dark green Range Rover he'd seen there before.

Curious to know who owned the Mini, Tanner immediately decided to ignore Forrester's order, continuing to rumble his way down the pot-holed broken track.

Coming to a halt between the two cars, he climbed out to see Hambleton's familiar face, grinning like a Cheshire Cat at the top of the grandiose stone steps whilst saying goodbye to a lanky young man dressed in an ill-fitting black suit.

With the lad turning to head down the steps, Tanner nodded at him as he passed before raising a hand up to Hambleton, only to see his previous cheerful demeanour slip instantly away.

'What is it now, Inspector?' Hambleton demanded, his arms folding resolutely over his chest.

'Sorry to bother you again, Mr Hambleton.'

'Are you, now?'

'I just wanted to have a quick word with you about your car.'

'What about it?'

'It appears that it – or at least one very similar – was seen recently at Potter Heigham.'

Hambleton's mouth fell open in sardonic horror. 'No! Really?'

'Anyway,' Tanner continued, forcing himself to ignore his irreverent sarcasm, 'we were just wondering if you'd been there recently?'

'Sorry, where was that again?'

'Potter Heigham.'

'Yes, of course. I can remember exactly the last time I was there.'

'Which was?'

'When I was twelve, just before we left for South Africa.'

Tanner could feel his fists clench together with frustrated annoyance. 'Did you use your car at all yesterday morning?'

Hambleton stared thoughtfully up at the cold slate-grey sky. 'Yesterday afternoon I did, but not yesterday morning, not as far as I can remember.'

'Do you know if anyone else did?'

'I'm sorry?'

'Have you lent it to anyone recently?'

'Why on earth would I have done that?'

'Nobody's taken it without your permission?'

'You mean, did anyone steal it in order to do some shopping at Potter Heigham to then bring it safely back again an hour later?'

The sound of the lanky young man in the suit starting his car to begin driving away had Tanner glancing around. 'May I ask who your friend is?'

'He's an estate agent. I've just commissioned him to put the house up for sale.'

'You know, it's funny,' Tanner continued, turning back, 'but when we first met, you seemed adamant that you were going to give the place a go.'

'No doubt I did, but that was before the estate agent the boy works for called to let me know how much the place was worth. Then there's the weather, of course. Had I known it was going to be quite so bloody cold all the time, I doubt I'd have even bothered flying over. Anyway, as much as I enjoy standing here talking to you whilst freezing my nuts off, I don't. So, if you'll excuse me.'

'There's just one more thing,' Tanner continued, leaving Hambleton theatrically rolling his eyes.

'Go on then.'

'We understand you arranged to have lunch today with a certain Mr Marcus Brookes?'

Hambleton folded his arms over his chest to begin eyeing Tanner with wary suspicion. 'And how, may I ask, do you know about that?'

'We also understand you then called the restaurant to cancel the reservation, shortly before you were due to arrive.'

'And...?'

'I was just wondering why that was?'

'Why I was going to meet him, or why I decided to cancel?'

'Well, both, I suppose?'

'I wanted to talk to him about the possibility of selling. He's the solicitor who dealt with my grandfather's estate. I suppose I was in two minds about the whole thing, but when I woke up this morning I'd reached the decision that I definitely didn't want to live in this God forsaken place anymore, so I cancelled, calling the estate agent instead.'

'Without bothering to tell Mr Brookes?'

Hambleton bored his eyes down into Tanner's. 'I think you'll find that I left a message with someone on reception.'

Tanner quietly pulled out his notebook.

'You still haven't told me why this is all so important, inspector?'

'Because, Mr Hambleton,' Tanner replied, glancing up, 'the man you were due to meet was found dead in the restaurant's carpark this afternoon, only a few minutes after you were supposed to meet. Regretfully, he didn't appear to have received your message.'

- CHAPTER FORTY NINE -

THANKING HIM FOR his time, Tanner made his way back down the steps to his car, leaving Hambleton watching him from between two of the hall's four giant pillars.

With the car door closed, he made a surreptitious note of the Range Rover's number plate before reversing out to begin rumbling his way back the way he'd come, occasionally glancing into the rear-view mirror until he saw Hambleton unfold his arms to make his way back inside.

Returning his focus to the broken road, he saw the estate agent's car parked just beyond the twisted gates ahead. With no immediate sign of the person behind the wheel, Tanner pulled up to make sure he was OK, only to find him standing on his tiptoes, endeavouring to attach a large For Sale sign to one of the gates.

Taking the opportunity to have a chat, Tanner stopped the car to step quickly out. 'Do you need a hand?'

'All done,' the young man replied, stepping back to admire his work. 'Not exactly straight, but neither are the gates!'

'Do you mind me asking how much he's selling it for?'

The estate agent turned to cast a calculating eye over Tanner's XJS before taking him in with an ambiguous smile. 'Are you in the market?'

'I suspect it's a little beyond my reach,' he replied, digging out his ID. 'Detective Inspector Tanner, Norfolk Police.'

'Oh, right, sorry,' the young man replied, suddenly not knowing where to look. 'I had no idea.'

'I think it's the car that throws people off,' Tanner replied, trying to put him at ease. 'So anyway, how much is he asking?'

'We've agreed to give it a go at just under five million.'

Tanner raised an eyebrow, rotating his head to stare back at the crumbling mansion. 'Is it really worth that much?'

'It will be if we can find the right buyer.'

'One with deep enough pockets to have the place renovated.'

'Oh, I suspect it's a little beyond that. It will probably go to one of the larger property developers. The house itself sits on approximately thirty acres of land. This has the potential to become one of Norfolk's largest new build developments.'

'Does he know that's what the intention is – to knock it down to build a giant block of flats?'

'That was the proposal he put to us.'

'After you contacted him?'

'Er...he was the one who contacted us.'

'Oh, right,' replied Tanner, once again searching for his notebook.

'He seems to be in a bit of a hurry as well,' the estate agent continued. 'We told him he could probably get five and a half if he was prepared to wait, but he seems keen to push it through as quickly as possible.'

- CHAPTER FIFTY -

THE SOUND OF his phone ringing from the depths of his coat had Tanner tugging it out to see it was Townsend, calling from his mobile. Pivoting quickly around, he answered the call.

'I just wanted to let you know that I've found Christine's car, or at least I think I have.'

Tanner felt the pace of his heart quicken. 'What do you mean, you *think* you have?'

'Its number plate was picked up going into Norwich Station's carpark. It wasn't seen driving out, so the assumption is that it must still be there. I've called the station office, asking for someone to verify if it is or not.'

'And...?'

'I'm still waiting for them to come back to me.'

'Did you ask if anyone saw her entering the station at the time in question?'

'I did.'

'So...what did they say?'

'Apart from laughing at me, not much.'

'I take it that was a no, then?'

'Something like that, but he gave me access to their CCTV cameras for the platforms and outside the main entrance. So far I've only had a chance to go through the footage immediately after her car was seen driving in, which only made me realise why the guy on the phone was laughing at me. The place was heaving with people, so it's going to take me longer than I thought to go through it.'

'What about her finances?'

'I've applied for access but haven't heard back.'

'When they come through, we need to know if she bought a train ticket, and if so, to where?'

'Understood.'

'Any news of Whitaker and his men?'

'Not a word.'

'I'm not sure if that's good or bad,' Tanner muttered to himself. About to end the call, he heard Townsend's voice come back over the line.

'Before you go, sir, I did see someone on the CCTV footage whose face was immediately recognisable.'

'Please tell me it was Baines?'

'Unfortunately not. It was the person we were just talking about.'

'Superintendent Whitaker?'

'The one and only.'

'Was he going anywhere nice?'

'Not that I could see. One of the cameras caught him talking to someone through the window of a car in a way that I could only describe as being suspicious.'

'In what way?'

'He kept glancing about, as if looking to see if he was being watched.'

Tanner raised an intrigued eyebrow. 'I don't suppose you saw who he was talking to?'

'I couldn't. The camera was facing down at them, but I was able to see the number plate. It would appear the car is owned by another one of our special new friends. The Clinical Services Director at Bradfield Hospital, Dr Michael Copeland.'

- CHAPTER FIFTY ONE -

WITH A BURNING curiosity to know what the Superintendent of Norfolk Police had been doing in Norwich Train Station's carpark, talking to the Clinical Services Director of Bradfield Hospital in a manner described as being suspicious, Tanner decided to head straight over to the hospital in question to see if he could find out.

Half an hour later he was pushing open the doors to make a beeline for the reception desk, digging out his formal ID as he did. 'I don't suppose I'd be able to have a very quick word with Dr Copeland?' he asked the woman he found sitting there.

Taking a cautious moment to study his ID, she eventually reached for her phone. 'If you care to take a seat, I'll see if he's free.'

Tanner glanced around at the chairs being offered only to see the very man he'd come to see, marching along an adjacent corridor with his pristine white lab coat billowing out behind him. 'Dr Copeland!' he called, his voice cutting awkwardly through the otherwise peaceful waiting area.

Seeing him stop to stare furtively about, Tanner held up his hand to help garner his attention before hurrying over. 'Sorry for the unannounced arrival.'

Copeland's eyes immediately began searching Tanner's face with fretful desperation. 'Have you found my son?' he demanded, the words flying out of his mouth.

'Not yet, I'm afraid.'

Copeland's face sagged with forlorn desolation before his eyes flashed with resentful anger. 'Then what is it? What do you want?'

'I – er – firstly wanted to talk to you about something you mentioned when I was here last,' Tanner began, lowering his voice, 'About how one of your employees was caught having relations with Jason Baines.'

'Yes – and – what about it?'

'I was hoping you'd be able to tell me who that person was?'

Copeland's head jolted back in disgust. 'I'm sorry, but that would be highly unethical!'

'I appreciate that, but this has now become a double-murder investigation.'

'That doesn't mean I'd be able to divulge such sensitive information.'

'Would you at least be able to confirm if it was the person who's been recently named in the news?'

'Am I to assume that you're referring to Christine Halliday?'

'Is it true?' Tanner asked, his voice rising in desperation. 'Was she caught with Baines when she was working here?'

Copeland's mouth remained firmly closed.

'Would it help if I was to tell you that I'm not asking purely from a professional perspective?'

'I take it you know her?'

Tanner replied with a hesitant nod. 'We live together. We have done for some time. I found a box of her letters shortly after she disappeared. Most of them were from him.'

'It sounds like you've already uncovered the answer to your question.'

'So, it's true? She *was* the person you were referring to?'

Copeland cast his eyes around the empty corridor they were standing in the middle of before lowering his voice. 'If it's any consolation, I don't believe she was entirely to blame. As I said before, Jason can be a particularly beguiling individual. I doubt there'd be many women who'd be able to resist his seemingly inexhaustible charms. In Christine's particular case, I suspect there were things going on in her life at the time which would have made her even more susceptible.'

'Like what?'

'She'd been struggling with post-natal depression, something her husband seemed unable to understand. I think she probably came back to work after her maternity leave far sooner than she should have, probably to escape problems at home. Then there was the accident, of course.'

'Was she still working here then?'

Copeland nodded. 'With all that had happened, I wasn't at all surprised to hear that she ended up having therapy herself.'

'The letters she wrote in response to the one Baines sent her,' Tanner continued. 'I don't suppose you kept copies of them?'

'I'm afraid it's not our policy to keep such items on file.'

'But someone would have read them before they were given to Baines?'

'Which would have been me.'

'Can you remember what they said?'

Copeland shrugged. 'To be fair, there weren't that many. Two, maybe three? From what I remember, they were all very similar. She clearly felt guilty for what she'd done, always ending them by asking him to stop writing to her.'

Tanner took a moment to let that sink in. 'I would ask if you knew how that made him feel, but from what I understand, people like him don't feel much of anything.'

'I think you're misunderstanding the mindset of a psychopath, Inspector. They may struggle to understand how other people feel, but that doesn't mean they don't experience emotions themselves.'

'OK, so do you know how he felt about Christine, after she left?'

'He hid it well, but I'd say he felt that she'd abandoned him, in much the same way he felt his parents had.'

'I'm sorry, but how could he blame his parents for abandoning him when he was the one who cut them up with an axe?'

'His sense of abandonment came long before he killed them. Were you aware that they kept him locked in a cage; no lights, no heating, just a blanket and barely enough food to live on?'

'I – I didn't know that,' Tanner found himself forced to admit. 'Do you think it's true – what the newspapers have been saying – that they've managed to resume their former relationship?'

Copeland's eyes rested gently on Tanner's. 'I don't believe it would have happened straight away, but if Jason was able to find the opportunity to speak to her alone, possibly asking her to help convince him to do something she felt he should do, like for him to continue with his treatment, for example, then I'm afraid I'd have to say the answer is probably yes.'

Tanner's eyes fell to the floor as he remembered what the Broads Ranger had told him, that he'd seen her talking to Baines in the carpark before watching her climb into the passenger seat.

With the conversation seeming to have come to an end, the doctor looked beyond Tanner to the end of the corridor. 'If that's all, Inspector, I really must be getting along.'

It was only then that Tanner remembered what he'd actually come to ask. 'Sorry, Doctor, but there was one more thing.'

'Make it quick. I'm already late for a meeting.'

'You were filmed by a CCTV camera, talking to a senior official of Norfolk Police, in the carpark outside Norwich Station yesterday.

'Assuming you're referring to my informal meeting with Alan Whitaker,' Copeland replied, holding Tanner's eyes, 'what about it?'

'I was wondering what you two were talking about?'

'Our missing children! What did you think?'

'Sorry, yes, of course. I suppose I just didn't realise that you two knew each other.'

'We went to Oxford together. We were both reading Psychology before he made the switch to Law. I was asking if there was anything else that could be done. Begging, really.'

'Right, I see.'

'Now, if that's all, I really must be getting along.'

'But if you knew each other,' Tanner continued, 'couldn't you have just phoned him up?'

'I felt it was important enough to meet face-to-face, being that both our children have vanished off the face of the Earth and nobody – including yourself I may add – seems to be doing a damned thing about it!'

- CHAPTER FIFTY TWO -

THE MOMENT HE was back in the carpark, Tanner pulled out his phone to put a call through to the office.

'Townsend, it's Tanner. How've you been getting along?'

'Not much to report, really. I've got Higgins helping me go through the CCTV footage, but neither of us have seen any sign of Christine.'

'How about her financial records?'

'Still nothing from her bank account, but we have been given access to her credit card.'

'Anything?'

'Nothing in relation to her buying a train ticket. In fact, there hasn't been any activity on it since the day she disappeared.'

Tanner felt his stomach tighten. Despite what Dr Copeland had said, that Baines could have easily seduced Christine into helping him, that and all the evidence continuing to pile up against her, he still couldn't believe it. But the longer she remained out of contact, the more guilty she appeared. 'OK, drop the CCTV for now. I need you to do something else for me.'

'What's that?'

'I want you to find out anything you can that might link Superintendent Whitaker to Dr Copeland. Start with Oxford University. Copeland told me they were both there at the same time, with him reading Psychology and Whitaker Law. I'm not sure what year, but that shouldn't be too difficult to find out.'

There was a pause from the other end of the line before Townsend's voice came whispering back. 'Are you saying that Whitaker is now a suspect?'

'I'm not sure. All I know is that he was the SIO for the investigation into the murder of Baines' parents, and I'd certainly like to know what they were *really* talking about in such a clandestine manner outside Norwich Station. I doubt it was what Copeland just told me.'

'What was that?'

'That he was asking Whitaker if any more could be done to help find their sons.'

'You don't believe him?'

'Oh, I'm sure he did, but that couldn't have been all. If it was, he'd have simply picked up the phone. No, there's something else going on between them. Whatever it is, I can almost guarantee that Jason Baines is involved, and that's the real reason why he's targeted their children.'

'OK, will do.'

'Speaking of our superintendent, has there been any sign of him?'

'He came in with his men about five minutes ago. Judging by the look on his face, I don't think they had much luck. By the way, you should probably know that he was asking after you, in particular as to your location, so don't be surprised if you get a call from him straight after this one.'

'OK, that's fine. If he asks again you can tell him that I'm heading back to the office now.'

- CHAPTER FIFTY THREE -

WITH DAYLIGHT FADING fast, Tanner sped past the various news media vans cluttering up the pavement along Stalham Road before braking hard to make the sharp turn into Wroxham Police Station. As his headlights swept over the front of the building he saw Townsend, pacing up and down outside the entrance, both hands buried deep inside the pockets of a heavy winter coat.

Stepping out into the freezing night's air he found the young detective constable was now staring directly at him, his hands cupped around his mouth, clouds of moisture billowing out between his fingers.

'Taking a break?' he called, closing the door to make his way over.

'I wanted to catch you before you went in.'

Tanner raised an intrigued eyebrow. 'What's up?'

'As you asked,' he began, sending a fretful glance through the glass entrance doors behind him, 'I've been doing some digging into what connects Whitaker and Copeland.'

'Go on.'

'Well, they did go to Oxford together.'

'And...?'

'Dr Copeland was an expert witness for the prosecution at Jason Baines' trial,' Townsend eventually continued, his voice nothing more than a whisper. 'It was his testimony that helped secure

Baines' conviction – that he was a sociopath who was more than capable of murdering his parents. However, his testimony was in clear contradiction to two expert witnesses brought by the defence. They both stated that Baines was no more a sociopath than they were, concluding that it was highly unlikely he'd have been able to commit such a crime, no matter how badly he'd been treated.'

Seeing someone walk past the door inside reception, Townsend led Tanner down the side of the building. 'The defence also had fingerprint evidence that suggested someone else had been at the scene,' he eventually continued, 'together with a witness who said she'd seen a large heavy-set man leaving the house in question; his hands and face covered in blood.'

'So why the hell was Baines convicted?'

'The fingerprint evidence went missing halfway through the trial, and the defence's star witness retracted her statement the second she took to the stand. She ended up saying that the man she'd seen hadn't come out of the house but had only been walking past, and what she thought had been blood could have easily been something more innocuous, like engine oil, being that the road was lit by florescent yellow streetlights making colours difficult to differentiate, that and the fact that a car had broken down at the bottom of the hill.'

Tanner snorted with contempt. 'In other words, someone got to her.'

'I think it may also be worth noting that it was Whitaker's first murder investigation, and records show that he was promoted up to DCI shortly afterwards. Furthermore, Dr Copeland went on to appear as an expert witness in numerous murder investigations, all again led by Whitaker.'

Tanner thought for a moment, his eyes drifting over to where he could see Whitaker's car. 'I assume he's inside?'

Townsend nodded. 'That's why I'm out here, freezing my balls off.'

'OK, we'd better go in before someone wonders what we're up to, but I suggest you don't mention this to anyone else, and again that includes Sally, even if she does manage to pin you up against the fridge. Is that understood?'

'Yes, sir,' Townsend replied, blushing slightly as he turned to follow Tanner inside.

- CHAPTER FIFTY FOUR -

HEAVING OPEN THE door, Tanner stepped inside only to nearly walk straight into the very man they'd only just been talking about, marching out the other way.

'Detective Inspector Tanner!' he heard Whitaker exclaim. 'Where the hell have you been all day?'

Having hoped to avoid him, Tanner cursed under his breath as he pulled himself up to attention. 'I've been tracking down leads, sir.'

'Leads! What leads?'

'Into the location of the escaped convict, Jason Baines, with the hope of being able to then find your son.'

'Would you care to enlighten me as to what these leads actually are?'

'Well, sir, I was speaking to a witness earlier today who said he thought he'd seen Baines behind the wheel of a Range Rover.'

'When was this?'

'Yesterday morning.'

'I assume you've checked to see if one's been reported stolen?'

Realising he'd forgotten, Tanner shifted awkwardly from one foot to the other. 'I was just heading inside to do so, but first I had to see if the car belonged to the owner of Long Gore Hall, as he has one very similar.'

'And did it – belong to him?'

'Well, the car was still there, and he said it hadn't moved since he'd last used it.'

'So that's a no then. Right. So...what else have you been up to?'

'We – er – managed to locate the car belonging to Christine Halliday as well, sir,' Tanner replied with grudging contempt. Having spent what had remained of the day investigating the very man he was currently talking to, he couldn't think of what else to say.

'Christine who?'

'Halliday, sir. The Broads Ranger whose DNA was found at the scene of Norman Gibbs' murder.'

'You mean that girlfriend of yours?'

'It had been left in the carpark outside Norwich Station,' Tanner continued, deliberately ignoring the question. 'We believe she must have caught a train somewhere after her name was mentioned in the press.' It was a lie in that he didn't believe she had, but it was better than telling Whitaker about how a witness had seen her talking to Baines before climbing into a car with him.

'That's not a lead, Inspector, it's a loose end!'

'An important one, though, as it means she hasn't been helping Baines as we first thought.'

'What the hell are you going on about? I thought we'd already established she hadn't?'

'Well, yes, but...'

'Then why have you been looking for her car when you haven't even bothered to see if the one Baines was seen driving has been reported stolen?'

'As I said, sir, I was just about to.'

'And what about my son? You are still aware that he's gone missing, I hope?'

'Of course, sir. As I just said, that's why we're working so hard to find Baines.'

'You've just told me you've spent half the bloody day trying to find your girlfriend!'

'Yes, but only because if she had been with Baines, then finding her would have led us straight to him. But as that doesn't seem to be the case, she's now another missing person, just like your son.'

'But she's not though, is she!'

Tanner could feel his blood rapidly begin to boil. 'Are you suggesting that your son is more important than the woman I'm currently in a relationship with?'

Whitaker's cold grey eyes bored silently down into Tanner's.

'I suppose he's more important than Dr Copeland's son as well?' Tanner continued, unable to stop himself.

'I want Baines found,' Whitaker began, leaning his sunken angular face in towards Tanner's to expose the ends of his crooked tea-stained teeth, 'and I want him found now. I don't give a shit what it takes. And if he does have my son, and you find him in anything other than the best of health because you spent your entire time looking for your girlfriend instead of an armed psycho-nutjob, I'll have your head on a fucking platter. Am I making myself clear?'

'I believe you are, sir,' Tanner replied, returning to him a thin cold smile, 'and may I say thank you for taking the time to do so.'

Whitaker glowered at him for a moment longer before snorting through his nose.

Watching him stomp over towards his car, Tanner caught Townsend's eye. 'Do me a favour, will you? See if you can dig up the name and phone number for that witness from Baines' trial, the one who opted to change her story at the very last minute. But before you do, ask Sally to run a quick check to see if any Range Rovers had been reported stolen. Just don't tell her why.'

'OK. No problem. Assuming I'm able to find the witness's number, do you want me to give her a call?'

'Better not. I'll contact her after I've spoken to Forrester.'

'About what?'

'I think I need to spend a few quiet moments with him discussing some alternative motives as to why our Superintendent Whitaker is *really* out searching for Jason Baines with such unusual determination.'

- CHAPTER FIFTY FIVE -

RAPPING HIS KNUCKLES on Forrester's office door, Tanner nudged it slowly open. 'May I have a word, sir?'

'For Christ's sake, Tanner. Where the hell have you been?' Forrester demanded, slamming a pen down onto his desk.

'Not you as well.'

'You do know that Whitaker's been looking for you?'

'Don't worry, he just found me.'

'And – what did you tell him?'

'Nothing I wanted to.'

'What's that supposed to mean?'

Tanner made a point of making sure the door was closed before placing his back against it. 'I think I know why Baines specifically targeted Whitaker's son; Dr Copeland's as well.'

'But – we know why,' Forrester replied, staring at Tanner with an expression of indignant confusion. 'Even if we didn't, what the hell does it matter?'

'Townsend found CCTV footage of Whitaker talking to Copeland in the carpark outside Norwich Station.'

'I'm sorry, Tanner, you've already managed to lose me.'

'So I went to see Copeland; to ask what they were talking about.'

'What on Earth do you mean? Wasn't it obvious?'

'It turns out they were at Oxford together. Copeland was also the expert witness for the prosecution at Baines' trial. It was his testimony – claiming Baines to have been more than capable of murdering his parents – that helped secure his conviction, despite evidence to the contrary from the defence.'

'Right, OK, but what's any of that got to do with Whitaker?'

'The court notes also state that fingerprint evidence for the defence mysteriously vanished halfway through the trial. It was going to prove that someone else had been at the scene. On top of that, an eyewitness said she'd seen someone leaving the house covered in blood, but decided to change her story the moment she took the stand, saying instead that she wasn't sure if he had left the house or not, and that the blood she'd seen may instead have been engine oil.'

Forrester continued staring over at him. 'Are you trying to tell me that Baines was innocent?'

'More that Whitaker had been doing whatever he could to prove he wasn't, including hiding material evidence, intimidating a key witness, and installing one of his Oxford University chums into the witness stand to say whatever was necessary to secure a conviction. It was Whitaker's first murder investigation as the SIO. He must have been under considerable pressure to see Baines convicted. The fact that he did led him to being immediately promoted up to DCI. It also saw him continue his relationship with Copeland, using him as a so-called "expert witness" right up until his appointment as Superintendent.'

'This is all fascinating, Tanner, really it is, but

apart from the fact that it would be virtually impossible to prove, what the hell has any of it got to do with our current investigation, that of Baines being suspected of murdering no less than two people in as many days whilst kidnapping two more as well?'

'It provides motive, sir.'

Forrester took a moment to steeple his fingers against his mouth. 'Yes, I see, but does it help us to find him?'

'Well, no sir, but...'

'THEN SO FUCKING WHAT?' the DCI bellowed, his fists crashing down onto the table with such force, his desk phone's receiver nearly jumped out of its cradle.

The hollow silence that followed had Tanner opening his mouth only to find himself closing it again. Forrester was right. It didn't make the slightest difference to the current investigation, only to his moral sense of right and wrong. He was still no nearer to finding Christine, nor Baines for that matter, let alone the two missing teenagers.

With his eyes losing their focus as they drifted slowly down to the floor, Forrester let out an exasperated sigh. 'OK, look, why don't we go over what you have so far.'

'Nothing,' Tanner replied, his voice becoming a despondent whisper, 'at least, nothing worth reporting.'

'What about Hambleton? Did you ask him about a Range Rover being seen at Potter Heigham?'

'Only briefly. His car was still parked outside Long Gore Hall, so it seemed unlikely to have been his.'

'Do you know if any other Range Rovers have been stolen?'

'I've asked Sally to find out.'

Forrester made a point of glancing down at his

watch. 'And she still hasn't come back to you?'

'Well, no, but in fairness, that was only about thirty seconds before knocking on your door; via Townsend as well.'

Forrester shook his head from side to side, his eyes remaining fixed on Tanner's. 'Then I suggest you see how she's getting on. If we can find its number plate, then it shouldn't be too difficult to track down, hopefully in time to find Baines still sitting behind the wheel.'

- CHAPTER FIFTY SIX -

L EAVING FORRESTER'S OFFICE, Tanner made his way over to Sally's desk only to find her giggling to someone on the end of the phone. Rolling his eyes with bewildered impatience, he instead looked over to where Townsend was sitting, just in time to see him end a call to begin hurrying over.

'I've just got off the phone to the witness from Baine's trial,' he started, his voice a clandestine whisper. 'She's supposed to be ex-directory, but her number came up in a Google search.'

Tanner found himself sending a surreptitious glance over his shoulder at Forrester's office. 'I thought I told you not to call her.'

'Yes, I know, but I wasn't sure if it was her number or not.'

'OK, so, what did she say?' he asked, leading him towards the kitchen.

'I asked if she'd be willing to talk to someone about the events surrounding Jason Baines' trial.'

Finding the kitchen thankfully empty, Tanner steered them both inside. 'I assume you told her who you were?'

'Of course, but it didn't make any difference. She refused to say anything about it, so I left her your name and number, asking her to give you a call if she changed her mind.'

'OK, well, no harm done, I suppose.'

Hearing the sound of a woman clearing her throat in the kitchen's doorway, they whipped their heads around to find Sally, batting her heavily-mascaraed eyelashes at them with a curious frown. 'I hope I'm not disturbing you?'

'Not at all!' Tanner stated, offering her a disarming smile. 'Can I – er – get you a coffee?'

'I'm good, thanks. I just came over to tell you that nothing's been reported.'

It took a full moment for Tanner to understand what she was referring to. 'You mean...the Range Rover?'

'You did ask me to see if one had been stolen?' she questioned, her dazzling blue eyes flickering briefly over at Townsend.

'Sorry, yes, of course,' Tanner replied, noticing the young detective constable blush ever-so slightly beside him.

'Anyway,' she continued, 'the last one reported stolen was over two months ago, and that was pulled out of a river in Suffolk a few days later.'

'Then it must be Hambleton's!' stated Townsend, the colour of his skin returning to normal. 'Baines must have taken it without him noticing.'

An uncertain frown rippled over Tanner's forehead. 'And to bring it back immediately afterwards? I'm not sure that's very likely.'

'Then we must be looking at this from the wrong angle,' Townsend continued. 'What if it's not Baines we're looking for, but Hambleton?'

'I'm sorry, but why would we be looking for Hambleton?'

With both Tanner and Sally now staring at him, Townsend swallowed before re-opening his mouth. 'You remember when we first met him, and how he openly admitted to having shot the intruder?'

'You mean the intruder who turned out to be Jason Baines?' added Tanner, hoping for Townsend's sake that he wasn't about to say something stupid in front of a girl who he evidently, and perhaps unsurprisingly, found rather attractive.

'Well – what if he really *had* shot him?'

Tanner did his best to suppress a condescending smirk. 'Er...yes, Townsend, we know he did, hence the shotgun pellets we found embedded into the kitchen island, that and all the blood, of course.'

'I mean, what if he didn't just injure him. What if Baines died, right there in his kitchen?'

Tanner could feel his mind come juddering to a halt. 'But – we have a witness who said he saw Baines get up to follow Hambleton inside the house?'

'Someone who was likely to have been drunk at the time. For all we know, what he actually saw was Hambleton lifting Baines' body up in order to move it.'

'So you're suggesting *Hambleton* killed the homeless guy?'

'Why not? I mean, he had just witnessed him shooting an intruder in the middle of his kitchen, something that could have easily led to a charge of manslaughter. Maybe Hambleton's original plan was to hide the body and clean up the mess to pretend it had never happened, but when he discovered there'd been a witness, he was forced to change his mind. So instead he hid the body, leaving the blood where it was. He then called us to openly admit to having shot an intruder, saying the man had only been injured and had escaped the same way he'd come in. That would explain why our sniffer dogs kept coming back to Long Gore Hall, and why Hambleton became increasingly reluctant to let us anywhere near the place after we'd searched it the first time. It would also explain why he changed his mind about giving his ancestral home a go, choosing instead to sell it as quickly as possible to enable him to leave the country.'

'I suppose he could have planted Baines' DNA on the homeless guy's body as well?' nodded Tanner, unable to be anything but impressed with his junior colleague's imaginative thought process, 'although, it doesn't explain his motive for murdering the solicitor, that's assuming the same person killed the homeless guy.'

'Maybe he was worried that we were about to figure out what really happened, more so after our second visit, so he killed the solicitor to again make it seem like it was Baines. Don't forget, he was the one who booked the table, only to cancel it a few minutes before his intended victim was due to arrive.'

It was another plausible explanation, but Tanner knew something Townsend didn't, at least not yet; that Christine's fingerprint had been found on the body. As much as he didn't wish to believe it, he knew it was possible for Christine to have been helping Baines, but for her to have been working alongside Hambleton instead...?

As Tanner began shaking his head from side to side, another objection came skulking into his mind. 'There's something else we're forgetting: the missing teenagers. I suppose it's possible for Hambleton to have killed the solicitor, to keep our focus on Baines instead of him, but there's no reason for him to have kidnapped them as well.'

'Maybe their disappearance has nothing to do with any of this? Maybe they just happened to be friends and simply decided to run away together?'

'And what about Christine,' Tanner heard himself

ask, 'and the fact that we have a witness seeing her climb into a car with Baines behind the wheel?'

'I – I don't know,' Townsend replied, beginning to sound flustered. 'But we've never been exactly sure what Baines looks like. The photographs we've been given have either been old or grainy. Maybe the witness simply thought it was Baines when in fact it was Hambleton? All I know is that everything keeps leading us back to Long Gore Hall. Don't you think it's time we applied for a search warrant, to have a more thorough look around the place?'

Finding both Townsend and Sally offering him the same imploring look, Tanner let out a reluctant sigh. 'I suppose there's no harm in trying, but I doubt one will be granted. Unfortunately, there's no physical evidence connecting Hambleton to any of this.'

Seeing the look of despondent rejection in Townsend's eyes, Tanner thought he'd better throw him a bone. 'Tell you what, why don't you run his number plate through the ANPR. That should at least give us an idea as to his movements. You never know, we may then be able to pick him up on CCTV, climbing either in or out, telling us if it's Hambleton or Baines behind the wheel.'

- CHAPTER FIFTY SEVEN -

TAKING THE OPPORTUNITY to pour himself a coffee, Tanner had barely made it to his desk when he again heard the demanding tone of his mobile. With his mind immediately jumping to Christine, he ditched the mug to stare down at the screen. But it wasn't her, just some unknown number. For a full second he considered declining the call before realising that it could have still been her, forced to have to use someone else's phone.

'Tanner speaking!' he replied, standing bolt upright beside his desk with a look of anxious anticipation.

'Is that Detective Inspector John Tanner?'

Hearing the unknown woman's voice on the other end of the line, his face crumpled as he sank slowly down into his chair. 'Speaking.'

'It's Patricia Ward,' the woman continued, in a way that suggested he should know who she was. 'I had a call from someone earlier today. I think he said his name was Townsend?'

A furtive glance around the office had him ducking his head under the desk's partition. 'Are you the witness from Jason Baines' trial?' he eventually asked, pressing the phone hard against his ear.

'He said you wanted to talk to me – about what happened. Is now a bad time?'

'No – no – not at all, but it's probably best if we

don't talk over the phone. Perhaps if I could come over to see you?'

The phone went strangely silent.

'Mrs Ward?' Tanner questioned, pulling the phone away from his ear to check the signal.

'I'm sorry,' came her voice again, 'but I'd rather not give out my address. It's not that I don't trust you, but...'

'OK, well, how about if we meet in public somewhere? Where abouts do you live?'

'Near Ranworth.'

Tanner checked his watch, wondering if he'd be able to drive there and back without anyone missing him too much. 'How about outside The Maltsters? I can be there in about twenty minutes.'

More silence followed. 'OK, I'll meet you there, but I really can't be away for long.'

'Me neither,' Tanner muttered to himself.

Ending the call, he grabbed his coat to hurry over to see Townsend. 'How've you been getting on?'

'Hambleton's number plate was picked up heading down the A149 towards Potter Heigham on the morning when he was seen talking to Christine, and the following day, when the solicitor's body was found at the back of that restaurant. I think it's time we applied for that search warrant. Don't you?'

Tanner checked his watch again. He knew it still wasn't enough. He also still couldn't see how it could have realistically been Hambleton, not when Christine's fingerprint had been found on the murdered solicitor alongside her former lover's. 'Look, it's getting late. How about checking CCTV footage in Stalham at around the time of the solicitor's murder. If we can find his car parked nearby, ideally with him climbing out of it, then I suggest you tell Forrester your theory: that

Hambleton killed Baines and is now endeavouring to cover it up.'

'OK, I'll see what I can find,' Townsend replied, with tired despondency, casting his eyes down at Tanner's coat. 'And you?'

'I'm off to see a man about a dog. I shouldn't be long, but if I'm not back in an hour and you haven't found anything else, I suggest you call it a day.'

- CHAPTER FIFTY EIGHT -

SWINGING HIS CAR into Ranworth's public carpark, Tanner climbed quickly out to stare over at the whitewashed walls of The Maltsters pub, situated on the opposite side of a quiet country road. There he could see a tall middle-aged woman standing just to the side of a large lantern-styled light on the pub's corner, her hands buried inside a nondescript sailing jacket.

Zipping up his own, he checked the road was clear before hurrying over. 'Mrs Ward?' he enquired, the moment their eyes met.

Seeing her offer him a nervous nod, he pulled out his ID to hold it under the light. 'DI Tanner, Norfolk Police. We spoke on the phone.'

'I really can't stay long,' she replied, casting a jittery eye over at the pub's entrance.

'I'd like to ask about the trial, if I may? You gave a statement to the defence, saying that you saw a large man covered in blood leave the house where Jason Baines' parents lived, only to retract it the moment you took the stand.'

'I didn't retract it, I just said I wasn't sure.'

'But in your statement you said you were.'

The woman's eyes danced erratically between the pub's entrance and the road before eventually settling onto Tanner's. 'I'll tell you what I know, but it *has* to be off the record.'

'You have a legal obligation to tell the truth, Mrs Ward, especially if what you know could help clear the name of someone who may have been wrongfully convicted of murder.'

'Which is why I'm here, talking to you, but I'm not prepared to put my name to a witness statement, and I'm certainly not going to take to the stand in court – not again!'

Tanner stood in silence, waiting for her to continue.

'I had a visit from someone from the police,' she eventually sighed, 'the day before I was due to testify. It was the same man who'd originally questioned me. He said he wanted to go over my statement. We were sitting in my living room, my children playing at my feet, when he laid a particularly lethal looking knife down on the table in front of me.'

'Go on,' Tanner prompted.

The woman's face started to tremble slightly as the first sign of tears began shimmering in the corners of her eyes. 'He then began telling me that I *hadn't* seen a man come out of the house as I'd said, but that he'd only been walking past, and that it wasn't blood I'd seen on his hands and face but was more likely to have been engine oil from a car that had broken down at the bottom of the hill.'

'Did he say anything else?'

'He didn't have to. He just put the knife away and left. I've never been so terrified in all my life!'

'This man – do you remember his name?'

'I doubt I'll ever forget it, his name nor his face. Whitaker. Detective Inspector Alan Whitaker.'

Asking her to call him again if she changed her mind, Tanner turned to head back to his car only to hear his phone ringing once again.

'Good evening, Tanner,' came Forrester's unmistakable voice from the other end of the line.

'Oh – er – hello sir. How are you?'

'Never mind all that. Once again I've stepped out of my office to find that you're not at your desk.'

'I'm just making my way back now, sir,' Tanner replied, his feet crunching over the carpark's gravel.

'I see, well, before you do, I don't suppose you'd mind dropping in to see a building surveyor over in Stalham for me?'

Tanner came to a halt beside his car. 'A building surveyor, sir?'

'Yes, that's right; if it's not too much trouble?'

'No, it's – er – fine. It's just...is there something you'd like me to pick up?'

'No – no – nothing like that. The poor man has returned from a business trip only to find his junior partner has been shot through the head. Inconvenient I know, given the time of day, but if you wouldn't mind taking a look for me, I'd be most terribly grateful.'

- CHAPTER FIFTY NINE -

L EAVING TOWNSEND A quick message to meet him there, by the time Tanner arrived Stalham's normally peaceful high street was already lit by half-a-dozen blue flashing lights, each one ricocheting off shop window fronts as a bustling crowd of locals craned their necks behind a line of Police Do Not Cross tape.

Surprised to see Dr Johnstone's car was already there, he nudged his XJS onto the kerb behind it to step quickly out.

Once through the crowd, he ducked underneath the tape to find himself being ushered through an arched doorway into a surprisingly spacious open-plan office, a desk at the furthest end surrounded by overall-clad forensics officers.

Seeing Dr Johnstone staring into the wide open blue eyes of a smartly dressed young man resting his head against the back of a chair, seemingly unharmed but for a halo of congealed blood splattered against the wall behind him, Tanner cleared his throat to make his way over.

'Evening doctor. You made it here in good time.'

'Ah, Tanner,' Johnstone replied, straightening himself up. 'I was wondering when you'd show up.'

Tanner took a moment to study the body. 'So, what do we have, apart from the obvious?'

'As far as I can tell, what you see is what you get.

The only slightly unusual aspect would appear to be the entry wound.'

'Which is...where?'

'At the back of the throat.'

'You mean...the gun was placed inside his mouth?'

'Nothing like that,' Johnstone replied, shaking his head. 'I don't think it was deliberate. I think the victim just happened to have his mouth open when he was shot. But the exit wound is pretty standard. The bullet ended up in the wall behind him, so forensics should be able to give you a decent enough ballistics report. The only other aspect worth noting are the blood-covered fingerprints.'

Tanner stopped to stare over at him with an expression of tired, angst-ladened dread.

'You can see them quite clearly on the victim's shirt,' Johnstone continued, directing Tanner's gaze. 'They're also scattered around the desk, as if the culprit was looking for something. What I fail to understand is how the blood managed to find itself on the culprit's hands to begin with. I mean, the body hasn't been moved, not like before.'

'I assume you're suggesting that they've been placed their deliberately?'

Johnstone pushed his glasses up the ridge of his nose. 'My job isn't to speculate, Tanner. I'm just trying to provide you with an alternative explanation, just in case they end up belonging to one of the same people as last time.'

'Yes, sorry, of course,' Tanner replied, his eyes drifting vacantly over the scene.

'Whilst on the subject,' he heard Johnstone continue, 'I suppose I'd better warn you that my post-mortem report into the solicitor's death is ready to be sent. I actually finished it this afternoon, but I'll wait until tomorrow before sending it out. I won't be able to delay it any longer, I'm afraid.'

Tanner quietly nodded his understanding. 'I don't suppose you know if the person who found him is still here?'

'I believe he's been asked to wait for you in an office at the back.'

'Has there been any sign of young Townsend?'

'Not that I've seen. Was he supposed to be here?'

'I left a message for him to come,' Tanner replied, lifting himself up onto the balls of his feet to cast his eyes over at the crowd outside. 'Don't worry, he's probably still on his way. Right then, I suppose I'd better have a word with the guy who found him. Any chance you can get those fingerprints fast-tracked again?'

'Well, I can try, but I think it's unlikely, given the hour. I suppose you're going to ask for the same discretion as last time?'

'Only if they end up belonging to the same person.'

'OK, then I'd better give you a call as soon as I know.'

- CHAPTER SIXTY -

L EAVING JOHNSTONE TO continue with his work, Tanner made his way to the back of the building to find a small storage room piled high with boxes, in the middle of which sat a frail-looking elderly man with hollowed-out cheeks and pale paper-thin skin.

Catching the eye of the police constable standing in the corner, Tanner pulled out his ID to sink slowly down into the chair next to him. 'Detective Inspector Tanner, Norfolk Police. I understand you found the body?'

'Matthew,' the old man replied, staring down at the floor. 'Matthew Cunningham.'

'That was his name?' Tanner enquired, exchanging his ID for his notebook.

'He was just a boy,' the old man nodded. 'Straight out of university. I even met his parents. Christ! What am I going to tell them? I promised I'd take care of him. I couldn't even do that!'

'None of this is your fault, Mr...?'

The man raised his watery blue eyes to send Tanner a confused questioning look.

'May I ask your name?' Tanner enquired, with a benevolent smile. 'Mr...?'

'Sorry, of course. How stupid of me. Charles Godfrey. I'm the senior partner. Actually, I'm the only partner,' he continued, his eyes drifting slowly away.

'I had hoped to have retired by now, but...well, you know how it is.'

'And what time did you find him?'

'It must have been around eight o'clock, I was late back from a meeting. I was going to go straight home, but then I remembered I'd forgotten something, so I came back only to find...'

'I don't suppose you know what he was working on at the time?'

'Nothing if any importance,' he shrugged. 'It's been very quiet recently. It often is at this time of year. I told him he could go home at five if nothing else came in.'

Tanner thought for a moment. 'I don't suppose you've heard of an estate not far from here called Long Gore Hall?'

'Of course. I'm sure most people around here have.'

'Have you ever done any work there?'

'We have, but that was years ago. From what I understand, the place isn't much more than a ruin. I was half-expecting it to have collapsed during that last storm we had, but apparently it's still standing. I've no idea how.'

'So you haven't been commissioned to do anything there recently?'

'As I said, not for years, although we did get a call from the new owner last week.'

Tanner looked up from his notes.

'Nothing came of it, of course,' Godfrey continued. 'To be honest, I knew it wouldn't. As Matthew said when he came back, the place really is beyond repair. From a financial perspective, it would be far better to simply knock it down and start again.'

'You sent Mathew over to take a look?'

'He asked if he could go. He's always been good at

that sort of thing – talking to clients. Not something that's ever been one of my strong points.'

'So, he would have met the new owner, Lawrence Hambleton?'

'I assume so. Matthew said he seemed keen to undertake a full renovation, so he must have done. We then spent some considerable time coming up with a quote for us to assess the building's structural integrity, but as is often the case, we never heard back.'

Tanner thought for a moment. 'Did *you* ever meet him?'

'There was no need. We emailed the quote over and that was the last we heard of it.'

'Just one more question, Mr Godfrey. I don't suppose you've seen a dark green Range Rover parked outside your office recently?'

'You mean, one of those monstrous SUV type things? Not that I recall, but to be fair, I'm about as good with cars as I am with people.'

- CHAPTER SIXTY ONE -

STEPPING OUT INTO the cold bustling street, Tanner forged his way through the crowd to make a beeline for his car. With a hand cupped under its chrome door handle he glanced briefly around for any sign of Townsend before climbing inside to put a call through to the office.

'Forrester, sir, it's Tanner again. It was the junior surveyor who was shot. Young chap as well.'

The line fell momentarily silent. 'Any idea who did it?'

'I'd say the same person who killed both the homeless guy and the solicitor, but I'm becoming increasingly convinced that it might not have been Baines.'

'You think it could have been Hambleton?'

Forrester's question had Tanner immediately asking another. 'Did Townsend speak to you?'

'About an hour ago. He managed to unearth CCTV footage of Hambleton climbing out of his car near the restaurant, twenty minutes before the solicitor's body was found. He went on to explain his somewhat outlandish theory: that Hambleton killed Baines when he broke into Long Gore Hall and has been attempting to cover his tracks ever since.'

'What did you think?'

'That what it lacked in material evidence was made up for in creative thought. I don't suppose you've discovered anything else that could add flesh to its bones?'

'Only that a set of blood-covered fingerprints were found on and around the young building surveyor's body, which Johnstone thought was strange, being that he hadn't been moved, that and the fact that the victim met Hambleton last week. According to the firm's senior partner, he went over to Long Gore Hall to provide an estimate for some work to be carried out.'

'You think the fingerprints were planted?'

'If they turn out to belong to Baines, then I'd say there was an above average chance.'

'OK, but they still don't provide proof that it was Hambleton.'

'Maybe not, but the circumstantial evidence certainly seems to be piling up. We know Baines broke into his kitchen, Hambleton openly admitted to having shot him, there was a witness to the event who ended up dead, bodies are now turning up covered in an unusual number of fingerprints – each victim having a connection to Long Gore Hall, and the only person who's seen Baines since he was shot was a Broads Ranger, but that was behind the wheel of Hambleton's car.'

'But would Hambleton really have murdered a solicitor and a building surveyor for no other reason than to try and misdirect us into thinking that Baines was alive and well?'

'If it was to cover up a charge of manslaughter, then I think it is – possibly more so than Baines, that's if what I found out earlier is true.'

'And what was that, may I ask?'

Tanner drew in a fortifying breath. 'I met the defence witness from Baines' trial – the one who'd changed her story at the last minute. She confirmed what the trial notes had alluded to. Someone *had* managed to get to her, so confirming her original statement – that she had seen someone coming out of Baines' family home covered in blood, and it wasn't the person who ended up being locked away in a mental institution for being a deranged axe-wielding psychopath. If what she said is true, and there's no reason for her to have been lying, then not only is Baines innocent of murdering his parents, but it's unlikely that he's capable of killing anyone, making it even more likely that Hambleton is the one behind these recent events.'

Tanner could almost hear the cogs of Forrester's mind whirring inside his head.

'What about Christine?' the DCI eventually asked.

'Maybe she found out what Hambleton was up to?'

'And Whitaker's boy, and the hospital Doctor's?'

'I admit, I don't know, but if Whitaker and Copeland are old friends, there's no reason to think that their sons aren't as well. If that's the case, then what Townsend also suggested could again be correct. They could have simply decided to run away together. To be honest, if I had the misfortune to be Whitaker's son, I'd be quite keen to run away as well. For all we know, the two boys are gay, and their parents had just banned them from seeing each other. Either way, I think it's time we had a more thorough look around Hambleton's estate.'

'That's pretty much what Townsend said.'

'I assume you said no?'

'I told him to go home; possibly not in the most diplomatic fashion, either.'

Assuming that must have been why Townsend hadn't bothered to return his call, Tanner started the engine. 'So, is it OK for us to apply for a search warrant?'

There was a pause from the other end of the line. 'Can it wait till the morning – to see if anything else turns up?'

Tanner's mind immediately turned to Johnston's post-mortem report, the one that would provide evidence that Christine's fingerprint had been found on the body of the solicitor. 'I think it would be better to send off the application now. I can do it when I get home, if that's alright?'

'OK, fine. I'll leave it with you, but I don't think we should get our hopes up. The magistrate will be expecting to see at least some form of material evidence, and we don't have any!'

- CHAPTER SIXTY TWO -

WITH HIS MIND turning once again to Christine, Tanner glanced down at his watch. It was only half-past nine. The search warrant application would take him about half an hour, leaving him the rest of the night with nothing better to do than to pace from one wall of his house to another, a bottle of rum hanging from a despondent hand, all the while wondering if it was really possible for Baines to have beguiled her into re-kindling their former relationship.

Driving out of Stalham, his mind returned to the conversation he'd had with the witness; how she'd seen someone else creep out of Baines' family home all those years before. If it was true, and Baines wasn't the raging psychopath everyone had been assuming he was, maybe Christine already knew? Maybe she'd known all along, which was why she'd helped him escape. But if she had, why would she have waited for such a long time? Surely she'd have done so when she was still working at Bradfield Hospital. Then another thought began worming its way into his mind, that Townsend was right: Baines was dead, and she'd somehow found out that Hambleton had killed him.

He shook his head violently from side to side in a frantic bid to clear his mind, but it was no use. It had become nothing more useful than a maelstrom of twisting contradictions.

Desperate to avoid having to go back to his lifeless home he began driving from village to village, one eye on the road, the other staring into the depths of every shadow with the futile hope of seeing Christine's face suddenly appear. When his eyes began blinking themselves closed, he was eventually left with no choice but to head for home to pour himself a generous glass of rum. With his laptop open on the kitchen's breakfast bar, he spent a few desolate moments staring at a blank search warrant application form. Only when the glass had been drained and he'd poured himself another did he feel able to begin the tedious task of filling it out.

- CHAPTER SIXTY THREE -

Friday, 11th February

HAVING BEEN STUPID enough to stay up until the bottle was empty, Tanner arrived at work the next day with the lurking suspicion that he was still drunk from the night before, certainly enough to make him over the legal limit to be perched behind the wheel of a car.

As he drove past the various news teams preparing for their live morning broadcasts he cast his eyes over the station's carpark. Forrester's car wasn't there, neither was Townsend's. However, Whitaker's was. He could also see him, briefing his firearms officers at the furthest end as they busily checked over their lethal-looking carbine rifles.

Parking to climb slowly out, he saw Forrester's gleaming black BMW begin turning sedately into the carpark. With its owner endeavouring to catch his eye, Tanner felt obliged to remain where he was as the car came to a graceful halt beside him.

'Morning, sir,' he began, doing his best to keep his breath away from the window as it slid gracefully down.

'I just wanted to have a quick word before you went inside.'

Tanner knew what was coming and braced himself accordingly.

'Did you see Johnstone's post-mortem report,' Forrester continued, 'for the solicitor?'

'I didn't know it was expected,' he lied.

'It came through just as I was walking out the door. You better know that one of Christine's fingerprints was again found on the body. One belonging to Jason Baines as well.'

Tanner forced himself to remain calm. 'I think that only goes to prove what I've been saying, that someone's doing their damnedest to make it seem like they're responsible, when neither of them have had anything to do with it.'

'Unless, of course, the opposite is true.'

'I'm sorry, sir, but there's no way Christine is capable of such a thing. And as I said yesterday, I don't think Baines is, either.'

'You still think it's Hambleton?'

'More so with every passing minute.'

The two men fell suddenly silent when they caught Whitaker shooting an antagonistic glance over at them.

Making sure to keep his voice low, Tanner risked leaning his head in towards Forrester's open car window. 'There's something I need to tell you,' he began, endeavouring to hold Forrester's eye, 'about what Baines' defence witness told me yesterday.'

Forrester's attention drifted slowly back to their Superintendent.

'I said that someone had persuaded her to change her story,' Tanner continued, following his gaze, 'but I never said who it was.'

'I suppose you're going to tell me it was Whitaker.'

Tanner replied with a nod, just as the man they were discussing in such conspiratorial tones began lurching his way towards them. 'She said that he threatened her with a knife, telling her what she actually saw, all whilst her children were playing at her feet.'

Forrester's attention returned to Tanner. 'Did you manage to get that search warrant application off?'

'It was late, but yes.'

'Were you able to make a convincing argument?'

Tanner endeavoured to cast his mind back to what he'd written, but beyond entering his name and the date, he simply couldn't remember. 'I laid out the facts,' he eventually replied, hoping that was true, but suspecting that it probably wasn't.

'Then let's just hope it's approved.'

Once again they both turned to look over at Whitaker, marching over the carpark towards them.

'I don't suppose you've thought about what you're going to tell the man in question?' Forrester asked, his eyes remaining focussed on their Superintendent.

'Who, me?'

Forrester offered Tanner a sanguine smile. 'Don't worry, no doubt I'll be able to think of something.'

'What are you two whispering about?' came Whitaker's commanding voice, stomping to a halt beside them.

'Good morning, sir,' the DCI began. 'We were just discussing the plan for the day.'

'I thought that was obvious. To find Baines before he manages to kill anyone else.'

'To be honest, sir, at this stage we're not sure if it is Baines we're actually after.'

'What the hell are you talking about?'

Tanner watched Forrester's hand tighten around the top of his steering wheel.

'We believe it's possible that he may already be dead, and that the man who shot him has been endeavouring to cover his tracks.'

'The man who shot who?'

'Baines, sir, when he was caught breaking into Long Gore Hall.'

'You mean Lawrence Hambleton?'

Forrester nodded, only for Whitaker to return a look of frustrated bewilderment. 'You're not seriously suggesting that it's Hambleton who's been going around shooting people instead of a convicted psychopathic murderer?'

'That's the theory we're currently working on.'

'Please God, tell me you're joking!'

'Well, sir, he did admit to having shot Baines when he broke into his kitchen. Then the witness was found dead, closely followed by a solicitor, then a building surveyor, both of whom Hambleton knew; all of them found with Baines' fingerprints on them.'

'And that means it's Hambleton, does it?'

'Well, sir, it's certainly unusual to find quite so many fingerprints on a murder victim, especially in the case of the young building surveyor found yesterday. They were left all over both him and his desk, despite having been shot from several feet away and the fact that his body hadn't been moved.'

'Or alternatively, Baines is so deranged that he wanted to take a closer look at the person he'd just killed, not really caring if his fingerprints were found on his victim or not.'

Forrester eyes flickered over at Tanner. 'As I said, sir, at the moment it's just a theory.'

'Yes, I see,' Whitaker mused, placing a pensive finger against his clean-shaven chin. 'So, Hambleton killed Baines and has since been going around murdering people in some sort of bizarre attempt to convince us that he's still very much alive. Well, I suppose it makes sense, apart from one small matter.'

Tanner knew what was coming. Judging by the look on Forrester's face, he did as well.

'WHO THE FUCK TOOK MY SON?' Whitaker roared with such furious rage that just about every journalist on the other side of the carpark whipped their head around to see what was going on.

Forrester took a moment to clear his throat. 'We were actually wondering if your son – and Dr Copeland's – may have been friends, sir, and perhaps they may have simply run away together.'

'Friends? Why the hell would they be friends?'

Forrester opened his mouth only to close it again a moment later. Tanner knew what he was thinking. If he explained why he thought his son and Dr Copeland's may have known each other; that their fathers had gone to Oxford together, then he could easily end up having to explain just exactly how he knew that, and what else he knew, thanks to Tanner's unauthorised investigations into him.

'Well?'

'Well – we – er – just thought it was a possibility, sir,' Forrester eventually spluttered, his eyes falling to the ground.

'I think there's also a possibility that you're a complete fucking idiot,' Whitaker barked, 'one who's clearly incapable of doing his job. But putting that to one side for now, they're *not* friends, and there isn't a single reason as to why they would be.'

Hearing his phone ping out a notification, Tanner made a point of digging it out to stare down at the screen.

'Anything of interest?' he heard Forrester ask.

'It's an email from the local magistrate,' Tanner replied, glancing up. 'Our application's been approved.'

'What application's been approved?' Whitaker demanded, his steely blue eyes training themselves onto Tanner's.

'Last night I applied for a search warrant to take a look inside Hambleton's stately home.'

'With the evidence you've just presented to me?'

Tanner replied with a nod.

'And they approved it?

'Whether it's Baines or Hambleton,' Tanner began, 'what little evidence we have keeps leading us back to Long Gore Hall. That's where this whole thing started, and the local magistrate clearly agrees.'

Whitaker took a moment to stare at Tanner before transferring his gaze down to Forrester. 'OK, fine!' he eventually exclaimed, 'but if we arrive to find Baines has killed someone else, ten miles in the opposite bloody direction, don't expect to wake up with a job in the morning. And that goes for you as well, Inspector.'

- CHAPTER SIXTY FOUR -

L EADING A PROCESSION of vehicles along the twisting country roads that meandered their way towards Norfolk's ancient coast, Tanner turned onto a track to begin rumbling his XJS over a broken pot-holed surface. When he reached the lopsided rusting gates that marked the boundary to the Long Gore Hall estate, he slowed for a moment to stare through the windscreen at the crumbling mansion ahead, a thin veil of early morning mist creeping slowly around its base.

Remembering the convoy of cars and vans behind, he continued on to eventually see a rectangular removals van was parked to one side of the hall's four stone pillars. Struggling to believe he'd been able to sell the estate so quickly, Tanner pulled up next to it to see Hambleton limping out from the entrance to begin hurrying down the steps, one arm waving wildly above his head.

Curious to know what he seemed so desperate to bring his attention to, he climbed quickly out.

'I was about to call,' came Hambleton's breathless voice, as first Forrester's car, then Whitaker's came skidding to a halt behind him. 'I was wrong – about that man you've been looking for.'

'You mean Jason Baines?' Tanner queried, glancing around as his two superior officers appeared on either side of him.

'He must have been hiding here the entire time, him and that girlfriend of his. I caught them in my kitchen about ten minutes ago, helping themselves to the contents of my fridge. Then I found this.' Hambleton held out a crumpled old sleeping bag. 'It was in the conservatory around the back. I've hardly been in there else I would have found it sooner.'

'Which way did they go?' Whitaker demanded, lurching forward to snatch the sleeping bag from Hambleton's hands as the sound of van doors could be heard sliding open behind them.

'I'm not sure. They were heading over the marshes towards the coast. Then they disappeared into the mist. I lost sight of them after that. But before I did, I saw something I think you should be aware of.'

'What was that?'

'The man had my shotgun. He must have taken it last night. The girl was armed as well.'

'OK, thank you, Mr Hambleton. You've been most helpful.' With that, Whitaker snapped his head around to glare at first Tanner, then Forrester. 'You see,' he began, his mouth contorting into a dangerous snarl, 'I told you it was Baines!'

Tanner watched with a growing feeling of dread as Whitaker spun on his heel to begin marching over to where a couple of police vans had come to a halt behind them, the side of one becoming surrounded by his firearms officers, the other with dogs scrabbling out from the back. 'I don't like this,' he whispered over to Forrester, watching magazines being handed out to the firearms officers, 'not if Baines has got Christine with him.'

'If she's armed, like Hambleton says, then I'm sorry, Tanner, but I'm not sure we have much choice.'

'What if he's lying?' Tanner continued, leading Forrester away from the base of the steps.

'And why would he do that?'

Tanner shook his head in frustration. 'I don't know, but the facts haven't changed since we left. The only thing that has is that there's now a giant removals van sitting outside the stately home Hambleton said only a few days ago that he had no intention of selling, and that according to him, an escaped convict – a man who probably isn't the psychotic murderer everyone's been saying he is – has spent the last week camped out in his conservatory.'

The metallic click of ammunition magazines being loaded up into the base of snub-nosed carbine rifles had Tanner jerking his head around to see Whitaker hand the sleeping bag to one of the dog handlers. 'I want to have a chat with Hambleton,' he continued, keeping his voice low. 'Can you try and stall Whitaker and his men until I do?'

'Well, I'll try, but they look as if they're about ready to go.'

'Just tell him I need to clarify something first.'

Seeing Hambleton limp back inside, Tanner didn't wait for a response, spinning around to launch himself up the stone steps. 'Mr Hambleton?' he called, raising a hand. 'May I have a word?'

The estate's owner stopped where he was to offer Tanner a quizzical frown. 'Of course, but I thought you had an escaped lunatic to catch?'

'I just wanted to ask about the removals van.'

'Er – OK – are you looking for one yourself?'

'I was wondering if it meant that you'd already managed to sell the estate?'

'Oh, right. Unfortunately not. It just means I've had enough of living in a freezing cold crumbling mansion, one that leaks every time it rains and is located somewhere that seems to have more in common with the Arctic Circle than what I imagined England's so-called green and pleasant land to have been like.'

Tanner stopped where he was. 'Sorry, but I thought you said you grew up here?'

Hambleton held Tanner's eyes. 'Yes, I did, but as you know, that was years ago. Frankly, I'd forgotten just how utterly miserable it was.'

'Only in the winter,' Tanner replied, casting a casual eye up at the cold grey sky above. 'Does that mean you're heading back to South Africa?'

'That's the plan.'

'When are you leaving?'

'Oh, not until the morning. I've got to make sure that all my stuff is loaded up properly first, then I'm going to catch a train down to London. My flight isn't until tomorrow evening.'

'Heathrow or Gatwick?'

'Actually, it's Stanstead.'

Tanner took a moment to study his face. 'You know, you really should have told us you were leaving before making plans to do so.'

'I'm sorry, I forgot. It's not a problem, is it?'

'Well, it's hardly ideal, but as long as you leave us a forwarding address, I suppose it'll be OK. I assume you wouldn't have any objection to us having a look around the place before you go?'

Hambleton pursed his lips. 'If you must, but I've already told you. The man you want is out there.'

'So you said,' Tanner mused, his head turning to see Forrester having an animated discussion with Whittaker, as three Alsatian police dogs strained at their leads just behind.

As the harrowing image of a firearms officer aiming his rifle at Christine's head came crashing into his mind, he heard Hambleton's voice saying something behind him. Shaking his head clear, he turned quickly back. 'Sorry, what was that?'

'I was asking what you'd be looking for, if the man you're after is out there?'

Tanner offered him a smile of grim capitulation. 'As it turns out, we had a search warrant application approved this morning. I must admit, had I known you'd seen him before we set off, I doubt I'd have bothered bringing it with me. But now that we're here, I suppose we may as well take a look around, after we've captured our escaped lunatic, of course.'

Hearing the dogs begin barking behind him, he turned to see them dragging their handlers away with Whitaker and his armed men following after. 'Anyway, looks like we're off. I take it you'll still be here when we get back?'

'As I said, I won't be leaving until tomorrow.'

'OK, good. Then I'll save our goodbyes until then.'

- CHAPTER SIXTY FIVE -

SEEING FORRESTER WAS kindly waiting for him, Tanner left Hambleton to launch himself back down the steps.

'I couldn't persuade him to wait any longer, I'm afraid,' came the DCI's voice, as Tanner joined him on the overgrown drive.

'Don't worry,' Tanner replied, each taking to their heels to begin chasing after the already distant sound of baying dogs.

'Did Hambleton say where he was going?'

'He's booked a flight back to South Africa, leaving from Stanstead tomorrow night.'

'I assume you told him he couldn't leave, being that we're in the middle of a multiple murder investigation, one that seems to be centred around his sprawling estate?'

'To be honest, I actually said he could.'

Forrester shot him a sideways glance as they quickly caught up to their fellow officers. 'Are you sure about that?'

'Not really,' Tanner shrugged, glancing over his shoulder at the stately home behind them, already shrouded by the gently swirling mist. 'I don't know who, or maybe even what he's got us chasing after, but I'm becoming increasingly convinced that it's not Baines. With any luck, it's not Christine either.'

'So, why did you say he could go?'

'I thought it was safer to make him think that we didn't have an interest in him, not after he's just sent us on what is probably nothing more than a wild goose chase.'

A sudden series of agitated shouts erupting from the group ahead had them surging forward.

Catching up to Whitaker to find him staring into the mist ahead through a pair of over-sized binoculars, Forrester attempted to catch his eye. 'What's going on?'

'Looks like we've found them,' came the superintendent's eager response, the binoculars remaining pressed against his eyes.

'Are you sure?' Forrester questioned, endeavouring to follow his gaze.

'I can see two people out there, the taller one has what looks to be a shotgun, the other a pistol of some description.'

Peeling the binoculars from his eyes, he took hold of a megaphone slung over his shoulder to place against his mouth. 'This is Superintendent Whitaker, Norfolk Police,' came the unnatural sound of his voice, echoing out over the barren landscape beyond. 'A unit of trained firearms officers have you both in their sights. You need to put your weapons down and place your hands on top of your heads. Failure to comply will leave us no choice but to open fire.'

As his voice gradually dissipated into the surrounding mist, he took the megaphone away from his mouth. 'What are they doing?' he asked an armed officer to his side, a rifle pressed firmly against his shoulder.

The man closed one of his eyes to stare down its telescopic lens. 'Not what you told them to.'

'OK, then you have my permission to shoot.'

Tanner lunged forward, forcing himself between

Whitaker and the armed police officer. 'You can't do that!' he ordered, grabbing Whitaker's arm. 'You've got no idea who's out there!'

Whitaker stared down at Tanner's hand as if it belonged to a deformed leper. 'I suggest you remove your hand from my arm, Inspector, or you'll be facing a charge of assaulting a high-ranking police officer.'

'I'm sorry,' he apologised, snatching it away, 'but you can't shoot them. Not until we know who they are.'

'I appreciate that, but we do know who they are. One of them is Jason Baines, the other is his girlfriend. I'm sorry that she doesn't appear to be *your* girlfriend anymore, but I guess that's just the way the cookie crumbles.'

'But how do you know it's Baines? Because Hambleton told you?'

'Because Baines is a convicted psychotic murderer. Why else would he be attempting to flee with a shotgun in one hand and what I understand is his equally disturbed girlfriend in the other?'

'And what if it isn't him?'

'Then it makes no difference. They're both armed. We've told them who we are and what they need to do. As neither of them seems willing to do so, then I can't see that we have any choice but to open fire.'

The distant blast of a shotgun, echoing out from the mist ahead, had everyone ducking instinctively down.

The firearms officer beside them took to a knee. 'That was them,' he said, his voice lacking even the vaguest trace of emotion as he continued staring down his rifle's telescopic lens. 'Looks like they've taken cover. No. Hold on. They're up again.'

'Do you have a clear shot?'

'I do.'

'Then I suggest you take it.'

- CHAPTER SIXTY SIX -

BEFORE TANNER KNEW what was happening, the officer's rifle cracked twice in quick succession, leaving the explosive sound drilling mercilessly down into the side of his head.

Unable to move, he stared into the distance, his mouth hanging open as the firearms officer removed the gun from his shoulder.

'Targets are down,' the man eventually announced, his voice flat with professional dispassion.

As if slapped awake from a nightmarish trance, Tanner lunged forward to begin pelting his way over the soggy uneven ground, unable to shake the image from his mind of Christine; face down in the mud, blood oozing out from where her face used to be.

With the sound of dogs fast closing in behind, he continued on until out of the mist appeared two bodies, the first being a man lying face-up, a shotgun held firmly over his unmoving chest. The other appeared to be a woman, rocking gently on her knees, a tangled mop of greying-blonde hair directed down at a gun clasped firmly in her lap.

Tanner stopped where he was to take slowly to a knee. 'Christine?' he asked, his voice barely escaping his lips.

From immediately behind him came the stark shrill voice of a man, bellowing out with furious intent. 'DROP THE GUN AND PUT YOUR HANDS ON YOUR HEAD!'

Tanner watched as she slowly raised her eyes to look at him, tears streaming down her dirt-encrusted face. It was only then that he was able to complete the picture being presented. Her mouth had been covered with beige-coloured gaffer tape. The same tape had been used to fasten her hands around what at first glance had appeared to be a handgun, but was in fact nothing more threatening than a broken piece of wood. And the body lying motionless next to her wasn't that of Jason Baines, it was young DC Townsend, the shotgun covering his chest also taped to his hands.

Leaping to his feet, Tanner spun around to confront the fast approaching armed officers, their carbine rifles jammed firmly against their shoulders. 'Stand down!' he commanded, stepping forward with his hands raised up in front of him. 'This is *not* what it seems!'

The armed unit stopped where they were, the barrels of their rifles aimed squarely at the woman behind him.

'Drop your weapon or we'll be forced to shoot!' the nearest one ordered.

'I SAID, STAND DOWN!' Tanner yelled, stepping back again, using his body to protect Christine.

'Step away from the target, sir, or we'll be left with no choice but to open fire.'

'This is *not* how it looks! You *must* stand down!'

'Then tell the target to drop her weapon!'

'You idiot! Don't you see? She can't! The gun's been taped to her hands!'

'What the hell's going on here?' came Whitaker's barking voice, elbowing his way through the line of armed police.

'The detective inspector is refusing to stand clear of the target, sir.'

Seeing Forrester emerge through the group, Tanner kept his eyes fixed on Whitaker. 'As I've been attempting to explain to your men, *sir*, what they think is a gun has been taped to her hands. She couldn't let go of it even if they shot her through the head. And the person they quite possibly already have is *not* your so-called axe-wielding lunatic, he's one of our own fucking men!'

Tanner's words, and the strained tone used to convey them, had the armed police hesitantly begin lowering their weapons, enough at least for Tanner to feel it was safe enough for him to step away.

'Jesus Christ!' came Forrester's thick baritone voice, barging past Whitaker to surge suddenly forward.

Easing himself alongside Tanner, he crouched down beside the man's unmoving body. 'It's Townsend,' he muttered, as if unable to believe what he was seeing. Snapping his head around, his eyes fixed themselves onto Whitaker's. 'You incompetent fucking moron,' he spat, his mouth contorting into a raging snarl. 'You've ordered your men to shoot one of our own!'

'But – I – I d-didn't...' the Superintendent spluttered, the skin hanging from his narrow bony face fast draining of colour.

'Well – don't just stand there!' Forrester continued, obviously not caring in the slightest that the man he was barking at was his immediate superior. 'Call a fucking ambulance!'

Leaving Whitaker to begin scrabbling around for a phone, Forrester turned to place two fingers against Townsend's neck.

'Anything?' asked Tanner, easing himself slowly

down beside him.

In the hollow silence that followed, Tanner saw the armed police officers abandon their weapons to come running to Townsend's aid.

'He's still alive – thank God!' came Forrester's eventual reply, searching the body for signs of injury. 'Looks like the bullet caught his shoulder. There's blood here, on the rock beside his head. I think it's more likely he's out due to concussion than anything else.'

With Forrester searching for something to plug the bullet wound with, Tanner gave his attention to Christine. 'Are you hurt?' he asked, peeling the tape from her mouth.

Taking in a deep juddering breath, she blinked the tears out of her eyes to stare into his. 'I'm alright,' she eventually replied, taking another stabilising breath.

With a broad smile of unabashed relief, Tanner focussed his mind on the task of undoing her hands and the piece of wood they'd been taped to. The moment they were free, he held them in his to look deep into her eyes. 'Who did this to you? Was it Hambleton?'

Christine shook her head, her eyes seemingly unable to remain focussed on his.

'You mean, it *was* Jason Baines?'

'It always has been,' came her fragile response, her head sinking slowly to the ground.

Tanner's forehead creased in confusion. 'Sorry – but – I don't understand.'

'Baines *is* Hambleton,' she eventually continued, lifting her eyes to meet with his. 'That's been his plan all along – to take his identity, that and everything he owns.'

It took a full moment for what she'd said to sink in. 'You mean – the person we left back at Long Gore

Hall – that was Jason Baines?'

'The real owner of the estate is dead,' Christine continued, allowing Tanner to help her to her feet. 'Jason showed me his body. He killed him the morning after he broke into his house. He's been pretending to be him ever since.'

'But – that can't be,' Tanner replied, turning his head to bring Forrester into the conversation. 'I met Hambleton after he called the police. We even took samples of his DNA and fingerprints.'

Christine wiped at an escaping tear. 'That was what he said was the genius of his plan. He deliberately waited for you to meet the real Hambleton in order for you to take those samples. Only then did he murder him. That way he could drive around in Hambleton's car killing just as many people as he liked, without you ever suspecting it was really him. As you already had Hambleton's prints on file, he knew you'd never think to take them again.'

Tanner turned to look at Forrester. 'That must have been why he killed the solicitor, and that building surveyor; because they'd met the real Hambleton and would have known Baines wasn't him.'

Leaving the other officers to attend to Townsend, Forrester stood up to take a firm hold of Tanner's arm, leading him away from Christine to whisper down into his ear. 'Careful, Tanner. Don't forget about the homeless guy – that he was responsible for the death of Christine's husband and child. It was her fingerprints found at the scene. Not only there, either.'

From behind them came the woman being talked about, lurching forward to attach her eyes onto Forrester's. 'I know what you're saying – and yes, I did find his body,' she began, her voice trembling with unchecked emotion. 'I saw him when I was patrolling the bittern's nest. I didn't know who he was until I took a closer look. Then I didn't know what to do. I knew what you'd all think if I called it in, so I just left him there. I didn't think about stuff like fingerprints and DNA until later, by which time I thought I'd look even more guilty. So I just kept quiet. I'm sorry, John. I know that was wrong, but I just didn't know what else to do.'

'What about Baines? You were seen getting into a car with him?'

'He told me he was desperate to talk. I'd no idea he was going to drive me off to Long Gore Hall to have me locked up in a cellar.'

Tanner wanted nothing more than to take her in his arms and kiss away everything he'd been told about her over the last several days: how she'd been seen motoring away from the body of Norman Gibbs, her endless trail of blood-covered fingerprints, and most upsetting of all, her intimate relations with Jason Baines.

Remembering what he'd found beside the sink in their bathroom his gaze fell to where he knew an unborn baby peacefully slept, free from the evils of the world outside. 'I found letters,' he eventually muttered, his eyes lifting to rest once again on hers, 'in a shoebox, at the top of the wardrobe.'

Christine didn't reply.

'I spoke to Dr Copeland. He told me about what had happened between you and Baines, and the real reason why you left Bradfield Hospital.'

'It was a mistake!' she suddenly spat, her lips tightening around her teeth, 'and I've paid for it in more ways than you can possibly imagine.'

'Why – because you lost your job?' Tanner heard himself scoff.

The skin around Christine's nose lifted as fresh tears began tumbling down her face. 'Jason was the reason why I lost my baby Annabella. I was telling Anthony, my husband, about us when we were on the motorway. I was saying how sorry I was, but he was angry – so very angry. I don't think he even saw the truck turning over in front of us. My relationship with Jason cost me *everything!* So yes, I've paid for what I did, and if you're not able to understand that, then I guess we're done.'

Forrester's voice came floating towards Tanner as if from another world.

'I'm going to get Cooper and Vicky to get themselves over to Long Gore Hall to make sure Hambleton, or Baines, or whoever it is doesn't make a run for it, but I suggest we head back there ourselves.'

'Of course,' Tanner replied, with absent obedience, his eyes being held captive by Christine's acrimonious glare.

'Ms Halliday,' Forrester continued, daring to catch her eye, 'I don't suppose you know what happened to the two teenage boys who went missing? Was it Baines who took them?'

'All I know is that he has them locked inside that abhorrent mansion.'

'But – they're alive?'

She glanced away to begin shaking her head. 'I'm – I'm sorry. I don't know.'

'OK, thank you anyway. I'm sure you understand that we'll be needing a full statement from you, but before we do that I suggest you get yourself checked over to make sure you're OK. There's an ambulance heading over to Long Gore Hall as we speak. Do you need help getting there?'

'I'm fine!' she replied, her bloody-minded

265

response aimed more at Tanner. 'You two had better get yourselves after Jason. I'll stay here to look after your detective constable.'

- CHAPTER SIXTY SEVEN -

WITH THE SOUND of a solitary siren drifting over Norfolk's wide open landscape, Tanner and Forrester joined the police dog unit to begin pelting their way back over the uneven waterlogged ground. As Long Gore Hall gradually began re-appearing out of the mist ahead, they arrived in time to see the ambulance they'd been listening to lurch one way, then the other, as it careened down the broken track towards them.

Leaving Forrester to lead the emerging paramedics over the marsh to where Townsend remained, a frantic glance over at Long Gore Hall's moss-covered stone steps had Tanner re-taking to his heels, over to where a couple of removals men could be seen wrestling a sofa into the back of the truck. 'Where's the car – the Range Rover?' he breathlessly called, only to find his question met by two vacant blank expressions. 'The car that was here?' he repeated. 'Where'd it go?'

'Er...Mr Hambleton drove off in it about 'alf an 'our ago,' the larger of the two eventually replied. 'He said he'd already told you – that he'd decided to 'ead off early.'

'Did he say where he was going?'

'Some 'otel near 'Stanstead Airport.'

'Shit!' Tanner cursed, his eyes staring wildly up at the vast Palladian pile. 'Did he say anything about there being anyone else inside?'

'How d'ya mean, "anyone else"?'

'The man you just watched drive away – that was Jason Baines – the serial-killing psychopath who escaped from Bradfield Hospital. He's kidnapped two teenagers. They're both supposed to be in there somewhere.'

The two men exchanged a look of befuddled bemusement before staring back at Tanner. 'I'm sorry, mister,' the larger one continued, 'but the guy who was here – that was Mr Hambleton. We ain't seen no serial-killing psychopath.'

Tanner could feel his body tense with helpless frustration. He could hardly blame them for being unable to understand what he was saying. He himself had had countless conversations with the man he'd thought to have been the estates true legal owner without realising for a single moment who he really was, and that was after he'd stood face-to-face with the original version, albeit just moments after the estate had been plunged into darkness.

Hearing the sound of a police dog bark suddenly behind him, Tanner spun around to find himself staring at its handler. 'The owner has gone,' he began, 'and we don't have a single sodding clue where the missing boys are. All we know is that they're in there somewhere. Can you organise your team to start a search?'

'Well, we can, but we'd need something belonging to at least one of the boys if we're to stand a chance of finding them.'

Tanner tore his eyes over the driveway to see Whitaker stumbling his way aimlessly over the gravel, binoculars in one hand, a carbine rifle in the other.

'Superintendent, sir!' he called out, raising a hand to help garner his attention. 'We think your son is inside the house.'

As if a veil had been lifted from his eyes, Whitaker looked first up at the mansion, then over at Tanner. 'Where's Baines?' he demanded, his mouth twisting into a contorted snarl.

'It looks like he's made a run for it. He drove off about half an hour ago, heading for a hotel near Stanstead.'

'Then it looks like I'll be heading off after him,' Whitaker growled, turning on his heal to begin charging towards his car.

'But – your son,' Tanner called, forced into a run. 'We think he's still alive.'

'All the more reason for me to ask that murdering bastard where he is,' Whitaker replied, reaching the boot of his car to heave it open, 'which will also give me the opportunity to spend a few pleasant moments smashing his face in with the butt of my Heckler and Koch.'

With the rifle still in his hand and a look of primordial rage etched onto his face, Tanner knew better than to question the man's distorted priorities. 'The dogs should be able to find him, but they'll need something with his scent on.'

Tossing the rifle into the trunk, Whitaker picked up a faded red buoyancy aid. 'This is his,' he said, handing it to Tanner, as if it was of no further use to him.

Tanner stared down at it as Whitaker slammed the car boot closed to storm around to the driver's side.

'If you find my son alive before I find Baines,' Whitaker continued, tugging open the door, 'then I suggest you give me a call. But if he turns up dead, it will probably be better if you don't.'

- CHAPTER SIXTY EIGHT -

TANNER STEPPED BACK from Whitaker's car as it spun around in a giant arc, spewing gravel out from its tyres as it roared its way towards the estate's rusting iron gates.

Remembering the buoyancy aid, he glanced around to see the dog handler he'd been talking to before, standing at the base of the worn stone steps. 'This belongs to Superintendent Whitaker's son,' he said, having hurried his way over. 'Will it do the job?'

'You don't have anything else?' the handler asked, turning it over in his hands with an uncertain eye.

'That's all we've got, I'm afraid.'

'Then I suppose it will have to.'

Leaving him to begin introducing the item to his team of dogs, Tanner gazed around, first at the ambulance, then over at the mist-covered marsh. When he saw the shadowy outline of a group of people emerging slowly through the swirling mist, he was about to run over to help guide them back when his eyes were blinded by the incandescently bright headlights of a rapidly approaching car.

Assuming it was Whitaker, having come to his senses to help find his son, he held up a hand against the light only to realise it wasn't a Mercedes, but a sleek bullet-grey Audi saloon, with Cooper behind the wheel and Vicky perched in the passenger seat.

As it skidded to a halt, Tanner remained where he

was to watch them climb out.

'Was that the Superintendent we just passed?' he heard Cooper ask.

'Quite possibly.'

'Bloody idiot! The guy nearly ran us off the road. Where's he going in such a hurry, anyway?'

'He came to the rather peculiar decision to set off after Baines, instead of staying here to help find his son.'

'So, Baines was behind everything after all?'

'Something like that.'

'How's Townsend?' Vicky enquired, catching Tanner's eye with a look of deep concern. 'We heard he'd been shot.'

'We think the bullet only caught his shoulder, so hopefully he'll be OK.'

'And Christine?'

The question had Tanner casting his eyes over once again at the slowly approaching group. 'She seems fine; all things considered. Hambleton must have sent them wandering into the marsh to give him time to make a run for it.'

'You mean Baines, don't you?' questioned Cooper.

'Yes, sorry, of course. Apparently, Hambleton's long dead. Baines murdered him the morning after he broke in.'

'But – he can't be,' Cooper continued, shaking his head. 'A call came in just after we left. His Range Rover has been seen heading north, up the A149.'

It took a full moment for the meaning behind Cooper's statement to sink in. 'Shit!' Tanner eventually cursed. 'That must mean he's not heading for Stanstead Airport after all.'

Cooper's face was now a mask of total bewilderment. 'Who isn't heading for Stanstead Airport - Hambleton?'

'I just told you. Hambleton's dead. Baines murdered him. That was his plan all along.'

'To kill Hambleton?'

'To take his place. That's why one minute he was ready to make a go of Long Gore Hall, the next he was desperate to sell, killing everyone who'd know that he wasn't the person he was pretending to be before buying a one-way ticket to South Africa.'

'So...what's he doing heading north if he's intending to fly out from Stanstead Airport?'

'He could be going to Norwich Airport?' Vicky proposed. 'He'd at least be able to get a connecting flight from there.'

'Fair enough,' continued Cooper, 'but that still doesn't explain why he's heading north. The only thing at the end of the A149 is Cromer. After that, it's just the North Sea.'

'Does Cromer have a marina?' Tanner questioned. 'Somewhere he could charter a boat?'

Cooper shook his head. 'Not that I know of. All it has is a pier, and not a very long one at that.'

'There *is* an airport up there,' interjected Vicky, catching Tanner's eye.

Cooper turned to stare over at her. 'Since when?'

'Well, I suppose it's more of an airfield than an airport. My dad used to take me there at the weekends. Baines may not be able to fly to South Africa from there, but he would at least be able to get over the Channel.'

Tanner's eyes drifted over towards his car. 'Do you remember where it is?'

'I should do. Assuming it's still there, of course.'

'OK. Vicky, come with me. Cooper, you stay here.'

'And do what?'

'We still need to find the missing boys. Baines apparently has them locked inside the hall somewhere, but we've no idea where, and all we have to find them is an old buoyancy aid that Whitaker's son apparently wore at some point in his life.'

The rumble of what sounded like distant thunder had them all turning to stare at the hall. There a cloud of dusty grey smoke could be seen billowing out from the entrance through which stumbled three removals men, coughing and spluttering their way down the narrow stone steps.

'Christ! That's all we need,' Tanner muttered, as the entire building seemed to groan for one long anxious moment before becoming ominously still.

'What the hell happened?' he shouted, running over to make sure the men were OK.

'We were taking the chandelier down – in the main hall – like Mr Hambleton told us,' the larger of the three began, still choking at the air. 'Before we knew it, the whole fucking ceiling came down on our heads. We're lucky to be alive!'

A bark from a dog had Tanner spinning around to find its handler, skidding to a halt beside him. 'Am I right in thinking that the whole place is about to collapse?'

'It was just the ceiling.'

'*Just* the ceiling?' the man repeated, staring at him with a look of unamused scepticism.

Tanner glared back. 'There are still two teenage boys inside!'

'Do we even know that they're still alive?'

'There's no reason for us to think that they're not.'

'But we don't know for certain?'

Tanner didn't reply, turning his attention instead to the hall's vast crumbling structure.

The dog handler looked first at the removals men, then up at the entrance. 'OK, we'll have a quick look, but if there's so much as a tremor I'll have no choice but to abort. I'm not risking the lives of both my men and dogs on the off-chance that the boys are still alive, especially not when just about every other of Baines' victims seems to have ended up otherwise.'

- CHAPTER SIXTY NINE -

ADVISING COOPER ONLY to risk entering the hall if the dogs picked up a firm scent, Tanner hurried around to the back of the ambulance to find Christine and Forrester, anxiously watching the paramedics stretcher Townsend inside. 'Is he going to be all right?' he asked quietly beside them.

'They've yet to say,' Forrester replied. 'I suspect it's too early to know.'

Tanner's eyes attempted to rest themselves on Christine's. 'And how about you?'

'As I said before,' she replied, her focus remaining fixed on Townsend, 'I'm fine!'

'They gave her the once over,' Forrester interjected. 'Just cuts and bruises. I assume Baines managed to do a runner?'

Tanner nodded in response. 'Whitaker's gone after him.'

'What about his son?'

Tanner shrugged as he turned to look back at the hall. 'He seemed more interested in finding Baines. The dogs are about to head inside to take a look, but there's another problem. The removal men brought the foyer's ceiling down when they were dismantling the chandelier. A supporting beam must have been dislodged at the same time, as the whole place looks as if it's about to collapse.'

Forrester joined Tanner in staring over at Long

Gore Hall, one of its four pillars leaning precariously over to one side. 'Is it even safe to go in?'

'I didn't think we had any choice?'

'No, I suppose not.'

'It would help if we knew where to look,' Tanner continued, his attention drifting over towards the hall's solitary black gates, 'so I'm going to take Vicky with me to see if we can find the man responsible. I assume that's alright by you?'

'Of course, but – I thought that's what Whitaker was doing?'

'We suspect he's going the wrong way. Hambleton's Range Rover was seen heading north up the A149. Assuming it's Baines behind the wheel, we think he may be heading for a small airfield near Cromer. I don't suppose there's any chance you could ask if there are any squad cars in the area who could take a look?'

'That's easy enough.'

'Without making it obvious as to who they'd be looking for?' Tanner added, turning to fix Forrester's eye. 'Whitaker took a carbine rifle with him. That and the demented look he had when he left, I think it may be better if he continues going the wrong way, for everyone's sake.'

- CHAPTER SEVENTY -

FOLLOWING VICKY'S DIRECTIONS, it wasn't long before Tanner was turning his XJS into a small airfield on the outskirts of Cromer, where a seemingly empty police squad car had been left next to the base of a modest two-storey control tower.

With no immediate sign of either Baines or the Range Rover, Tanner pulled up beside the car to climb quickly out. 'I don't suppose you can see him?' he asked Vicky, her head appearing on the opposite side.

'Nothing,' she replied, stepping up onto the Jag's stainless steel footplate to try and see above and beyond the dozens of single-engine aircraft crowding in around them. 'I can't even see his car!'

'Shit!' Tanner cursed, now staring wildly about. 'Then we must have guessed wrong.'

Glancing up at the tower to see two uniformed constables talking to someone inside, he jumped down to make his way over to its base. 'I'm going to ask if anyone's seen him,' he called back to Vicky, reaching a galvanised staircase fixed to the tower's side. 'You may as well wait there. I won't be long.'

Clattering his way up to a door at the top, he burst through to be met by the startled glare of the three people he found inside, the two constables he'd seen from the ground, and a shorter man wearing a stained roll-neck jumper.

'DI Tanner, Norfolk Police,' he stated, his eyes resting briefly on the man in the jumper before darting between the two constables. 'I assume you're here looking for Jason Baines?'

'That was the idea,' replied the nearest.

'Any luck?'

'Not yet. We've been asking Mr Dixon, here, about his car, but he doesn't seem particularly willing to cooperate.'

The man being referred to scowled back at the officer. 'All I said was that I haven't seen a Range Rover, nor is it my job to. I'm an air traffic controller, not a bloody carpark attendant!'

'He's not helping much with regards to the location of Baines, either, despite having told him that he's an escaped psychopath wanted in connection with the murder of at least three people. The only thing he's told us that's of any possible use is that they provide piloted charter planes.'

'Do they keep records of everyone who hires one?'

'I've already checked,' Dixon huffed. 'The name Baines isn't there.'

'How about Hambleton?'

The man offered Tanner a blank stare before shrugging his shoulders. 'It doesn't ring a bell.'

Tanner let out an exasperated sigh. 'Can you at least check?'

'If I must,' he replied, turning reluctantly on his heel to plonk himself down behind the control tower's desk, 'but I'd have remembered if we had.'

'Well?' Tanner demanded, a fractured moment later.

Dixon swivelled the monitor around for Tanner to see. 'As I said, nobody named either Baines or Hambleton has chartered one of our planes, neither today nor at any time over the last three years.'

A speaker fixed to a shelf above the desk came crackling into life. *'Cromer Tower this is Cessna 491AF at Beta 2, ready to taxi with Alpha.'*

'What was that?' Tanner demanded.

'My job!' Dixon stated with an indignant snort, pressing a button on the desk to lean his head in towards a microphone. 'Cessna 491AF, Cromer Tower. Taxi two right via Alpha Omega.'

'Two right via Alpha Omega, 491AF,' came the immediate response.

'I meant,' Tanner continued, 'what did it mean?'

The man folded his arms to offer Tanner a look of imperious condescension. 'That the aircraft Cessna 491AF has checked the latest weather forecast and was ready to approach the runway.'

Tanner lifted himself onto the balls of his feet to stare out through the control tower's windows where a small white plane could be seen trundling out towards a long wide strip of tarmac. 'Is it a piloted charter?'

'It is,' Dixon replied, returning to his monitor, 'but it wasn't booked by either a Baines or a Hambleton. The name given was Halliday, paid online by credit card yesterday evening.'

'That's him – the cheeky bastard,' Tanner muttered, his eyes remaining fixed on the plane. 'He's using one of his victim's names. Probably her credit card as well. Can you stop it from taking off?'

'I suppose that depends on how desperate they are to leave.'

No sooner had the question been answered did the speaker crackle back into life.

'Cromer Tower this is Cessna 491AF, holding short of Beta 2, right crosswind departure.'

'That's them again, asking permission to take off. What do you want me to say?'

279

'Something that would be reasonable enough to delay them.'

With a sagacious nod, Dixon leaned into the microphone again. 'Cessna 491AF, this is Cromer Tower. We have a, er, flock of birds sighted in the immediate area. Please standby.'

'*Cromer Tower, Cessna 491AF, standing by.*'

'That should hold them, for a few minutes at least, but if there is a deranged murdering psychopath on board, the second he sees you lot approach I can't imagine he won't be forcing the pilot to take off, at which point there'll be nothing more I can do.'

Tanner pushed himself away from the desk to glare over at the two police constables. 'Right you two. I want you down by your car, but under absolutely no circumstances are you to approach that plane until I tell you. Meanwhile, I'm going to see if I can persuade Mr Baines to come quietly. You never know, he might even agree!'

- CHAPTER SEVENTY ONE -

'**L**OOKS LIKE BAINES is here after all,' said Tanner, climbing back into his car to find Vicky waiting for him in the passenger seat. 'We think he's chartered the plane that's currently sitting at the end of the runway, waiting for permission to take off.'

'You're telling me he can fly a plane?' questioned Vicky, staring over at him with her mouth hanging open.

'Not unless he did an online course during his stay at Bradfield Hospital.'

'Does that mean he can, or he can't?'

'It's a piloted charter,' Tanner clarified, 'although I wouldn't put it past him. The traffic controller has told them to wait. He can't stop them from taking off, but he's attempting to delay them by saying that a flock of birds has been spotted in the area. It should give us a few minutes. So I thought we'd use the time to drive up to where they are without raising too many alarm bells to park the car in front of them, hopefully preventing them from taking off.'

Vicky continued gaping over at him. 'And that's your plan, is it?'

'Well, yes. Something like that.'

'What about the squad car?'

'We thought if Baines saw that driving up, he'd force the pilot to take off.'

'And if Baines sees a 1980s jet black Jaguar XJS trundling down the runway towards them, he's going to think that's normal, is he, especially when he must know by now that the car belongs to you?'

'I must admit, it's times like these when it would be more useful to be the proud owner of a Ford Mondeo, but it's still less threatening than a squad car.'

'Couldn't we just walk?'

'As long as you're happy to stand in front of the plane whilst I endeavour to persuade Baines to give himself up, then that's fine by me.'

Vicky thought for a moment before reaching for her seatbelt.

'Does that mean we can take the car?' asked Tanner, watching her clipping it into place.

'Naturally,' she replied. 'Besides, I've never been one for walking. It's always much more fun taking the car!'

Starting the engine with a smile, Tanner eased his XJS past the squad car to begin following the tarmacked road around. Steering carefully around the dozens of small fixed-wing aircraft parked on either side, he eventually saw the one he'd seen, stopped at the end of the runway. It was only when he began thinking about what he was going to do when he got there, other than to stop the car in front of the plane, did he consider what Baines had gaffer-taped to Christine's hands, or more to the point, what he hadn't.

'So, what's the plan again?' Vicky queried, shifting uneasily in her seat as they grew ever-closer to the awaiting plane.

'First-up, to hope Baines isn't currently staring at us through one of the windows.'

'You mean that he hasn't spotted your car driving

suspiciously slowly towards him over a stretch of tarmac normally reserved for small fixed-wing aircraft?'

'And secondly,' Tanner continued, 'that he forgot to bring his gun.'

'I'm s-sorry!' Vicky spluttered. 'Nobody said anything about guns!'

'Don't worry, there should only be one.'

'I don't care how many there are. If someone had mentioned the "g" word before we left the control tower, I'd still be there, watching events unfold through a pair of binoculars.'

'Tell you what. Why don't you stay in the car?'

'You mean...this one?'

Tanner couldn't help but laugh. 'Honestly, you'll be fine. The worse that can happen is that the plane will try to shove you out of the way. And if it does come down to a pushing contest between a two-and-a-half tonne car built out of solid British steel and a plane that weights no more than a slice of bread, I know which one I'd put my money on.'

'It's not the plane I'm worried about,' Vicky continued, staring out at its propeller, whirling around at the end of its nose. 'It's the guy inside it. The one with the gun – remember?'

'Don't worry about Baines. I'll take care of him.'

'And just exactly how are you going to do that?'

With the noise of the plane's engine growing increasingly loud, Tanner eased his car cautiously around its propeller to come to a halt directly in front of it.

Tugging on the handbrake, he offered Vicky a victorious smile. That's us over the first hurdle.'

'You didn't answer my question.'

'Sorry, which one was that?'

'You said you were going to take care of him. I was

just curious to know how you were going to do that?'

Tanner reached for the door handle. 'To be honest, I'm not exactly sure, but no doubt something will spring to mind.'

- CHAPTER SEVENTY TWO -

TANNER STEPPED OUT into a vortex of noise to see the pilot wrench a pair of bulbous grey headphones off his head to start mouthing what looked to be a string of obscenities at him. Giving the whirling propeller a wide berth, he edged his way along the port-side wing to see a shadowy face staring out at him through a side door window. As he rounded the wing's tip, stepping out through the door emerged a man Tanner had until then thought of as being the owner of Long Gore Hall, Lawrence Hambleton, one hand hidden inside the pocket of a high-collared sheepskin coat, the other holding firmly onto the door's white plastic handle.

'Mr Baines, I presume?' Tanner called over to him, lifting his voice above the heavy drone of the aircraft's engine.

Stepping cautiously out onto the wing, Baines offered Tanner a self-amused smirk. 'Honestly, Inspector, I thought you'd have been on to me the moment we first met. You remember that, don't you? When you came over that morning to ask if I was OK, having just discovered that a man convicted of butchering his parents with an axe some ten years before was the same person who'd broken into what has since become my ancestral home. All I had to do was to turn the generator off at the appropriate time, put on a slight South African accent and limp around for a bit.'

'I don't think anyone is going to be convinced that Long Gore Hall belongs to you anymore, Mr Baines.'

'Of course, and neither do I want them to be. I'm happy enough for them all to continue believing that the estate is owned by its rightful heir, Mr Lawrence Hambleton, and you're going to have a hell of a job proving that that isn't me.'

'I'm sorry, but why do you think that will be difficult to prove?'

'Well, for a start, there's no evidence to suggest that Mr Hambleton is anything but alive and well. Forgive me if I'm wrong, but I think you'd need a body to prove otherwise. It will be even more of a challenge once he's taken up his new residence in the Cayman Islands, where he's recently opened up a bank into which the proceeds from the sale of Long Gore Hall will eventually go. I'll be honest with you, Inspector, personally I believe that I'm fully justified in being able to live out the rest of my life in what most people would consider to be opulent luxury. My parents may have kept me in a cage, abusing me in ways you wouldn't want to imagine, but despite what your Superintendent Whitaker made everyone believe at the time, I didn't kill them. Neither was I a deranged psychotic lunatic, no matter what his friend Dr Copeland testified to. Actually, saying that, I must admit, I'm not so sure now. Ten years of being strapped to a table to undergo unimaginably painful electrotherapy treatment may have had the opposite effect of what I believe its intended purpose was.'

'I know what Whitaker did,' Tanner began, edging his way around the aircraft's wing, 'and that you didn't kill your parents. I spoke to the defence witness who'd originally claimed to have seen someone else leaving your house on the night in question. She also confirmed that it was Whitaker who forced her to change her story. Between you and me, had you not escaped from Bradfield Hospital to end up murdering no less than three innocent people, I'd have been happy enough to let you go.'

'You know, from what you're saying, it almost sounds as if you think you can stop me.'

'Well, my car *is* parked directly in front of your plane, which I suspect will make it a little more challenging than normal for it to take off.'

'And what's to prevent me from shooting you in the head, and whoever else is in your car, to then simply push it out the way?'

Tanner felt his heart lurch inside his chest as his eyes fell briefly down to the pocket inside which Baines' hand was buried. Doing his best to disguise his growing apprehension, he looked up to offer him a shrug of nonchalant indifference. 'Then you'd be wanted for the murder of two police officers as well. And when word gets out that you're not the mentally disturbed clinical psychopath Dr Copeland made you out to be, I sincerely doubt you'll be sent back to the relative comfort of Bradfield Hospital. I think it's far more likely that you'll find yourself spending the rest of your life locked up inside the far less tolerant world of a maximum security prison, inside which you'll be beaten by the guards during the day and gang-raped by its sexually repressed inmates at night.'

'I think you're forgetting something, Inspector.'

'Oh yes, and what's that?'

Baines offered Tanner a callous grin. 'You're going to have to catch me first, something you'll find even more challenging with a bullet lodged inside your brain.'

Tanner returned the smile to run his eyes over the aircraft's fuselage. 'You do realise that you can't fly all the way to the Cayman Islands in this, don't you? You'll be lucky to make it to France.'

'Who said I'm going to France?'

'The pilot's flight plan will tell us where you're going, Mr Baines.'

'Gosh, you're right!' Baines exclaimed, raising a hand to his mouth in mocking consternation. 'I hadn't thought of that. Then I suppose I have no choice. I'll just have to give myself up. Unless, of course,' his eyes drifted slowly up to the sky, 'the pilot just happens to alter course at some point during the trip and forgets to tell anyone. Do you think that would work?'

'You'll still need to find yourself a connecting flight to the Cayman Islands.'

Baines shook his head with such violent frustration that he nearly managed to lose his balance on the aircraft's smooth sloping wing. 'Enough of this shit!' he eventually spat, finding his balance to pull the handgun out of his pocket that Tanner feared had been there. 'Now, are you going to move that car of yours, or am I going to have to shoot you to do it myself?'

With the gun pointed at his chest, Tanner could feel his heart thumping at the base of his throat. 'Tell you what,' he began, struggling to keep his eyes off the end of its barrel, 'how about I make a deal with you?'

'You want to make a deal with me?' laughed Baines. 'You seem to be forgetting, Inspector, I'm the one with the gun.'

Tanner drew in a fortifying breath. 'I'll move the car in exchange for you telling me where the missing boys are. It will be quicker than having to shoot both me and my colleague,' he added. 'It would also save you having to serve an additional two life sentences, were you to ever be caught, that is.'

Baines eyes danced briefly between Tanner's. 'Tell you what, how about if you move the car after which you can tell everyone that it was someone else on the plane, and that you don't have a single idea as to where I am, or where I'm likely to be?'

'If the boys are where you tell me they are, and they're still alive of course, then you'll have yourself a deal.'

'OK. Move your car and I'll tell you.'

'Tell me, and I'll move my car.'

Tanner held his breath as he watched Baines narrow his eyes.

'If I ever find out that you've lied to me, Inspector, you'll be waking up one morning to find your throat's been sliced open, much like Lawrence Hambleton did.'

Tanner swallowed involuntarily at the thought of opening his eyes in the middle of the night to find Baines leaning over his head with a knife pressed against his neck. 'Understood,' he eventually managed to reply, finding his mouth had become as dry as sandpaper.

'Very well,' Baines eventually responded, returning a smile that Tanner found so disturbing, he wished he was back at home. 'You'll find them...'

The sudden blast of a siren had Tanner whipping his head around to see the squad car he'd left back at the control tower come screeching around the corner. As it tore up the tarmac towards them, he was about to launch himself over to head them off, when he realised why they'd decided to disobey his direct order. Careening around the bend directly behind them came a dark blue Mercedes Benz, Superintendent Whitaker's face leering out at them from behind its black leather steering wheel.

- CHAPTER SEVENTY THREE -

A S THE BUFFETING air from the aircraft's engine filled with the noise of wailing sirens and screeching tyres, Tanner turned to look back at Baines. 'You can still tell me where they are,' he blurted, his eyes burning with pleading desperation.

'It's a little late for that, don't you think?' came the man's sardonic response, lifting the gun to aim directly at Tanner's head.

'You don't have to do this!' Tanner heard himself cry, holding a hand up as if it alone could stop the bullet from blowing out the back of his skull.

'Oh, I think I do, Inspector.'

'Jason Baines!' came an all-too familiar voice, as the sirens' blare came grinding to a lackadaisical halt. 'This is Superintendent Whitaker, Norfolk Police!'

From around the fingers of his still out-stretched hand, Tanner watched in fretful hope as Baines' eyes trailed over to the man he knew must have been standing on the tarmacked surface behind him.

'I know who you are, Superintendent, thank you.'

'I need you to drop the gun and place your hands on top of your head.'

'Right. Yes. I see. And what if I don't?'

Tanner forced himself to turn his head, just enough to see the man responsible for the entire Norfolk Constabulary jam a carbine rifle firmly against his shoulder.

'Then I'll be left with no choice but to shoot you,' he heard him say, 'but not before you've told me where my son is.'

'You know, it's funny, I was just this minute about to tell your Detective Inspector here, but now I'm not so sure.'

'I don't see that you have much of a choice, Mr Baines.'

'I think you'll find that everyone has a choice, Superintendent, just as you did when you had me carted off to a mental institution for a crime I didn't commit.'

'I think your stay at Bradfield Hospital has allowed your imagination to run away with you.'

'Has it, now?'

'Either that or you're looking for someone else to hold accountable for what you did.'

'I don't know who killed my parents, but I know it wasn't me, and there's no way I'm going back to Bradfield Hospital for Dr Copeland to resume his electro-fucking therapy treatment.'

'Put the gun down and tell me where my son is!' came Whitaker's barking response, his tone dripping with lethal intent.

'Or what? You'll shoot me?'

'Don't think I won't, Mr Baines.'

'But then you'll never find out where your son is.'

'Who said I'd be aiming for your head? I think I'm far more likely to start with your kneecaps before working my way up. The moment I reach your genitalia, I doubt there'll be much you wouldn't have told me, and for what? You'll still end up back where you came from, except this time to find yourself having to be pushed about in a wheelchair.'

Struggling for breath, Tanner watched Baines'

eyes begin filling with tears as they shifted erratically between him and the policemen behind, all the while keeping the gun aimed squarely at his head. With the only sound being the drone from the aircraft's engine, he glanced around again, just in time to see Whitaker adjust the angle of his rifle.

'It looks like you're running out of options, Mr Baines,' the Superintendent continued, his face cracking into a smile. 'Either you tell me where my son is, or you can say goodbye to the use of your legs.'

'You seem to be under the impression that you've won again, Superintendent,' Baines continued, pulling his shoulders back to stand tall and straight, 'but you're forgetting what I told you earlier. *Everyone* has a choice.'

'And you're down to two.'

'I hate to disagree, but you seem to have forgotten one.'

In the blink of an eye, Baines removed the aim of his gun's narrow bead from Tanner's head to press firmly against the temple of his own.

'NO!' Whitaker screamed, but too late to change the man's deadly intent.

As the sharp crack of the gun ripped through the air, a dense cloud of blood billowed out from the side of Baines' suddenly deformed head. With his body collapsing over the edge of the aircraft's wing, Whitaker threw himself forward, barely reaching Tanner before what was left of Baines' skull smacked into the tarmac, splitting it open like an over-ripe melon.

Dropping to his knees, Whitaker heaved the body up by its coat's lapels to begin screaming down at the unblinking eyes staring up at him. 'TELL ME WHERE MY SON IS, YOU PSYCHOTIC FUCKING BASTARD! DID YOU HEAR ME? I SAID TELL ME

WHERE HE IS!'

Watching Whitaker begin shaking the lifeless body with such animalistic rage that globules of blood began flying out from the side of his head, Tanner crouched down discreetly beside him. 'I'm sorry, sir, but – I think he's dead.'

'He's not dead,' came Whitaker's sobbing response, his hands gradually easing their grip on the coat's lapels. 'He can't be. He hasn't told me where Adam is yet.'

Seeing tears begin tumbling their way down the side of his face, Tanner laid a steadying hand on the man's trembling shoulder. 'Try not to worry, sir. We still have dogs searching the estate. For all we know, they may have already found him.'

'They'd have called if they had.'

Knowing he was right, Tanner stood slowly up. 'Then if it's alright by you, I'm going to make my way back to help with the search.'

With the only response being the wretched sound of gentle sobbing, Tanner took one more look at the man he'd spent the last few days believing to be Lawrence Hambleton. Struggling to accept his mistake, and the fact that the only person who knew where the missing boys were was now dead, he shook his head from side to side. With Vicky casting a look of concern over at him from beside his car, he held up a hand to let her know he was OK before lowering his head to begin trudging his way over.

- CHAPTER SEVENTY FOUR -

WITH DARKNESS FAST closing in, Tanner careened between Long Gore Hall's rusted lopsided gates to see the entire front of the Palladian mansion lit up by a series of tall portable floodlights.

Skidding to a halt behind a police van, he stepped out with Vicky to the sound of raised voices, echoing out from inside. A quick glance over the car's roof had them both racing up the steps to meet a paramedic at one end of a stretcher, hauling it out the other way. With what was left of an arm hanging out from underneath a long white sheet, its skin burnt to a blackened crisp, Tanner looked quickly away to see Forrester come hurrying out from inside. 'Is it one of the missing boys?' he asked, bringing the DCI to a halt with his eyes.

'Johnstone thinks it's more likely to be Hambleton, but he's not sure. The body was found on top of a smouldering bonfire, so he won't know until he's been able to match his dental records. I don't suppose Baines told you where they are?'

Tanner shook his head, turning to watch the stretcher being lifted into the back of the ambulance. 'Nor is he likely to.'

'Dare I ask why?'

'Whitaker showed up. He threatened to shoot first his kneecaps, then his testicles, unless he told him where his son was. Baines ended up shooting himself, straight through the head.'

'Jesus!'

'What's worse was that he was about to tell me, just before our Superintendent's untimely arrival. I left him sobbing like a child, struggling to believe the man was dead.'

Tilting his head, Tanner peered over Forrester's shoulder. 'I don't suppose the dog team has had any luck?'

'Just a lot of false leads. Nothing more.'

'And Townsend?'

'He's been taken to Wroxham Medical Centre. Christine went with him. She said that if I saw you, to ask if you could pick her up.'

Tanner's eyes drifted over towards his car.

'You can head off now, if you like,' Forrester continued, following his gaze.

'Will you call me if they find anything?'

'Of course, but to be honest, at this stage, I don't think we should hold out much hope.'

- CHAPTER SEVENTY FIVE -

WITH NO SIGN of Christine in the carpark, Tanner took the steps up to Wroxham Medical Centre's main entrance to find himself nearly walking straight into Sally Beech, coming out the other way.

'Oh, er, hi Sally,' he began, stepping to one side. 'I don't suppose you've seen Christine?'

'She's in reception,' she replied, her eyes shining above a whimsical smile.

'You seem happy.'

'Don't I normally?'

'Sorry, of course,' Tanner replied, unsure what else to say. 'I suppose you just seem particularly so.'

Sally's face flushed ever-so slightly. 'Mark – I mean DC Townsend's awake. I was worried, so I drove over to see him.'

Tanner made a somewhat obvious deduction from the evidence at hand. 'Does that mean that the two of you are...?'

'He asked me out. Well, technically, I asked him out, but he said yes, so I think that must mean he's alright about it.'

'Oh, I'm sure he is. May I ask what happened to that other boyfriend of yours, the one I saw dropping you off at work the other day?'

'Oh, him! It turns out that he was only after one thing.'

'I thought *all* men were only after one thing?'

'Not that – silly,' she replied, nudging him away with coy rebuke. 'I found out that he was a reporter for the Norfolk Herald. He'd only asked me out so that he could pump me for information.'

Tanner did his best to suppress a devilish smirk. 'Am I to assume he did a lot of pumping?'

Sally's entire face erupted with colour. 'I don't believe you just said that!' she spluttered, her eyes widening with embarrassed shock.

Tanner cleared his throat. 'Sorry, that was unforgivable. Anyway, I think you've made the right choice in Townsend. He's a good man.'

She glared at him for a moment longer before taking in a calming breath. 'Well, I hope so, but with my luck, he'll probably turn out to be an undercover reporter working for The Daily Mail.'

'Oh, I doubt it. He may be a good detective constable, but he can't write for shit. Have you seen his reports?'

Sally let out a cackle of a laugh as her eyes drifted up towards the cold star-filled sky.

'Anyway,' Tanner continued, glancing through the glass doors to spy Christine, sitting on her own at the end of a line of empty chairs, 'I'd better head in. All the best again with Townsend. I'm sure you've made the right choice.'

- CHAPTER SEVENTY SIX -

'What on Earth did you say to that poor girl?' Christine asked, as Tanner came strolling up. 'I'm not sure I've ever seen anyone go quite so red.'

'Nothing I should have,' Tanner muttered in response. 'I hear Townsend's awake. Have the doctors said anything?'

'Not to me.'

An awkward silence seemed to lodge itself between them as Christine turned to stare down at the floor.

'How're you holding up?' Tanner found himself asking, unsure whether to take the seat beside her or to remain standing where he was.

'I've already told you.'

Tanner's mind took him back to their last conversation, and then to what he'd found next to their bathroom's sink. 'And the baby?'

He watched in silence as a single tear began rolling its way down the side of her nose.

'How d-did you know?' she eventually asked, looking slowly up.

'Something I found in the bathroom.'

'And...what do you think?'

'About you being pregnant?'

Christine nodded, her eyes shimmering with fretful apprehension.

Blinking against tears of his own, Tanner sucked in a juddering breath. 'I think it's the most amazing news I've ever heard in my entire life.'

She continued to stare at him for a moment longer before her mouth seemed to tear itself apart, rivers of tears tumbling freely down each side of her face.

With absolutely no idea what was wrong, Tanner sank slowly down into the chair beside her.

'I'm sorry,' she eventually mumbled, using the backs of her hands to wipe her face dry. 'I am happy, it's just – it's just – I didn't know what you'd think. I thought that maybe you'd say you weren't interested, and I'd never see you again.'

Tanner could feel himself becoming overwhelmed with compassion. 'Why on earth wouldn't I be interested in having a child with the woman I love?'

As fresh tears welled up in Christine's eyes, Tanner took her in his arms. And there they stayed, holding on to each other as if their lives depended on it, until the sound of a woman clearing her throat brought them fumbling apart.

'I don't suppose either of you is a Detective Inspector Tanner?' questioned the stern middle-aged nurse they found standing in front of them, her hands clasped firmly together.

'That's – er – me,' Tanner replied, climbing to his feet.

'Mr Townsend is asking to see you,' the nurse continued, in a matter-of-fact tone of voice. 'If you could follow me, I'll take you to his room.'

- CHAPTER SEVENTY SEVEN -

TANNER CREPT INTO a small dimly-lit private room to find Townsend, propped up in bed with his eyes closed. Assuming he must have fallen asleep, he began heading back out when he heard the rustle of bed sheets.

'Is that you, sir?' came his rasping voice.

Turning, he saw him peering over at him through a pair of half-open eyes. 'How's the shoulder?'

'I can't feel a thing,' the young DC replied, glancing down at the arm lying over his chest in a blue NHS sling.

'That must be the drugs. Don't worry, it will hurt like hell when they wear off.'

'That's certainly good to know. Thank you.'

Tanner smiled as he perched himself on the edge of the bed. 'I saw Sally outside. She said she'd been in to see you.'

A touch of colour rose to Townsend's otherwise deathly pale face. 'She asked me out. I said yes.'

'You'd have been a fool to say anything else.'

'Do you think Forrester will mind, being that he's her uncle and everything?'

'By "everything" I assume you mean that he's also your boss, the Detective Chief Inspector for Wroxham Police Station?'

Townsend looked away. 'That's what I thought.'

'Don't worry. There's a simple answer.'

'What's that?'

'Don't tell him.'

Townsend laughed, immediately grabbing his shoulder, his face grimacing with pain.

'I told you it would hurt like hell when those pain killers wore off.'

The room fell into an awkward silence, leaving Tanner struggling to think of something else to say. 'Did you hear about Baines?' he eventually asked.

'Sally told me. Is it true – he ended up shooting himself?'

Tanner nodded slowly in response. 'I had hoped for a different outcome.'

'What about the missing boys? Has there been any sign?'

'Nothing. They think they've found Hambleton, what was left of him, but nobody else. I was kind of hoping that you might have either seen or heard something when you were there. Something that might help us find them?'

'I didn't have much of a chance. I went over after Forrester bawled me out about getting a search warrant. Stupid, I know. I'm not even sure what I was hoping to achieve. All I knew was that I couldn't just go home and forget about it.'

'Did you see anything – anything at all?'

'Nothing worth talking about. I didn't go inside. I just peered in through some of the windows. The only thing I did see was Hambleton – sorry – I mean Baines, stepping out of what looked to be some sort of larder at the back of the kitchen. He didn't let on, but he must have seen me, as the next thing I knew I woke up tied to a chair with one hell of a headache.'

'Sorry, but – did you say you saw him coming out of a larder in the kitchen?'

'As I said, it looked like one. It wasn't the entrance.

That was on the other side.'

- CHAPTER SEVENTY EIGHT -

'HOW IS HE?' Christine enquired, sitting up in her chair as Tanner approached.

'He seems fine. Just his shoulder. Right! Are you ready to go?'

'Well, I was hoping to be able to stay a little longer,' she replied, gazing around at the blank sterile walls, 'but if you insist.'

Tanner held out a hand to help lift her to her feet. 'Don't worry, we can always come back. Besides, I need to make a very quick stop at Long Gore Hall.'

Christine stopped where she was to stare up at him. 'Not seriously?'

'It was something Townsend said just now,' Tanner replied, glancing briefly over his shoulder, 'that when he was there he saw Baines coming out of a larder in the kitchen.'

'Is that significant?'

'Only in that it doesn't have one, at least not one I know about. I think it might be what Hambleton mentioned when I first went over to see him – that the house had a hidden passageway. With everything that's been going on I'd forgotten all about it. I think it's possible that Baines found it and that was what Townsend saw him coming out of, which was why he ended up being bashed over the head. If there's even the vaguest chance that there is, and the missing boys are tied up at the end of it, I'm going to have to take a look.'

- CHAPTER SEVENTY NINE -

'**S**HIT!'' TANNER CURSED, lurching through the dilapidated gates to find Long Gore Hall shrouded in darkness, the emergency vehicles gone, all but for a solitary squad car.

Skidding to a halt behind it to leave Christine cocooned in the passenger seat, he grabbed a torch from the glovebox to lever himself out.

'Where the hell is everyone?' he called over to the two uniformed constables he found pacing lackadaisically up and down at the base of the moss-covered stone steps.

'A section of the roof came down,' the nearest replied, 'so they decided to call it a day.'

'What about the missing boys?'

'Not a sign. The guy in charge of the dogs said that they couldn't have been there, else they'd have found them.'

Tanner took a moment to stare up at the vast shadowy edifice. 'I don't suppose you're going to be around for a while?'

'We're on night duty. We've been told to stay until the morning.'

'Lucky you.'

'I know. It's going to be a blast.'

'It will if the building falls down.'

'Which is probably why we've been told not to go inside.'

'Shame. I was hoping one of you would like to join me.'

'You mean - in there?' the constable replied, casting a concerned eye up at the pillars, each one now looking as if it would come crashing down in the lightest of winds.

'Is there anywhere else?'

'No – but – unfortunately, we can't, and I'm not sure you should, either.'

'Don't worry, I won't be long. I just want to take a quick look inside the kitchen.'

Turning to launch himself up the stone steps, he nudged the front door open with his foot to lean his head cautiously inside. With the torch held in his hand, he brought the beam to bear on what was left of the ceiling. As a billion particles of dust began dancing in its light, he traversed it around the hollow empty space, all the while listening to the building groan like an old man clawing his way out of some ancient antique bed.

With no obvious sign that anything was about to collapse on top of him, he stepped inside to head down to the kitchen. Apart from a layer of dust that covered every surface like a thin delicate veil, it was very much as he remembered.

He took a moment to shine the torch over at the window, the one Baines had supposedly used to climb inside, then over at where Townsend had said he'd seen him emerge. It was just as he'd remembered. There was nothing there. Just a blank wall divided by a single dado rail, yellowing white paint flaking from off its surface. Wondering if there could be any footprints left in the dust to offer him some clues, he swung the beam down to find the floor around the wall covered in paw prints. *The dogs must have sensed something was there*, he mused to himself, *but not enough to bring anyone's attention to it.*

Stepping carefully over, he used the beam to study the wall's surface, searching for anything that could indicate where a hidden door might be. But there wasn't a single crack, nor could he see any sort of a latch hidden along the rail.

A scuffling sound from over his shoulder had him spinning around to find Christine, standing behind him, her face like a rabbit's caught in the headlights of an oncoming car.

'What are you doing here?' he demanded, his voice harsh but low. 'I thought I told you to wait in the car.'

'Er, no, you didn't.'

'Well, I meant to. You still haven't answered my question?'

'Your colleagues told me about the roof, and that the entire place could collapse at any moment.'

'So you thought you'd come inside to take a look?'

'I wanted to see if you were OK.'

'You do realise that makes absolutely no sense, don't you?'

'Does to me,' she shrugged. 'Anyway, I'm here now. How can I help?'

'I'm not sure you can,' Tanner replied, returning his attention to the wall. 'Townsend said he saw Baines coming out from a larder that's supposed to be here, but as you can see, there isn't one.'

'Could it be one of those secret door things?' she asked, stepping up to stand beside him. 'Houses like this used to be full of them, didn't they?'

Tanner began re-examining the surface with his torch. 'That's what I was looking for. Hambleton mentioned something about there being a hidden passageway somewhere. I thought it might have been here, but I can't see one.'

'Have you tried the rail?'

'Of course,' Tanner replied, tracing the torch beam along its length.

'Let me have a look,' Christine said, grabbing the torch from out of his hand to nudge him briskly out the way. As she crouched down beside the wall, she tilted her head to focus the light up underneath the rail. 'The problem with men,' she soon began, standing up to hook a hand under its furthest edge, 'is that they never look!'

Hearing something click, Tanner stood back in surprise as she pulled back a section of the wall to reveal a set of wooden steps leading down into what must have been some sort of unlit cellar.

'Good job you're here,' he muttered, taking back the torch to direct it into the inky blackness below. 'Ladies first?'

'Fat chance!'

The sound of a sudden gust of wind left the whole house groaning underneath its own immense weight.

'Honestly, Christine, I really think you should wait outside. The whole place could come down at any minute.'

'Then I suppose we'd better stop wasting time, hadn't we?'

Knowing he'd be unlikely to change her mind, he scrabbled around for some form of light switch. Unable to find one, he called down into the darkness. 'Hello?' Adam? David? Is anyone there?'

Remaining where he was, he held his breath to listen for the smallest of sounds. But the only thing they could hear was the torturous noise of the house, creaking and groaning directly above their heads.

'What was that?' he heard Christine whisper.

They waited in silence again.

'All I can hear is the house about to collapse,' Tanner replied, lifting his eyes to the ceiling above.

'There,' she said, placing a hand gently down on his arm.

She was right. There was a noise. The lightest of sounds, like a door being dragged open and closed by an undulating breeze.

'Are you sure you don't want to wait outside?' he asked, glancing around.

'Not really, but as I said, I'm here now.'

'OK, then stay close, but if the whole place comes down around our ears and we end up trapped down there, please don't blame me.'

'Don't worry, I will.'

With one hand held onto the torch and the other taking hold of a handrail, Tanner led the way down into what opened up into a large rectangular cellar, devoid of anything but an old stone fireplace and a myriad of dust-covered cobwebs.

'There's nothing here!' Tanner despaired, reaching the ground to begin spinning hopelessly around. 'It's completely empty!'

Then came the sound again, still faint, but a fraction louder.

'There is *something* here,' Christine murmured, joining Tanner at the base of the stairs.

Hearing it again, Tanner brought the beam to bear on the wall at the furthest end. 'The bricks are old but look, the cement holding them together isn't. The bastard must have bricked them up!'

Racing over to it, he called the boys' names again. 'Adam, David? Is that you?'

With the sound suddenly becoming more frantic, he handed Christine the torch to rest the palms of his hands against the cold hard bricks. Taking a half-step back, he surged forward, slamming his shoulder hard into the wall, but it didn't budge. Not even an inch.

'We need to find something to help break through,'

he muttered, glancing frantically about. 'The squad car outside might have something. Can you run and ask them?'

'I'll be as fast as I can,' Christine replied, handing the torch back to spin quickly away.

Watching her take the stairs two at a time, Tanner turned back to the wall. Then he remembered the fireplace.

Lurching around, he threw himself at it, falling to his knees to begin heaving out its heavy, soot-covered grate. Eventually able to lever it out, he hauled it back to the wall to lift high above his head before slamming it hard against the surface. Seeing one of the bricks move, he brought the grate down, over and over again, until the wall eventually began to give way, enough at least for him to see through to the other side.

Dropping the grate, he reached for his torch to shine through the jagged opening. At first, all he could see were clouds of swirling white dust. Then he saw them; two lanky figures, one squinting against the torch's glare, the other curled up in the corner.

With renewed urgency, he ditched the torch to again begin battering at the wall until the hole was large enough for him to squeeze his way through.

'Are you alright?' he asked the one staring over at him, ripping off the gaffer tape that had been flattened over his mouth.

Choking at the dust-filled air, the boy nodded briefly before his entire body began to spasm, tears bursting from his dirty blood-shot eyes.

'Are you Adam or David?' Tanner questioned, tugging at the tape used to bind his hands behind his back.

'David,' the boy spluttered. 'David Copeland.'

Hearing footsteps begin clattering their way down

the cellar's steps, Tanner looked over at the other figure, its body unmoving, its head facing the wall.

'I – I don't know how long it's been,' he heard David mutter, his voice rasping like a rusty saw, 'but I haven't heard him move. Not for ages.'

As the face of one of the policemen appeared through the wall behind him, Tanner turned his head to fix the man's eye. 'I need help! Tell your colleague to call for an ambulance. Then get in here. We need to get them out before the building collapses.'

- EPILOGUE -

IT WAS TWO days after the missing teenagers had been found when Tanner arrived at Wroxham Police Station to find himself staring curiously about. Despite being over half an hour late, and everyone else being already there, the open-planned office was unnaturally quiet.

Taking off his coat to hook over the back of his chair, he glanced down at his desk to see a copy of The Daily Telegraph, stuck to the top of which was a yellow Post-it note. He ran his eyes briefly over the broadsheet's headline and the photograph underneath. He didn't need to read the article itself to know the details. It had been on the news that morning. He'd also heard it on the radio coming in. The Post-it note, or what was written on it was, however, more intriguing. It said, simply, 'My office, please.' He knew who'd written it. That much was obvious. What struck him as odd was the unusual use of the word "please".

You wanted to see me, sir?' he asked moments later, having wrapped his knuckles on Forrester's already half-open door.

With his eyes remaining fixed to his monitor, the DCI beckoned him inside.

Closing the door behind him, Tanner turned to stand in front of his desk.

'I take it you've seen the news?' Forrester

eventually asked, glancing up to see the newspaper held in Tanner's hands.

'That the witness from Baines' trial has told the nation's press that the person in charge of the entire Norfolk Constabulary had threatened her with a knife,' began Tanner, 'forcing her to remain silent about what she'd really seen that night, the same man whose son was found dead inside a walled-up cellar underneath Long Gore Hall, after the apparently innocent Jason Baines had shot himself through the head?'

'The man who *was* in charge of the Norfolk Constabulary,' Forrester corrected, his tone solemn and low.

'So, Whitaker's been fired?'

Forrester shook his head.

'Don't tell me he had the good sense to resign?'

Remaining grimly silent, Forrester eased himself back into his chair. 'You may want to take a seat.'

Becoming even more curious, Tanner sank slowly down into the chair being offered.

'I had a call from Chief Superintendent Baxter on my way into work. It would appear that Whitaker's body was discovered in his study this morning. He'd shot himself with his old service revolver. A copy of that newspaper you're holding was found lying open on his desk.'

'Jesus Christ!' Tanner softly exclaimed.

'It was obvious he'd been hit hard by his son's death. This morning's news must have pushed him over the edge.'

With Tanner stunned into silence, it was left for Forrester to continue.

'Anyway, until his family has been officially informed, what I've told you is strictly between you and me.'

'Of course,' Tanner replied, finding himself staring absently down at the newspaper now lying on his lap.

'There *is* a reason why I brought you in here to tell you,' he heard Forrester continue, 'which is directly related to why Baxter called me this morning.'

At first Tanner didn't respond. His eyes had become transfixed to the photograph of Whitaker featured on the newspaper's front page, fighting his way out of Norfolk's HQ through a frenzied pack of overly zealous reporters.

Forrester leant forward to plant his elbows firmly down on top of his desk. 'Before they break the news to the press, they want to make sure that they're able to give the impression that his passing has in no way affected the smooth running of the Norfolk Police. A part of that is to ensure that a transition of power is already in place.'

Tanner looked up to begin gawping over at him in stunned silence, leaving Forrester clearing his throat. 'Baxter wants to promote me up to Superintendent, with immediate effect.'

Tanner first closed, then opened his mouth. 'And...what did you say?'

'I accepted,' came his forthright response.

'Then I suppose congratulations are in order.'

Forrester's face remained a mask of stone. 'What that does mean, of course, is that we now need someone to take over here as DCI. Baxter asked if I could recommend anyone,' he added, his eyes fixing themselves onto Tanner's.

'You couldn't possibly mean me?' Tanner heard himself say.

'You think I should recommend Cooper instead?'

'Well, no, but...'

'It would mean a significant pay rise, which I'm sure Christine wouldn't object to.'

'It would also mean more time spent at work, which I'm sure she would, not forgetting the additional responsibility.'

'Which you're more than ready for.'

Tanner shifted in his chair. 'I don't know, sir. I'm not sure it's really me.'

'Well, look, you don't have to decide now.'

'OK, that's good. How long do I have?'

'Baxter wants an answer by ten o'clock this morning.'

'I thought you said that I didn't have to decide now!'

'You don't,' Forrester replied, lifting his arm to make a point of staring at his watch. 'You've got twenty-minutes. You would have had nearly an hour had you made the effort to be at work on time.'

Grabbing both a coffee and his phone, Tanner unhooked his coat from his chair to make his way outside.

'Hi, honey, it's me. How are you doing?'

'I've gone back to bed,' came Christine's voice, purring at him from the other end of the line.

'And the baby?'

'I think it's a little too early to say, but do feel free to ask me again in about seven and a half months' time.'

A smile flickered over Tanner's lips before falling quickly away. 'I have some news I wanted to run by you.'

'That sounds intriguing. Go on.'

'Forrester's been offered the job of Superintendent.'

'Oh, right,' she replied, in a disappointed tone. 'I assume that means Whitaker's resigned?'

Tanner opened his mouth to tell her what had

315

happened before remembering what Forrester had said. 'Something like that,' he eventually responded. 'He's told them he'll take it, which means there's an opening for his position as DCI.'

'Oh, I see!'

'He's offered it to me, I'm just not sure I want to accept.'

'I assume it would mean more money?'

'Well, yes, but it would also mean more responsibility, and all the trappings that go with it.'

'OK, but you're going to have more responsibility whether you accept the job or not.'

'And why's that?'

'Er...because of the baby? Remember?'

'Sorry – of course,' Tanner spluttered, picturing Christine rolling her eyes.

'Well, if I were you, I think you should accept. You can't be a Detective Inspector for the rest of your life.'

'I was hoping I wouldn't have to be a detective *anything* for the rest of my life.'

'What else were you planning on doing?'

Without a clue how to answer that, Tanner remained despondently silent.

'Anyway, look, we can talk more about this over dinner.'

'They want an answer now.'

'Really? What's the rush?'

'I'll tell you when I get home.'

The line fell momentarily silent before Christine's voice came back over the line. 'So, anyway, what are you going to say?'

'To be honest, at the moment I'm not exactly sure, but no doubt I'll think of something.'

John Tanner
will return in
Weavers' Way

- A LETTER FROM DAVID -

Dear Reader,

I just wanted to say a huge thank you for deciding to read *Long Gore Hall*. If you enjoyed it, I'd be really grateful if you could leave a review on Amazon, or mention it to your friends and family. Word-of-mouth recommendations are just so important to an author's success, and doing so will help new readers discover my work.

It would be great to hear from you as well, either on Facebook, Twitter, Goodreads or via my website. There are plenty more books to come, so I sincerely hope you'll be able to stick around for what will continue to be an exciting adventure!

All the very best,

David

- ABOUT THE AUTHOR -

David Blake is an international bestselling author who lives in North London. At time of going to print he has written nineteen books, along with a collection of short stories. When not writing, David likes to spend his time mucking about in boats, often in the Norfolk Broads, where his crime fiction books are based.